KISS OF ANGELS

Also by CE Murphy

The Austen Chronicles
Magic & Manners * Sorcery & Society (forthcoming)

The Heartstrike Chronicles
Atlantis Fallen * Prometheus Bound (forthcoming)
Avalon Rising (forthcoming)

The Walker Papers
Urban Shaman * Winter Moon * Thunderbird Falls
Coyote Dreams * Walking Dead * Demon Hunts
Spirit Dances * Raven Calls * No Dominion
Mountain Echoes * Shaman Rises

The Old Races Universe
Heart of Stone * House of Cards * Hands of Flame
Baba Yaga's Daughter * Year of Miracles * Kiss of Angels

The Worldwalker Duology
Truthseeker * Wayfinder

The Inheritors' Cycle
The Queen's Bastard * The Pretender's Crown

The Guildmaster Saga
Seamaster * Stonemaster * Skymaster (forthcoming)

Stone's Throe
A Spirit of the Century Novel

Take A Chance
A Graphic Novel

Roses in Amber
A Beauty and the Beast story

The Lovelorn Lads
Bewitching Benedict

& writing as Murphy Lawless
Raven Heart

Kiss of Angels

COLLECTED TALES OF THE OLD RACES

C.E. MURPHY

a miz kit production

MKP

KISS OF ANGELS
ISBN-13: 978-1-61317-147-9

Cover Art: Tara O'Shea / fringe-element.net
Cover Design: C.E. Murphy / mizkit.com
Copy Editor: Stephanie Mowery/
                stephaniemowrey81@gmail.com

for Brian Nisbet

Author's Note

The author would like to suggest that the
OLD RACES UNIVERSE books are best enjoyed
in order of publication, which is as follows:

HEART OF STONE
HOUSE OF CARDS
HANDS OF FLAME

BABA YAGA'S DAUGHTER

YEAR OF MIRACLES

KISS OF ANGELS

Contents

FAMILY TIES

HE CAME FROM THE SPEAKEASY with blood on his hands.

Not literally; there had been no call for that. Not even to punish Eliseo, because the bulk of his wrath should be meted out on that man, and not the woman who had been his lover for a century or more. Vanessa had, in truth, deserved better, but she had understood all too well that she was a player in a game much older than herself, and Janx did not believe for a moment that she had truly lost the hand that had cost her life. Not when she'd won the hand, a hundred years earlier, that earned her the speakeasy; not when she'd confessed, years later, to the cheat that had won it. Vanessa Grey did not lose at cards, not unless she chose to. But he had blood on his hands, none-the-less, and that it was necessary made it no less unpleasant.

It was usually easier. They were so ephemeral, humans; they rarely survived long enough to gain his attention, much less for him to become fond of them. Vanessa had been different, though. Different for drawing Eliseo's eye and yet never once rising to Janx's flirtations; usually when mortal women fancied one of them, they found the other difficult—impossible—to resist. Vanessa, by all appearances, hadn't even *liked* him, and although Janx's ego was sufficient that he knew that could hardly be true, that she'd maintained the pretense convincingly over ten decades was admirable.

So yes, there was blood on his hands, and for the first time in a very long time indeed, real anger burned inside Janx's breast, that Eliseo Daisani had made it necessary. And that was how he went, with rage in his heart and blood on his hands, to meet the daughter Eliseo Daisani had stolen from him over a century ago.

Thrice in two centuries is not enough and too many times to see a creature such as Janx. Not enough, because his beauty is such that desiring him cost me my very life; too many, because I have stolen his daughter from him, or at least, not returned her when I might have, and if he did not know it before today, he most certainly does now.

She does not want me there, my Jana, but neither can she bring herself to send me away. She is too afraid and too forgiving both: afraid that her father will judge her for being the daughter of a witch, and not properly of the

Old Races at all; forgiving, that I have let that come to pass, and that she will protect me for it. I see him in her, in her emerald eyes and in the height and strength of her slim body, if not in her hair, which is as black as my own. The depths in her hair are red, not blue as mine are, or as her sister's are; those depths come from Janx, and from the dragon who was my daughter's mother. All I know of that one is her name: Fina, and I gave her daughter the best dragonly name I knew how, in homage to those I took her from.

Janx's presence is inimitable even at the best of times: he seems a man, but even the greatest and most charismatic of men would pay any cost to carry the weight and gravitas that a dragon can master. I do not know where a dragon's mass goes when it takes human form, but I know with certainty that they can call it to themselves to command a room, or indeed a city block, should that be their desire. Janx plays, mostly, at being frivolous and coy, which only heightens his power when he comes as he does now, rolling on fury and so laden with his immortal size that it is a wonder he can enter the room without damaging it.

But that is why we have chosen a church, an old and familiar place with room enough even for a dragon to stretch his wings. The gargoyle called Alban Korund slept beneath this place for over a century; it is, in so far as anywhere human-built can be, a sanctuary for the Old

Races, and perhaps for those like myself, who are born of human magic, but are in no wise human themselves. A priest, white-haired and with a wild beard, watched us come in, but did not approach, and it is not my imagination that he spoke with those few humans lingering here late into the night, nor that they departed with more haste than they might otherwise have intended. I might like to speak with him, for his gaze had something of the uncanny about it; I do not think we are secrets to him, for all that he may not know exactly what any of us are. But that is for later; now there are other things to attend to.

Their first sighting of one another is as powerful as waves crashing on the shore. She rises, my sweet, shy daughter, and Janx comes to a stop, his anger bleeding away into awe. Jana is strengthened by that, and lifts her chin until she meets her father's gaze. Were I my mother, I could feed off the magic of that meeting for a hundred years, but instead I hold myself still, hardly daring to breathe; hardly able, as if the air has been pushed away by the invisible mass of two dragons.

They do not move, not for long and long and long again, and in that stillness it comes to me that I do not, in fact, belong here. Jana does not, in the end, need my protection, and my presence can only disrupt their introduction. I step back, and Janx finally moves. Only the turn of his head, his eyes finding mine in the quiet light of the church. "You," he says, softly, and if it is not a threat, that is only because I am born of human magic, and beyond the Old Races' grasp, "you I will deal with later."

I bow my head and leave, but the last thing I hear are the first words my daughter says to her father, in her clear light voice: "You will not."

She'd never met another dragon; they were too scarce, too old, and too canny to expose themselves, and she wasn't raised among any of the Old Races at all. But even if she had been brought up amongst the Old Races, unless she'd been raised by her birth mother, the black dragon called Fina, Jana thought meeting her father would probably be terrifying. She wasn't like Emma, half-vampire, half-witch, and easy with the world and its ways, letting them flow and ebb around her. She wasn't like their mother, either, who saw events and people as things to be shaped to make a better place. Jana only wanted two things: to keep her mother and sister safe, and to wreak unforgiving revenge on Eliseo Daisani and his people, for stealing her from the family she'd been meant to know. Very little else mattered, and beyond fighting for those two things, she knew perfectly well she was tentative and shy where she, a dragon in human form, had no need or reason to be at all.

Of all the things she had no reason to fear, the red dragon Janx was probably first among them. She was his daughter, the only pureblood dragon born in centuries, and it was by no means her fault she'd been stolen from him before she'd even hatched. But he was *Janx*: he was immeasurably ancient, a leader—perhaps *the* leader—among their people. He cared, in broad and spectacular strokes, very little for humanity; and it was amidst humanity—more or less—that Jana had been raised. In the details he was worse: he could love and admire individual humans profoundly, which might seem a safety net for them, but was not. It would be better if he didn't care at all. Then she could understand his ruthlessness, but Jana had read stories of the dragonlord Janx for a very long time, and he *did* care. He cared deeply.

And yet as he entered the church, Jana could smell Vanessa Grey's death on him, and when he spoke, it was to threaten her mother. "*You,*" he said to her, "*you I will deal with later,*" and Jana's own voice broke over his, calm and very certain: "You will not."

Her stomach knotted as she spoke, and her heart became a cold fist pounding in her chest, but her hands fisted too, and preposterous thoughts darted through her mind: she was small, perhaps quick compared to his vastness; she could hardly defeat him in a fight but she could at least prove she was willing to try. She might do him some little damage, with her litheness, and she put away the knowledge that he would never actually hurt *her*, the last daughter of a dying race. Perhaps he would treat her as an equal, if she fought for it. She had to try, because Emma and their mother were Jana's hoard, and she would protect them at all costs.

Janx turned his regard to her, jade eyes bright in the church's dim late-night light. Amusement glittered in that green gaze, but so, perhaps, did admiration. "You remind me of your mother."

"Which one?" Jana threw the question down as hard as she could, sending it bouncing off the stone walls and flickering the flames of what candles danced in their holders.

Janx smiled, full of daggered teeth and delight. "Both of them, now that you mention it, but I was thinking of Fina. You look...almost nothing like her," he conceded after a moment's examination. "But you have her ferocity. Baba Yaga's daughter is less fierce, if no less implacable. I expect that's in you, too. Very well. I will not...deal with her at all, if that's your wish. Will you tell me your name?"

"Jana. Spelled with a J."

"*Yana.*" He repeated the sound, but his smile grew as she told him the spelling. "Jana. Well, damn the witch, I could hardly have named you better myself. Did she know what she was doing?"

"She's read her mother's grimoires," Jana replied. "She knows as much about the Old Races as anything human can."

"So instead of dealing with her, I shall have

to thank her." Janx sighed theatrically, then let the pretense fall away; inside a breath he was no longer human, much less mocking. His eyes were very serious indeed, and he took a single step forward. "May I call you daughter, and claim my bloodline as your own? Do not mistake me, Jana: I do not ask only for my own sentimental satisfaction. You are the first of our children in eight hundred years, and to be your father is to command more power among our people than even I might have dreamed. We are living on the cusp of change, and I—we —will need every shred of leverage we can get. I will use you to that end," he said, and the flagstones of the church floor shivered with the depth of his voice, "and I will protect you at all costs. At *all* costs, Jana. I've lost you once; that will never happen again."

"And if I don't let you call me daughter? What then? Will you still protect me? Will you still imagine that my safety is actually yours to command? You couldn't keep me from being stolen when I was in the shell. What makes you think that now, when I have wings and a mind of my own, that you could keep me if I wanted to go? You don't get to decide whether you lose me or not. That's not how the world works." Jana's jaw thrust out, either petulant or challenging; even she didn't know which, but whichever it was, or her words, gave Janx pause, and then a sigh.

"You *are* like Fina. I stand corrected in the face of modern women, or dragons, or both.

You're right. I cannot protect you. I *can* teach you to fight as a dragon, which I suspect you have little experience at, and in so doing I can offer you the skills to protect yourself. I can also lend you the measure of my name, which you bear in part already, damn the witch," he said a second time, more softly, as if he admired Baba Yaga's daughter and didn't want Jana to know it. "To be Jana is a great deal; to be Jana, daughter of Janx and Fina, renders you—"

"A target," Jana interrupted thoughtfully. "You already said you would gain power by being my father, but I'd be painting a target on my belly to be your daughter, wouldn't I? And it might not be that helpful to you, for it to get out that you lost me to a vampire and a witch before I even hatched."

Janx's eyes glittered. "I'm supposed to be the clever one, lass."

"Try harder." Fire burned through Jana's mind, lighting pathways that had remained unknown until she stood before another dragon. Emma was the quick one, always putting things together that left Jana behind. That had never disturbed her; she'd been content to be quiet and slowly thoughtful, but she understood suddenly why Janx *liked* to be the clever one, and found delight in out-thinking him now. "And I was so afraid of meeting you," she breathed, then said, "The story would have to be that you've done it on purpose. Hidden away the last dragon child until she grew into her power, so chance or mishap couldn't take her from the world. Where better to hide me than with a witch? Human magic clashes with our kind's. No one would ever be able to find me, even if they were looking, if a witch raised me."

"And who would be looking," Janx asked softly.

"No one," Jana answered truthfully. "Humanity, perhaps, but not in this century, or the last. Not in my whole lifetime, not really. And Daisani," she said with venom, "knew where I was all along."

Janx's face hardened. "I've made the first cut in retaliation for your loss, Jana. It's hardly enough to make amends for losing you, but that is a revenge to be extracted over centuries."

"She didn't deserve to die."

"No." Janx dropped into a pew, suddenly long bones of regret and weariness. "No, she didn't, but she chose to, and she died well. I can't strike at him directly; it's against our strictures. Our laws."

"Laws are for the law-abiding." Jana remained where she was, studying the man sprawled in the pew. He looked almost nothing more *than* a man, just then, though if she softened her gaze she saw the shadows and weights that accompanied him, as if they were spectres drifting in another world. "You liked her."

"Very much."

"And you killed her for a daughter you'd

never met. What if it turned out you preferred her to me?"

"Oddly," Janx replied softly, "it had almost nothing to do with you. Not as a person, at least. It was about the game. We've been in stasis a long time, he and I. Ever since—" He stopped as if he hadn't expected himself to say what he was saying, and Jana glanced where Baba Yaga's daughter had gone.

"Ever since my mother?"

Janx shook his head. "Long before that. He rescued me from the old witch, but he had to. We can't play the game alone. No, it was London, and the fire, and Sarah. We both lost too much with her, I think, and then the world began to change very quickly. Humans spread faster and faster, and we began to play closer and closer to our chests. But then there was Chicago, and it seems he made a move after all. He took a piece too valuable to ignore, once I finally learned it was him, and now…" Janx shrugged. "I take his piece in return. Regrets are immaterial. Do you want my protection?"

"No. Not the way you're offering it, as a cloak to hide beneath. I might like to learn to fight, but mostly I'd like to *know* you, and my birth mother. I want to belong in the world," Jana said, almost surprising herself. "Emma does, in her way. Mother does. But they're more like each other than I'm like them. They have magic, human magic, as well as Emma's other gifts. I…" She turned her palms up, as if she could call her dragonly hands to life around them. She couldn't; there were no halfway stages of transformation, not for a full-blooded member of the Old Races. Emma was more fluid, but Emma was only half a vampire. "I'm very human," she said to her hands, "for a dragon. You, though. You're very dragon, for a human." She looked up with a smile and found Janx grinning lazily back at her.

"I am. It's served me well enough. What do you want, Jana? To inherit my empire?"

"I'd make a terrible criminal."

"Give it time, my dear, give it time." Janx rose and sauntered to her, though his expression was far more serious than his stance. "Your mother went into the long sleep, after your egg was lost. It was that or wreak havoc on the world, and none of us could afford that. I'll try to awaken her, if you wish. It may be that you would have more luck. She would know your voice, I think, even in dreams. And I must ask one more thing, Jana: you don't like that I've killed Vanessa Grey. What would you have done to Eliseo Daisani?"

"I want him dead. Him, and all his kin."

"He has no kin, save your sister. Would you sacrifice her, in your vengeance? No," Janx said softly, as Jana recoiled. "I thought not. We Old Races are very difficult to kill, Jana, and vampires are perhaps impossible to end. I would take everything from him save your sister, in retaliation for losing you, and count that a high enough cost; better that he should live, having lost, than you should die trying to murder the master of a race. And now you're angry," he murmured, which was true; Jana's hands were fists at her sides and her skin felt hot and flushed with suppressed rage, "but sometimes we're angriest when we fear someone's insight is right. I promise you myself," he said with an air of ritual. "I promise you your mother, and I promise you your revenge, my daughter. On my honor as a dragonlord, you will have these things." He tilted her chin up, jade gaze intense on her face. "Do you believe me?"

"Yes." Jana's voice shook on the word, and as swiftly as he'd slipped it on, Janx threw off the weight of vows.

"Splendid. There's an all-night diner a few blocks away, my dear. Shall we retire to its well-padded booths and see if they can feed us enough pie to satisfy two dragonly appetites whilst we catch up on a century or so's worth of important life events?"

Jana stared at him, then laughed. "Are you usually this mercurial?"

"Always."

"No wonder my mother likes you."

"My dear," Janx said, injured, "*everybody* likes me. And I call dibs on the lemon meringue."

"You can have it. Restaurant lemon meringue is horrible."

Janx stopped short of offering her his elbow. "You can't possibly be related to me."

Jana slipped her arm through his anyway. "One's children are supposed to have more refined tastes than one's self. Emma makes amazing lemon meringue pie. If you're very nice, maybe she'll make you one and you can see what I mean about restaurant pie."

"I *have* had homemade pie before, Jana," Janx said dryly. "That's no reason to reject what's more readily available."

"It is when what's available isn't worth eating. Father," Jana said more quietly, more carefully, as they exited the church, and Janx looked down at her with a gaze so unguarded she squeezed his arm, almost a hug, as she whispered, "Thank you."

"Not at all, Jana. Not at all. That's what family is for."

21st CENTURY GHOST

i have an awkward
question

Oh, this should be good.

how do you ask a ghost
on a date

...you want to ask
"Grace" out?

is that so weird

I'm sorry, this requires
more than a text. Call
me. No, never mind, I'll
call you.

The phone rang, blaring R-E-S-P-E-C-T. Tony made a face and answered it with, "If I'd been brave enough to discuss it out loud I would have called you in the first place."

"Don't be ridiculous. Nobody ever calls anybody anymore if they can possibly avoid it.

Seriously, you and Grace?"

"You've got to admit she's kind of a...hell of a woman, Grit."

"Ghost. She's a hell of a ghost." Margrit's voice sparkled, if that was even possible. "Yes, she is. Where do you want to take her out?"

Tony groaned, sinking into his chair. Technically it was his lunch break and discussing his love life aloud in the precinct wouldn't draw attention. In reality he worked with detectives who worked lunch at their desks, dealing with overdue paperwork, so he mumbled deliberately, instead of speaking clearly. "I was thinking Cam and Cole's wedding."

On the other end of the line, Margrit Knight squeaked like she'd swallowed a Life Savers whole. "You want to take her to a *wedding* as a *first date*? Damn, man, are you just gonna go straight to putting a ring on it? I didn't know you two had even talked to each other!"

"There was some down time between all the...excitement." Tony pulled a hand over his face, then kicked his feet onto his desk and tilted back in his chair, staring at the ceiling. There had been a leaky pipe in it sometime before he'd started working there, and a brown watermark still stained the tiles. Once in a while he considered getting a can of white spray paint and painting it over, but the faint yellowing of age on all the other tiles would suddenly be obvious if he did that. The guerrilla tactic of having the whole squad sweep in some night, repaint the whole ceiling, and swoop out again had occurred to him recently, but he chalked that up to too much exposure to the Old Races. Or maybe just to having *learned* about them; finding out there were dragons and djinn and gargoyles — "Oh my," he breathed aloud, and Margrit, on the other end of the line, said, "Yeah," with a rueful note in her voice, as though she'd understood his whole thought process perfectly.

And maybe she had. She'd always been an astute lawyer, but something had changed in her recently. More than Tony knew, probably, but he knew for sure she'd been given two sips of vampire blood, gifts of health and life. It might have made her telepathic, too, although he gathered that was more a gargoyle's forte. Not that they were telepathic, exactly, but they communicated within an...over-mind...and Margrit had slipped between the cracks, found her way into that shared mind somehow. So he didn't know; she *could* be telepathic now. "You'd better focus on prosecuting, then."

"What?" Margrit sounded amused, and clearly didn't know what he meant, which suggested it was only long familiarity, and not telepathy, that had allowed her to understand the *oh my* comment. Tony shook his head like she could see him. "Nothing. Never mind. Do you think she'd go out with me?"

"I have no idea, Tony. You'd have to ask her."

"I don't even know where she lives. Or how to find her."

"Go down to the speakeasy. I bet she keeps a scout there, just in case anybody comes looking for her."

"I'm a NYPD detective," Tony said after a moment's silence. "You'd think I might have come up with that on my own."

"I'm sure you would have, if you were acting in your capacity as one of the city's finest," Margrit said cheerfully. "However, when you're reduced to calling ex-girlfriends to ask for dating advice, you have slid firmly into hopeless romantic territory, and nobody expects a hopeless romantic to be able to do detective work."

"That doesn't make me feel reassured."

"I'm not at all sure that's what I was trying to accomplish," Margrit said, still cheerfully. "Go get 'em, Tiger."

Tony muttered, "For God's sake, Margrit," and hung up to the sound of her cackles.

No one—almost no one—knew who'd built the speakeasy into an unused subway tunnel a hundred or so years ago. Maybe more; maybe it hadn't always been a speakeasy. But it was recognizably one when Grace O'Malley, the Big Apple's favorite leather-clad vigilante, had quietly informed historical preservation societies and city officials that she had 'discovered' it beneath the city streets. It had become a tourist destination since then, and most of the room was cordoned off, keeping it safe from oily fingers and sweaty hands.

He hadn't been to the speakeasy before—first it was too popular as a new tourist site, and then it was too late: he was a New Yorker, and never habitually went to what visitors regarded as touristy spots. The only reason he'd been to anything on Broadway was Margrit, who liked musicals, although in his secret heart, Tony admitted he wouldn't turn down tickets to *Hamilton* if they fell his way.

The photos he'd seen of the speakeasy almost did it justice. It had been built into the subway tunnel itself, out of some kind of golden wood that had been polished until it gleamed. There were electric light fixtures so closely matched in color they seemed to grow out of the wood, and thick clouded glass made the lights throw a gold glow everywhere. There were abstract Tiffany windows set into the back wall of the speakeasy, random patterns of brilliant colors. Tony had seen the pictures they made when overlaid, and tried to find the shapes of dragons and selkies hidden in the splashes. He almost could, but only almost. That was probably part of how the Old Races stayed hidden: not even people who knew what they were looking at could quite see it.

The rest of the room—it really was only a room, only one single curved tunnel through time—held lounges and velvet chairs, chess sets and glasses he assumed were also Tiffany in origin, with thick red and gold carpets under dark red hardwood tables. Everything about the room, except the stained glass windows, was done in red and gold, like someone wealthy had waltzed through dripping richness and left it to lie where it fell.

This space had been shared territory between the dragonlord Janx and the master vampire Eliseo Daisani, Tony remembered sourly, and thought that was *exactly* how the speakeasy had been decorated. Even the modern velvet cords that kept people away from the antiques looked unusually expensive, as if the city hadn't wanted to bring the tone down. There were a number of people, some of them guards, filtering through the narrow paths made by the cordons. Most of them had cameras and phones out, one or two trying to get a signal to post their selfies right away. Tony chuckled and stepped back out of the door, watching the entrance that led back up to the streets. A teenage girl with her hair done in cornrows watched him with a look that said she figured he was a cop, even if he was in jeans and a base-ball jacket. Tony lifted his chin in greeting and she edged back without really moving. Not quite afraid of him, but wary. After a minute, Tony poked his head back into the speakeasy and got one of their informational flyers, scrib-bling a note on it. Then he turned it into a paper airplane and threw it toward the girl.

'Toward' was generous. It flew a few feet, spun in a couple of circles, and skidded to the

floor a lot closer to Tony than the girl. He pulled
a face and went and got it, throwing it again. It
did the same thing and he collected it, exasperated, to try to improve its aerodynamics. Before
he finished, the girl, looking amused instead of
wary, came over, took the flyer from him, and
folded it into a completely different airplane that
flew from one end of the hall to the other without so much as a twirl. Tony watched it bump
into the far wall, crinkling its nose, and turned
an admiring look on the girl. "You must be good
in your engineering classes."

"I am. What'd it say?" The girl nodded toward
the distant plane and its note.

"It asked if you knew Grace."

The girl backed up a step. "Why does a cop
want to know?"

"I'm a friend of Margrit Knight's. I know
Grace. I just don't know how to get ahold of
her." Tony lifted his hands, fingers spread.

"How come you want to?"

Tony wrinkled his face. "To ask her out."

Sheer glee and a bright white smile split the
girl's face. "I'll let her know."

"Y—" There was no point: the girl darted off,
leaving Tony behind with his head hanging
and a rueful smile pulling at his lips.

Once upon a time, it had been unusual for
someone to come knocking at the balcony door.
The balcony, after all, was nine stories up,
roughly the size and shape of a fire escape grill,

and had no exterior access. Never-the-less, Grace O'Malley — rangy, bleach-blonde, leather-clad; basically everything top modeling agencies were looking for — stood out there, leaning on its waist-high railing. She'd knocked, which was observing protocol, by Old Races standards; most of them could rip doors off their hinges, if they wanted to. Not that Grace was actually *of* the Old Races, but she belonged in the same headspace, as far as Margrit was concerned: not human, imbued with magic, living a secret life.

There wasn't anything particularly secretive about arriving on the balcony to say, "He wants to *what*?", though. Margrit, both exasperated and amused, threw her hands up.

"I don't know why you're talking to *me* about this. I'm not a matchmaker. Come in, it's cold out there." It wasn't, or at least, she didn't feel the cold the way she used to, and Grace, as far as Margrit knew, didn't feel it at all. The ghost drifted inside to lean against the kitchen counter instead of the balcony railing anyway.

"People don't ask Grace out, love. I reckoned you'd know what was going on in his mind. I also know where you live."

"Oh, that's reassuring. You're a ghost. Can't you find out where he lives through some kind of secret network?" Margrit got water from the behemoth of a fridge, patting it fondly as she lifted the jug to ask if Grace wanted any. The ghost nodded, took the glass she was offered, and said, dryly, "I'm using my secret network right now, lawyer."

"Oh, pfft. I'm not secret."

"No, love, you're just the core holding all the Old Races' secrets in the city together."

Margrit rolled her eyes, but didn't argue, that time. It had only been days since Janx and Daisani had both fled New York, and the ramifications of their empires falling to selkie and djinn hands were still rumbling. Not even rumbling, really; the truth was things had barely begun to settle, and it was likely to be months or years before both empires ran smoothly again. Until then, Grace was right: Margrit was the mediator. The Negotiator, a title she'd stepped up and claimed for herself, even knowing its costs. The truth was, by the time all the dust *had* settled, she would be irrevocably bound up in the Old Races' world, in their negotiations and their decisions about shaping their future.

As if there had ever been a moment, from the first time she laid eyes on Alban Korund, that that hadn't been true. Margrit smiled, shook her head, and said, "So what is it you want, Tony's address or his phone number? Because, for the record, I'm not handing over his address without his permission."

"Does Grace look like she carries a mobile?"

"Grace *sounds* like she's affecting 'mobile' because she's Irish-born, never mind that she came off the boat three hundred years before phones were invented." Margrit snorted as Grace gave a guilty-as-charged shrug. "How do you communicate in the modern day without a cell phone? Messages in a bottle? Graffiti? Morse code?"

"Believe it or not, lawyer, there are still functioning pay phones around this city, and name me a business that doesn't still have a land line. Why would someone like me want to carry a beacon for the cops to track? And reception is terrible in the tunnels anyway. You could call him for me."

"Are you *twelve*? I am not playing—" Margrit broke off to laugh. "Telephone. I am not playing telephone between two adults who are trying to set up a date. You know where he works. Send him a note by courier. I don't know, but don't put me in the middle of it."

Grace stared at her long and hard for a moment, then shoved away from the kitchen counter in a sharp, explosive motion that contained—not anger, Margrit thought, but perhaps *fear*. Which seemed absurd; Grace O'Malley was one of the most brazenly confident people she'd ever met, but she had an aura of real discomfort. When she spoke, it was without the usual devil-may-care edge to her voice. "It's been a long time since Grace has had a date, love."

Surprise curved a smile over Margrit's lips. "Well, Tony's a good guy to start with, then."

"Is he? You broke up with him."

"About seven times," Margrit agreed, still smiling, but it faded. She folded her arms under her breasts, studying her feet, and said, "I used to say we were too stubborn, too much the same and too different. Too rigid. Couldn't bend enough for one another. Our careers weren't compatible, and neither of us was going to give them up." She glanced up, meeting Grace's eyes for a moment, then looked away again. "Except he offered to give up being a cop for me, in the end. I was…this had all happened, by then. Or had started happening, at least." She made a gesture as if it could encompass all the ways the Old Races had changed her life, trusting that Grace would understand. The other woman nodded, and Margrit went on. "This world, this secret world…I wanted to be a part of it, and I never imagined Tony could handle it. I was wrong, but ultimately…the truth is he loved me more than I loved him. I was the rigid one. He was willing to bend. I wasn't. And now I've got a man of actual stone to dash myself against—"

"That's too much information, love."

Margrit laughed. "You know what I mean."

"I also know Alban Korund is mighty flexible, for a gargoyle. I think that's the thing about you, lawyer. You're so damn sure of yourself you'll stand against the tide—against the ocean—and say 'No. *You* move.' It's why they like you."

"It almost got me killed on at least three separate occasions, too. I wasn't trying to make a point about me, though. Or only about why

Tony and I didn't work out. I underestimated him. He loves that the Old Races exist. And if he's even thinking about asking you out, it's because he's more able to bend than I ever imagined. He's a good guy. I think you might like him."

"Is he sniffing around because I'm part of that world?"

"I'm pretty sure he's sniffing around because you're a tall leggy blonde in black leather, Grace. And—no offense, but you're only peripheral to the Old Races."

"I *was*, until you came around."

Margrit raised her hands in apology. "My point is that he's got easier access to the Old Races by dropping by here, and that if he wants to ask you out then he's okay with what you do. Even if he's a cop. It's not a bad start to a date. Or a relationship."

"Speaking of relationships." Grace gave her a sly smile. "How is he in bed?"

"Oh, no." Margrit lifted her hands again, this time warding the question off. "No way. We've already failed the Bechdel test with this conversation. I am *not* getting into intimate bedroom details."

Grace made a face. "That bad?"

"Grace! No! *Grace!*"

Grace laughed, and, her own hands raised in an apology she clearly didn't mean, faded backward through the balcony door, and drifted out of sight.

#

It wasn't that Margrit Knight was wrong. Far from it: the lawyer was right. Finding Tony Pulcella shouldn't have been—wasn't—hard for a woman like Grace. She could slip into the precinct building, leave a note, and disappear again without ever being seen.

It was that she lacked the nerve to do it without encouragement that troubled her. She was Grace O'Malley, Ireland's pirate queen, and she by god ought to have been able to accept—or reject—a date without getting another person involved, and never mind that the detective had involved someone else in the first place. Grace wasn't known for being easy to find, else she'd never be able to do her job, slinking around the city trying to help kids who had been thrown out of their homes or otherwise had nowhere else to go. The tabloids called her a vigilante, though that had a crime-fighting air to it that didn't suit. She'd been *known* to stop a mugging or a rape from time to time, but she didn't scour the streets looking for criminals to apprehend. Nor did she kid herself that anyone who happened along might be decent enough of heart and brave enough of soul to interrupt that kind of behavior, or even that she did it from the decency of her own heart. She did it in large part because they couldn't hurt her, no matter how hard they tried, and it was easy to be courageous and valiant when you were untouchable.

She wouldn't think somebody like Anthony Pulcella, whose actual life was on the line, would be interested in a showboat like herself.

That was the one part of her mind; the other said *sure and why wouldn't he, for I'm Grace O'Malley, the pirate queen,* and led her back around in a circle to the first thought.

Well, she thought a little while later, breaking *in* to a police station was a thing she hadn't ever expected to find herself doing, and yet there she was, leaving a scrap of paper on Tony's desk, and then ghosting out again as the sun began to rise.

Tony didn't find the sticky note for two days.

Paperwork had been dropped on top of it and it took him that long to get it cleared off. Half his coworkers laughed as he jolted to his feet, swearing, then fell back into his chair. *Meet me at the High Line Tuesday at 7,* the note said in old-fashioned, precise handwriting. No name, but it could only be from Grace. And Tuesday at 7 had been the night before. Somewhere between laughter and despair, Tony texted Margrit: *i accidentally stood her up. she left a note i didnt see.*

Oh my God, came the text back, a few minutes later. *You two are like teenagers.*

> yeah i know. so will u
> pass her a note 4 me r
> what

> We broke up, Tony. Why am I still involved in your love life?

bc yr a good friend

> I'm a good friend who's going to take all the shortcuts off your phone and make you text like an adult human being.

If I text like an adult human being will you pass her a note for me?

> OH MY GOD, TONY.

Thanks, Grit.

His phone buzzed again a couple of hours later. It couldn't actually have buzzed *irritably*, but picking it up to read Margrit's message, it *felt* like it had—and the tone of her text only confirmed the sensation.

> You have a date tonight at The Polo Bar. I am NOT available to chaperone.

First, you forget that I'm a lowly police detective & sandwiches cost like thirty bucks there. Second, you can't get reservations that fast at The Polo Bar.

I pulled in a favor and got Kaimana's assistant to make the reservations. You owe me. And by 'owe me' I mean I'm going to show up after your dinner and mash your faces together, yelling, "KISS! KISS!" like you're Barbie dolls.

Don't think I won't do it.

I think you WILL do it. That's why I'm horrified!

hahaha. Have fun, Tony. :)

#

"You stood me up, copper." Grace ghosted into step beside Tony Pulcella as he left work, taking a smirking pleasure in watching him startle half out of his skin.

Color flushed his cheeks—nice gold skin, summer-warm even in winter, complemented by black hair and eyes almost that dark as well —before he straightened his shoulders and tried hard to look like he hadn't flinched. His tone was as genuinely apologetic as she'd ever heard, though, which counted for quite a lot. "I know. I'm sorry. Your note got buried." He slid a glance at her, hang-dog and hopeful. "Thanks for giving me a second chance. And…sorry for sending Margrit, like we were in high school."

"She said junior high," Grace said, amused. "I went to neither, copper, so I wouldn't know."

"I bet even in medieval Ireland kids sent their friends to sound out a crush, though." Tony winced as soon as he'd said it, earning a ringing laugh from Grace.

"'Crush'? Am I your crush, Detective Pulcella?" She let him off the hook, though, matching him stride for stride and whistling as she slid her hands into her pockets. "That lawyer told me she got us a fancy dinner date. All Grace has got in her wardrobe is black leather, love."

"Nobody," Tony said, his voice dropping half an octave, "is going to object to you in black leather, Ms O'Malley. I need to change, though. A suit's okay, but this one's a little… rumpled."

Grace swung around in front of him, blocking him and the pedestrian traffic that had been moving behind him. People parted around them with mutters and dirty looks where they noticed at all, while Grace looked Tony up and down. Rumpled might be a fair enough word: her note might have gotten lost under stacks of paperwork, but the rest of his job took him out of the office for investigations that couldn't be solved through computer work, and his suit had the look of having been lived in for the day. She said, "Disheveled," anyway, flickering her fingers at hair that had probably been tidy in the morning, and at the scrub of a five o'clock shadow lining his jaw.

Tony glanced down at himself and back at her with a small smile. "I'll take it. I don't know if The Polo Bar would, though. What are you doing here? I thought we would meet at the restaurant."

"Well, sure and we might have, but a dinner date, copper. It's so...*human*." Grace lifted her eyebrows to match as his rose. "What would you say to something else tonight, Detective? Would you like to solve a mystery?"

"It's a tea shop, Grace."

"So it is."

Theatrical drama would have them lying on their bellies in the muck, squinting through binoculars at a scrub-hidden shack, but in fact they were comfortably seated in the window of a small Italian restaurant across the street from Grace's mysterious tea shop; Tony had insisted on *some* kind of dinner, if for no other reason than he was hungry. There were already garlic dough balls on the table, and the promise of pizza — not romantic, but fast — on the horizon. The tea shop catered to a wide variety of people — everyone from fashionistas to grubby college students had been through the door in the few minutes he and Grace had been watching

—and what glimpses could be seen inside the shop suggested a cheerful ambiance within. "Where's the mystery?"

Grace pointed a long finger toward the shop. "The mystery, copper, is that Old Races go into that shop and they don't come out."

"What?" Tony stopped with a dough ball halfway to his mouth. "*What*?"

"It's been going on for years," Grace said. "But here's the odd thing, copper: Grace can't get into the shop to check it out."

"But you're a—" Tony swallowed the word *ghost*, but Grace's eyebrows lifted in agreement.

"I am, and I've never met a room that could keep me out. Not until this one, at least. It raises an itch along my spine, it does. I want to know what's going on there. Could be witches."

A chill ran over *Tony*'s spine, raising hairs on his forearms and nape. "Witches?"

"Hasn't anybody told you, love? How do you think Grace ended up a ghost?"

"I don't know, I guess—" Tony broke off, staring at the blonde woman across from him. "I don't know. How did you?"

"A witch cursed me, love. Cursed me to walk the earth until I received the kiss of angels."

"What's that?"

"If I knew, I'd have found it by now." Grace nodded toward the tea shop, redirecting Tony's attention again. "Want to pop over for a cuppa, love?"

"What if it's a witch?!"

"You're not an Old Race, copper. She'd have no reason to look at you twice. Get us some breakfast tea, why don't you? And see if there are any suspicious books or statuary lurking about."

"What's breakfast tea?"

She gave him a gimlet stare. "It's tea you drink at breakfast, love."

Tony bared his teeth. Grace laughed, and, shaking his head, he got up and went across the street to duck into the tea shop. A cornucopia of scents hit him just inside the door, some of them sweet, many of them dry and musty, just like tea tasted. Coffee was bitter, but at least it smelled good. Tony wrinkled his nose, stepped out of someone's way, and slipped through the little shop, getting a feel for its layout.

Narrow shelves were laden with teas he'd never heard of, presented by country of origin in some places and by ingredients—for herbal teas—in others. There was just enough room in the aisles to squeeze by other customers, with people exchanging rueful, apologetic smiles that seemed to accept that the tea was worth the claustrophobic conditions. At the back of the little shop a door, hidden by a dangling curtain of beads, led into a store room that, after a peek through its window, proved to have comfortable-looking furniture and some small plants in it as well. Tony edged up another aisle, looking for Irish teas, and was well on the way to giving up when a small woman appeared at his elbow to ask, "May I help you?"

"I hope so. I'm looking for something for a friend who said 'Irish breakfast tea'. I don't drink tea, so..." He spread his hands helplessly.

"Are they Irish?" At Tony's nod, the small woman — she didn't quite make it to five feet in height, had grey hair pulled back from a wizened brown face, and looked vaguely familiar — took a green and black tin of Bewley's tea off the shelf. "This should do for them. Anything else?"

"I don't think so." Clutching the tin, Tony followed the proprietor back to the front counter, where she rang him up. A mirror behind the counter had a fanciful silver frame, leaves winding around it with tiny creatures peering from within them. Tony leaned closer, squinting at the frame. "Are those dragons?"

The woman looked over her shoulder. "Dragons and djinn and gargoyles."

Tony breathed, "Oh my," which earned him a smile, paid, and left the shop swiftly. A minute later he handed Grace the tin of tea and sat down just as their pizza arrived. He picked up a slice, burning his fingers, and said, "The woman running the place knows about the Old Races."

Grace tipped the box of tea, examining it with pleasure, then lifted her eyebrows. "What'd you do, love, just come right out and ask? Oh," she said after he explained. "No, she wouldn't say that accidentally, would she. Was she a witch?"

"How should I know? Do they have scarlet W's on their heads, or something? She was tiny and grey haired and...I don't know if she was Asian or not. She could have been Chinese, or...just old."

Grace's mouth thinned as he spoke. "Chelsea."

"Chelsea who?"

"Exactly right, love." Grace smirked. "Chelsea Huo. She used to run Huo's On Fi—"

"—On First. The book shop that burned down." Tony lowered his pizza without having taken a bite, and turned a blank expression toward the tea shop. "I thought she died. She *did* die. There was a murder investigation, it was—" He inhaled sharply. "Janx. Margrit had me—I *thought* she looked familiar. I'd never seen her alive, though. How can she be alive? Is she a witch?"

"Grace doesn't know what Chelsea Huo is, except a busybody. She's always got her fingers in the Old Races' pies. They call her a helper," Grace said grudgingly. "One they can go to, if they need it. A bridge between their world and yours."

"What about yours?" Tony picked his pizza up, finally taking a bite, trying to give Grace room to answer. She tilted her head questioningly, and he had to get through a mouthful of cheese and pepperoni before he could say, "The way you said that. Their world and mine. Where does yours fit in? Where do you fit in?"

"I'm not one of them, love, and I'm not one of you either. Your world is where the wealthy and the powerful rule. I belong in the secret places, far below the city streets. I've been there a long time, and I don't see much chance of leaving."

"Why do you do it? You're a ghost. Not just a ghost. The ghost of a famous pirate queen." Grace flickered a salute, smiling faintly, as Tony went on. "Don't get me wrong, I'd rather you were being heroic than knocking over banks, but...wouldn't it be easier to just be a criminal?"

"Would you ask anyone that, or only someone who had been called a pirate? The waters were mine, copper. I took tithes and taxes from those who sailed them, just as the English did. The only difference was I didn't have the power of a nation behind me, only a wee little kingdom of my own. Why aren't you a criminal?"

"I'm a terrible liar." Tony grinned as Grace lifted an eyebrow. "No, really, I am. God forbid anybody should ask me directly about the Old Races. I'd fumble the reply. Lucky that nobody's likely to. I'm sorry," he added after a moment. "Pretty obnoxious, asking why you didn't just default to criminal."

"To be fair," Grace drawled, "part of the reason I don't is it's harder than it looks, ghosting through vault walls with armloads of loot. Ghosts aren't much meant to carry things."

"Or eat?" Tony nodded at her half of the pizza, cooling, untouched, on the platter.

Grace lifted a piece, ate a bite, and shrugged. "I can. I don't have to." Amusement sparkled in her eyes. "It's easier than stealing, though. It's only affecting my own self, and that's easy enough. It's ghosting other things that's hard. Damn," she added, glumly, looking toward the tea shop. "If it's Chelsea Huo in there, she's helping those who go in, and if they don't come out again, it's of their own free will. There's no real mystery."

"Except what she's doing alive. And why you can't enter the shop. And why Margrit doesn't know she's alive. Or that there's an—a what? An underground railroad for the Old Races running in New York? I'd think the Negotiator should know that kind of thing."

"Are you trying to make a mystery out of a molehill, Detective?"

Tony pointed his pizza at her. "You're the one who promised me mysteries instead of meals."

"Well, you got a meal anyway, even if it's not much of a mystery." Grace finished her slice of pizza, watching Chelsea's tea shop idly. "Grace hates not being able to get in there, though. It doesn't matter that there's nothing I want. It's the principle of the thing."

"We could pop over, knock on the door, and ask what's up, after we're done eating. And there is something you want." Tony nodded at the tea tin she'd set aside. "Irish breakfast tea."

Her eyebrows drew down and she glanced at the tea, then back at Tony with a suppressed smile, like he'd surprised her. "So we'll go knock on the door."

Tony waited until a lull in customers before slipping into the tea shop again. Chelsea Huo looked up, eyes bright with interest. "The tea didn't meet with their approval?"

"No, it was fine, thanks. But my friend wants to know why she can't come in." He gestured at the door, where Grace—appeared. Faded into view, rather than stepping into it. Nobody normal could do that, not without a host of special effects that didn't follow people around in real life.

The genial pleasantry faded from Chelsea's eyes. "Oh. Grace O'Malley. I don't suppose she's ever been able to cross into my domains, Detective Pulcella. It's her nature."

Tony snapped to attention. "You know me?"

"I wouldn't be much of a helper if I didn't know who in this city could be trusted, would I? Of course I know you. Ah, hm, let's see." Chelsea pulled an electric kettle out from beneath the checkout desk and set water to boil as she rooted around for bags of tea. The door opened behind Tony and he swung around to see who was there: a slight Middle Eastern man, who gave him a tight smile and disappeared amongst the aisles. Grace stepped toward the open door and —stopped. She didn't quite bounce off; it was as though the doorway was stickier than that, preventing her from doing something as obvious as bouncing, but also not allowing her to move forward. Strain raced through her jaw and throat, then relaxed as she stopped pushing forward. Chelsea, without looking, clicked her tongue. "Patience, child."

Grace, incredulously, said, "*Child*?"

Tony bit back a laugh at her tone, and had to do it again at Chelsea's expression of long-suffering exasperation. Grace, seeing his stifled laughter, gave him a dirty look. He ducked his head, sheepish, and grinned at the floor. Tiles, old ones that shifted slightly underfoot, were bordered with leaves and berries, as if they'd always meant to be a tea shop's floor. The kettle boiled and Chelsea poured hot water over a mix that smelled earthy. A young woman, dark-haired and broad-shouldered, came in and went roving through the aisles; this time Grace didn't try to follow. Chelsea tottered out from behind the counter with a cup of steaming tea in hand, offered it to Grace, and returned to her perch behind the counter. She looked like a bird, sitting there. Like an owl, maybe, wise and purse-mouthed, except Tony had never heard of an owl faking injuries, and he would swear Chelsea's totter was an act. She seemed like the sort of fragile old lady who would turn out to be eighth *dan* in aikido and able to take down an entire gang of street punks.

"This tastes like dirt," Grace announced from the doorway.

"I expect it does," Chelsea replied airily. "But if

you want to come in, you'll have to drink every last drop."

Tony, as solemnly as he could, said, "Are you trying to ground her, Ms Huo?"

Chelsea's expression went flat, save for a twinkle in the depths of her eyes. "That's precisely what I'm trying to do, Detective. As I said, her nature makes entry into my domain extremely difficult. Grounding is exactly what she requires."

Grace, shuddering all over, edged a toe against the threshold. This time she was able to pass it, and a few steps later she plunked the cup onto Chelsea's counter. "I doubt it's worth it. What are those two skulking around the back for? What is she, a selkie?"

"You're very astute, Miss O'Malley. I expect they're waiting for you two to take your leave so they can disappear without being observed."

Tony twisted to look toward the back door. "She's a selkie? How could you tell?"

"It's all in how they move," Grace muttered. "He's a djinn, too, if I don't miss my mark. I thought the lawyer had settled all this, Huo. What are they hiding from?"

"He's to be an unhappy participant in an arranged marriage," Chelsea said. "The djinn are numerous enough that they've rejected, within themselves, the possibility of mating outside the tribes. Individually, however, there are many who disagree. Especially those like that young man, who has fallen in love with a selkie girl."

"What will happen to their children?" Grace asked in fascinated horror. "They're anathema to one another, the selkies and the djinn."

"Chimeras." Chelsea shrugged. "As are all of the half-blood children, no matter what their parentage."

"Chimeras," Tony said, "what's that mean?"

"That there's no predicting what they'll be," Grace said. "The minotaur was born of mixing Old Race parents."

"Th—" Tony bit his tongue, eyes bugging, and swallowed. Both the woman looked amused. "I hope they live happily ever after," he managed after a moment. "Can I ask another question?"

"You can," Chelsea said. "You may not get an answer."

"How are you alive?"

A smile lit up her old face. "I'm hard to kill."

"Your *body* was on the *scene* — "

Chelsea Huo looked down at herself, spread her hands, and looked up at Tony again with elevated eyebrows. "I'm loathe to quote Sam Clemens, Detective, but…"

"Who are you?" Tony asked quietly. "One of them? Someone…magical?"

"I'm a helper, Tony. I help, when and where I can. There's nothing magical in that."

Grace made a disputing noise that earned an arch look from Chelsea, though they didn't exchange more than that as Chelsea's attention came back to Tony. "Surely you know by now that a great deal is not as it seems, when you're dealing with the Old Races."

"Am I, though?"

"You certainly were when my bookstore burned down, and that should be answer enough. If it's not, Detective..." Chelsea held up a hand, stopping his protest. "If it's not, you need to either get used to disappointment, or withdraw from their world entirely, because you will spend your life entangled in frustration and dismay. I believe you've already made your choice, but if I'm wrong, you'd better think about it before this," she said with a swirl of her hand at himself and Grace, "goes any farther."

"'This'?" Grace asked, amused.

Chelsea rolled her eyes. "Please, Miss O'Malley. I've been helping lovers run away together for a long time now. I can certainly see a bit of romance bubbling when it's right in front of me. Now, if you'll excuse me, I do have a pair of nervous young people back there who are looking to escape to new lives, and I need to do what I can to ease their way. Grace, if you wish to make a habit of visiting me here, you'll need a box of my tea to brew and drink before you drop by."

"I can scrape a bit of dirt up and mix it with hot water anywhere, love."

"You could, but it wouldn't let you cross my threshold." Chelsea offered Grace a box of the tea, and after a thoughtful moment, the ghost took it.

"What *are* you," Tony blurted. "A witch?"

Dismay flashed across Chelsea's face. "I certainly hope not. Most witches aren't helpful at all. Now, run along, you two. I have things to attend to. Oh, do tell Margrit hello, when you see her again, Detective. I'd like to think she'll be pleased to know I'm still around."

"Maybe," Tony breathed as they left, "but she's like a dog with a bone when it comes to getting answers about the Old Races. I'm the detective, and I'm an amateur compared to her."

Grace patted his shoulder cheerfully. "Not at all, copper. I'm sure if Alban had revealed himself to *you*, you'd have been just as ardent as the lawyer was on his behalf."

"I like my blondes with more curves and fewer slabs." Tony glanced back at the shop, which had shuttered its windows and killed the lights in the minute since they'd left. "Do you think they'll be okay? Those two kids?"

"No idea, love. Does it really matter?"

"No, but yes. I like love to conquer all."

Grace gave him a slow, surprised smile. "Do you, now. What are you doing asking someone like me on a date for, then? There's no happy ending for Grace O'Malley, copper. She's already dead and lost to this world."

"That's not true, though, is it? There's always the kiss of angels."

"That's just a silly story, love."

"Can't be. I'm a good Italian Catholic boy, and I know there are angels." Tony offered Grace his elbow, and when she took it, smiled.

"After all, I've got one on my arm."

"Oh my God." Grace sounded like one of her teen runaways, though she followed it up with a laugh. "My god, and it's me who's Irish and should have the gift of the Blarney Stone."

"I'll share," Tony offered, "when you think you might want to kiss me."

Grace's eyebrows rose. "Will you, now."

"I hope so." Tony took a deep breath. "If you'd like to go out again, that is. I, uh. There's an event coming up that I'd...I should probably ask later. After a second date. Or a sixth. Otherwise Margrit says I should just put a r—" He bit his tongue to silence himself while Grace stared at him, obviously trying not to laugh again.

"Well, you can't leave me hanging, copper. What's the big event? The Policeman's Ball? A communion? Your best friend's wedding? Oh, lord, it is." She did laugh again, as Tony felt his expression go stricken, then leaned in to kiss his cheek. "Ask after the third date, love, and Grace will see."

AWAKENING

THE PAIN OF AWAKENING was exquisite. The weight of wet earth lifting away; the ash and oak driven through an unbeating heart now pulled free. The burning iron unwound from wrist and ankle no more than bone, and the hunger, *oh:* the raging hunger, awakening as did the desiccated flesh.

Strong slim arms to carry a weightless body: *female.* The savior was female. Wind rushed across filthy skin, though the air itself sounded still and so the wind spoke of speed. Great speed. Inhuman speed. The savior was vampire. One of their own. One who had escaped the betrayal.

Rage boiled up, fast and sweet as blood. So long. It had been *so long* since the betrayal, and only now did rescue come? But no: fury failed as fast as it had risen. Revenge could come later. Later, when strength had returned to dried-up muscle and blackened skin was once more flush with color. Flush with blood.

There were *so many* humans. The scent of their blood carried even on the speeding wind.

Blood pounding hard in fat bodies, lush for draining. The need to taste that wealth sent a spasm through a useless body, cracking fragile bones with its strength. A spasm, no more, from a frame that had once sped across continents in hours, had once ripped body from bone not through great strength but through terrible speed. A spasm: merely a pathetic response from dead flesh.

This was not life, oh no, but it was more than had been granted for years uncounted, and that would be enough.

The bodies were disgusting. More than a dozen of them, all twisted and broken and blackened from their time beneath the earth. They'd weighed almost nothing, but their stench made up for their lightness. Rotten soil, rotten flesh, rotten wood, rusted iron, scummy water. They *stank*, and Ursula thought that if she'd considered that possibility beforehand, she might not have retrieved the vampires at all.

But then, she didn't often think of consequences beforehand, which, as it turned out, was probably the most vampiric of her inherited traits. Well, that and the speed, but being quick never got her in trouble, whereas acting without thinking often did.

Poor impulse control. She could all but hear her sister mocking her with the words, light and teasing and fond. Kate was her own father's daughter, ridden with the dragonly lust for treasures. Ursula *was* Kate's treasure; Ursula and their human, if not exactly mortal, mother Sarah. There were few things in the world as safe as being a dragon's hoard.

She had left Kate behind, though. Left her behind with the red dragon who was Kate's father, and had come to Europe alone with a mind to rescue the vampires her own father had betrayed. "Daisani," she said under her breath, half-mocking. "Master of the vampires." Only half mocking, though, because in the end he *had* mastered them, *had* set them away from the world, and if anyone could claim mastery over killing machines harder to herd than cats, then it was probably the one who had hidden them.

The one who had betrayed them.

It shouldn't matter to her. She was half human, as was Kate. She kept to their mother's last name, Hopkins; they both did, because they were not of the Old Races, not the way the others were. Not bound by their antiquated laws, not when her very existence flaunted them. *Never betray our presence to humanity. Never breed children outside of your own race.*

And *never kill one of your own,* but there were none of her own, no other half-breeds with vampires for fathers, and so she had very little problem killing those who were almost like her. Not vampires themselves, for a host of reasons. For one, Eliseo Daisani, her father, was the first other vampire she'd ever met.

For another, these creeping, twitching lumps that were her kin should by all counts be dead, and they weren't. They had been buried in earth, soaked in holy water, staked by wood and bound by iron, and lain beneath the Vatican for over a century, and still they had life in them. It was possible that vampires could not die at all. In that case, her father had done an even crueler crime than Ursula might have otherwise imagined.

And she was perpetuating it now, leaving them to scream their thin airy screams as she sat and stared in fascinated horror at what living, breathing creatures could become. Stealing them from beneath the Vatican had been the work of a few hours. Finding enough blood to feed them, that had been harder.

If she'd been Kate—if she'd had the baubles and priceless jewels Kate collected as happenstance—Ursula would have left restitution for the farmers whose cattle she'd slaughtered to get the necessary blood. Gallons of it, stinking as badly as the vampires, in its own way. *She* didn't *need* blood, not the way vampires in legend did. She liked her steaks rare, and perhaps ate more red meat than most, but she'd never craved blood as sustenance. Nor had she had time to ask her father if he did, or if that, like so many other things, was simply part of the stories that had grown up around his people.

Poor impulse control, she thought again, but her impulses were well and truly under control now. There would be consequences to this, if she finished. But there were consequences if she didn't, too; the vampires had been taken from the world once already, and she was not the one to put them back away, not now that she'd begun. The blood waited; all she needed to do was drip—or pour—its thickening heat down dry throats, and they would waken fully.

And then, if necessary, she would run.

Blood. Not from a body, but from a bucket. Cold, compared to the heat pumped by a living heart. Warmer, though, than the wet earth had been; kinder than stakes and iron could ever be. Bitter in flavor. The blood of cattle, tasting of the grasses those beasts chewed. Horse blood was sweeter, tinged with oats and grains, and the blood of carnivores was richest of all, flavored by fat and living flesh. To be given the blood of cows would be an insult, if it had not been so long since there had been blood at all.

Strength returned far more quickly than reason might expect. Dried muscle burned as blood forced its way through shriveled veins. There was no digesting, not like lesser creatures did. Blood was all, life, sustenance, and shape, and it ran from the victim to the vampire as if they were one.

Of the brethren whom Daisani had betrayed in Rome, Lona had died last, and lived first. Pain and power ruptured through her, bones cracking with returning strength, and within a breath she changed from husk to healthy.

The girl feeding her leapt backward, clearing a dozen feet in a single motion, and betrayed herself as vampire with the action. Lona had known it anyway, had understood it from the moment slender arms had scooped her up, but this was truth, this was verification, and the girl now crouched across a room littered by bodies, and was poised to run.

She was clever, then, because no wise thing would trust a newly-wakened vampire, not even one who had drunk her fill of cow's blood and who needed nothing more for weeks. Days. Perhaps only hours, after the unknown length of sleep, but not *now*, not in this moment.

Clever but not pretty. Not a beauty, at least, with her dark hair and plain, forthright features that shifted and slid toward greater loveliness the longer Lona looked. Not the subtle change a vampire could command, but something more. Something that said the gaze had lied at first, had mis-seen shocking beauty as something ordinary. The girl was not—was *not* —that attractive, but the compelling lie of her face reminded Lona of another.

Lona bared her teeth—such flat ordinary teeth, such mortal teeth, because no vampire showed its true face until the kill was upon it— and the first words she spoke in over a century were accusation: "You are Eliseo Daisani's get."

"I am the one who released you from his

prison." Not a denial but most certainly a reminder. A challenge. Lona sank into a crouch of her own, two predators across from each other, and between them the others slowly came to life.

Most were gone within minutes, never so much as looking between Lona and the girl, never so much as questioning their fate, only escaping this last room, this stone house in the hills beyond Rome. Returning to a world that would not know them, and to revel in the power that granted.

"How long," Lona said when those who were leaving had gone. Two or three remained, besides herself. Made wiser, perhaps, by the years under the earth, or simply too weak and tired yet to go. But the girl, Daisani's daughter, was the important one here, and Lona would not leave until she had her answers.

"About a hundred and twenty years. Things have changed."

"You were there?"

"For the changes?" The girl nodded. "For the capture? No."

No: Lona knew that already. The wind brought Rome's scent, told her where she was, told her about the plants in bloom outside on scrubby hills, told her the distances her fellow prisoners had already traveled, but nothing about the girl's scent was familiar. There had been a human there that night, a man, a vampire killer, and *he*, Lona would hunt. His children, if not himself, and their children all the way down until no drop of his blood remained unspilled. But this girl had not been there that night more than a century past, and tonight she had freed Lona. They were allies, if not friends, at least for the moment. "Tell me."

Silence, as the girl studied that request. Searched it for answers, and finally said "There are eight billion humans now."

The vampire, so newly fed and flushed with blood, turned white. She was not like Daisani: not swarthy to begin with, and she had been buried beneath the earth for decades on end. Dirt stains had left her already, shuddered away as her flesh rebounded from its destitution, but even cleansed and milky from a lack of sun, she paled.

It had not, Ursula thought, been the kindest way to explain the changes of the past hundred and more years, but it may have been the only way. There were too many changes, too vast to number even though she'd lived through them, and the doubling and redoubling of the human population seemed the only way to encapsulate what a century of sleep had missed.

"We're everywhere in their stories," she said after a pause. "They make mistakes about us. They think we're bound to night, like the gargoyles, and some of them think we're…romantic. But none of them know what we really are at all."

"How many?" The vampire's voice was hoarse,

not with disuse but with shock.

Ursula shrugged. "You're the second vampire I've ever spoken with. I think he buried them all."

The vampire's lip curled. She wasn't pretty, Ursula thought, but even with her crouched naked and angry, with ragged hair falling around her shoulders in discolored lumps, she could be mistaken for beautiful. Daisani was like that too: not handsome, but he caught the eye. Perhaps it was a vampiric trait. Ursula had the sudden urge to look at herself in a mirror, but there were none in the house she'd taken, and it would be poor impulse control to leave this awakening vampire to assuage her own vanity.

"How did you escape? Favorite daughter?"

"Unknown daughter." There were so many more things she could say to that, confessions of blood, but that would be telling far more than she should. Even the admission of the unknown was dangerous; it could lead to questions of her bloodline.

Had led to questions of her bloodline: that was clear inside a breath. The vampire's black eyes narrowed and Ursula dropped her jaw in response, hissing. Warning. Threatening. *Different*. A vampire—a full-blooded vampire— had to start the shift into its natural form in order to feed. In order to threaten. Fluid black oil would swim over the skin, *under* the skin, removing all question of their false humanity.

Ursula's shift was no more human: men did not dislocate their jaws, drop them loose beyond the obvious stretch of muscle and sinew, nor did their teeth shape and shatter, new rows coming to sharp life like a shark's. But her coloration didn't distort, and somehow that difference was all, in the eyes of humanity. She had rarely slipped, had rarely let even a hint of her other face be seen by humans, but when she had, they had stared, shaken themselves, and stared again, then dismissed what they'd seen as a hideous trick of light.

Harder, though, to dismiss the black oil slick that crawled over a full vampire's face, and utterly impossible for a vampire to dismiss its lack in Ursula. The creature across from her hissed in return, but it was a wary sound, not challenging. "What *are* you?"

"Chimera." That was the name Janx had given them: children of two races, heir to some and all and none of what their parents were.

Shock passed over the vampire's face a second time. "Forbidden."

"Things," Ursula said dryly, "have changed."

Fear roiled in Lona's gut, base prey fear that told her to bolt. Told her to be like the others, to run, find blood, regain full strength. To become what she had always been: an apex predator. To start, maybe, with this wild thing in front of her, this girl who was half of one thing and half of another and altogether something else of her own. Lona's fingers curled against the stone floor, nails scraping old dirt. Her own old dirt, probably, shed from a healing body. She could pounce, rend, kill—unless the half of one thing, half of another, gave the girl unexpected strength or let her ghost away like a djinn. Wiser to wait and see what the girl was, what she could do, before moving to the kill.

When, Lona thought, bemused, had any vampire heeded wisdom? Wisdom, thoughtfulness, consideration: those were for slower creatures. For things that could not cross a continent at a run, moving from one ocean to another in days. Wisdom was for those who couldn't act, react, and act again as fast as thought. Wisdom—

—wisdom, or its brother planning, had captured and buried a dozen vampires beneath the Vatican, and more, if what this girl said, more the whole world 'round.

Lona undug her fingernails from the stone and hunched smaller. Held herself still and made herself *wait*. Wait, which no vampire ever did. Wait, and think of the changes she'd already learned about: eight billion humans, and a chimera not drowned at birth.

There were answers lying within those two things by themselves, if she had the wit to dig and discover them. It was *hard*, hard to think ahead, hard to listen without acting. But there were so many humans, and a chimera whose father was Eliseo Daisani, and that chimera had come to waken the vampires. There were smart questions she should ask, things she should consider and weigh and respond to. One, one stood out, one was most important of all: "Why?"

The girl huffed air through her nose, noisy snort of sound. "Because he betrayed all of us. All of you. Because nobody else was awake to undo what he'd done, and someone had to. Because the world is changing for the Old Races. The Negotiator has made sure of that. We're allowed to interbreed. The selkies have come out of hiding. There might be a future for all of us, now, and the vampires should be part of that."

"No." The word came slowly, painfully. A hundred years and more of sleep had ingrained patience, or a truth, in Lona's blackened bones. "We feed. We kill. We do not…moderate. And if there were so many humans coming…" Hideous truth, that Eliseo Daisani had been right to bury the vampires. That they couldn't be allowed to go on as they were in a world where humans reproduced by the millions every day.

It was not an argument Lona could have even imagined, much less imagined agreeing with, before the death of sleep.

"Oh," said the girl, "so I should have left you buried?"

Lona lifted a hand: *wait*. Not that vampires ever waited on anything. And yet: *wait*. Slow consideration, as if the water seeping into her body over a century had distanced the space between thoughts. "Your vision. What is it?"

She could see in a heartbeat that the girl had

no vision. That the impulse to free the vampires had been that and that alone: impulse, acted on as any vampire might act. Immediately and rashly. The girl was one of them, then, no matter what else she might be. "Revenge," Lona asked. *Said.* Not a question, not really. "Survival. Domination."

"Don't be stupid," the girl said without missing a breath. "There are too many humans, and they're better than ever at killing and capturing things. A few dozen vampires will never conquer them. Integration. If you want to survive, integrate."

"As *he* has done." Lona hissed the accusation, but whatever had prompted the girl to free the vampires, it wasn't disgust at Daisani's embrace of humanity. She shrugged, saying, "It's worked very well for him."

"And you?"

The girl turned her head. Quarter inch, no more. Show of throat. Vulnerability. Then she righted herself, letting one shoulder rise and fall. "I belong more to humanity than the Old Races. Integration is more appealing than genocide. Or suicide."

"And what is revenge?"

"Best served cold," the girl breathed, then met Lona's eyes. "This isn't about revenge. Not for me. Maybe for you, but for me it's about righting a wrong. He shouldn't have buried you. Maybe you didn't hear me. Things are *changing.* There's a future for us, for the Old Races, one that nobody saw coming. We have an impossibly long way to go to get there, but the vampires deserve the chance to be part of it."

"No." A second denial, when she would never have thought even one would pass her lips. Lona settled into her crouch, studying the girl, studying the blank walls, scenting the wind and the distance of her running brethren. "Some of us," she finally said. "Some of us, Daisani's daughter. Some of us deserve the chance. You have made a mistake, girl. You should not have awakened so many at once. We will have to hunt now."

"*We?*"

Lona's jaw elongated, oily flesh tearing through the veneer of her humanity. It had been far too long since she'd felt that. Far too long, and it re-awakened hunger in her. There would be meat, though, while they hunted. Hunted together, if Daisani's daughter chose to side with her, and not against. "We," she repeated. "Or I will hunt alone."

"You just said I shouldn't have woken you at all. Why would I let you hunt?"

Vampires were fast. Ursula knew that, of course: she was one of them. Half of one, anyway, and faster, far faster, than anything human could ever dream of being.

The newly awakened vampire was faster. Even dry and hungry, she moved so quickly Ursula didn't see it until she was upon her.

Black and sleek and oily, hard to grip and absolutely wretched of breath, she had Ursula's shirt in her hands, had Ursula slammed into the floor and breathless before Ursula blinked. Speed: that was a vampire's gift. Not strength, though momentum lent them the illusion of strength.

Speed was Ursula's gift, too, but she had shared a womb with a dragon's daughter, and thus was half of one thing, yes, and yet also something more, of another.

Blinding fast, fueled by anger, powered by a core of fire burning within, she grabbed the vampire's throat and threw her. Across the room, against the wall, a sick thunk of flesh meeting stone. Hard enough to stun, when a vampire's strength should only have been enough to shove the other away. Ursula was on her in an instant, long fingers turning to claws in the other's flesh. One shake, one hard rattle and the other's head would crack against the floor, rendering her insensible long enough to bind her. Dangerous knowledge, how to bind a vampire. But instead of shaking her, Ursula hissed instead. "Why," she said again, "would I let you hunt?"

"Because the vampires you need are the ones who have learned patience," the other replied. "The ones who ran? They are dangerous. Dangerous to humans and so dangerous to us. We cannot *integrate* if we are hunted by mortals, and so we must hunt those who are our kind but not our allies. Do not be a fool, Daisani's daughter. I am Lona, and I am what you need."

There should be a clock, Ursula thought: a clock ticking away the seconds, loud with its own importance, as she stared at the other. At Lona, whose matted hair had cleaned itself now and whose human veneer grew steadily more striking. Not beautiful, but beauty was overrated. She now looked like someone people would want to know; someone interesting, compelling, exciting. Dangerous.

"Hunt the vampires you've loosed," Lona said. "Waken others one by one, so we might find those who can be patient. And we will *integrate*, Daisani's daughter, and we will show your father the power he has wakened in you and in us through the dead sleep and the learning of *patience*."

"Coming of age," Ursula said, with almost a laugh. "Is that what you think this is? Me trying to get Daddy's attention? I'm four hundred years old, Lona, and Daddy's the bastard who locked the rest of my people away. I don't really think I need his approval, and if I did, this isn't how I'd get it."

"Not approval." The female vampire hadn't moved, though she could have. Could easily have thrown Ursula off, started their fight anew, maybe even killed her, but instead her eyes were bright with conviction. "Challenge. You have already thrown down a gauntlet, Daisani's daughter. You have undone what he began, made a statement of intent. His mastery is no longer accepted by all. You have proclaimed yourself his heir, and an heir must depose the father in order to survive. Is that not your aim?"

She had no ambition. Not that she was aware of, not in that manner. What she had, what she had always had, was anger. Not so Kate; Kate, for all her dragonly fire, was easygoing, casual, and more inclined to laughter. Her father Janx was like that too, perhaps, though his rage was all the greater for its charming mask. Kate, like Janx, flexed and changed to meet the needs of the day. It had fallen to Ursula, always, to move their little family when they were too young for the number of years they'd spent in one place; Ursula who had kept her mother and sister close and shared nothing of them with the world. Ursula who boiled with fury at how neither world, neither human nor Old, could accept them. And it was she who most clearly saw what Margrit Knight had put into motion, a changing of the guard, a chance for a future wherein Ursula, Kate, Margrit herself; where every chimera had a place in the world, and where so too would their fathers and mothers.

And she meant to make the vampires a part of that change, and that desire was against Eliseo Daisani's wishes, and that meant that yes, in fact, she had ambition after all, and that this vampire woman was right in what she saw.

She let Lona go and straightened. Stood over her, and thought of the vampires already loosed, and of the wisdom of Lona's words, and decided.

"Ursula," she said, and offered Lona a hand. "Ursula Daisani."

PERCHANCE TO DREAM

THE MASK WAS NEARLY AS BEAUTIFUL as the woman bearing it.

They were both dark: it of ironwood so old its chocolate hues had aged to black; she with lustrous skin that said no white men had bred into her aboriginal stock. She was small but strong: had to be to lift the mask's weight so gracefully, when it was more than half her size. It was never meant to be worn: its fist-sized opal eyes couldn't be seen through, nor were its interior struts intended to be placed over shoulders. It was to be carried, danced with, thrust forward so its size and exaggerated features could bring watchers into a world beyond their own.

Janx knew a thing or two about worlds that went unseen.

He had shed his bulky dragon form weeks ago and had taken a commercial flight, like any ordinary man, from Indonesia to the Australian outback. The necessity irked him, in a vague and distant way: a creature born to wings should not have to place himself in a long metal tube and trust another to guide his flight. On the other hand, satellites now watched every surface of the earth. It was perhaps unlikely that human eyes should look at just the right time to see a serpentine red dragon skimming across the surface of the ocean, but it wasn't a risk Janx was willing to take. He hadn't lived this far into modern society by being that particular kind of fool.

Watching the mask-bearer dance, he was quite happily reminded of what kind of fool he *was,* and how well-worth the price such foolishness could be.

"Go away," she said to him when he approached, and shouted a bright laugh at his astonishment. "You think I do not mean it, but I do. I am not for you, the mask is not for you. Go away, with your handsome smile and fiery hair and green green eyes."

"How," he said instead, and sat down in the red sand beside her, "how could you possibly know I want the mask?" The other was more obvious: men often wanted beautiful women, and she had great strength of personality in her round features. She was right, though. Women he could find a-plenty, but the mask was a rarity and he had nothing like it in his hoard. That was, as far as he was concerned, reason enough to desire it. "No, that's not the question I should have asked. What's your name?"

"Darri, and it is the question you meant to

ask. What are you called?"

Such a subtle difference in phrasing brought a quirk to Janx's lips. Not *what is your name, but what are you called.* There were those amongst the Old Races who hoarded their names close, and it was a mark of her wit that she asked the one question rather than the other. "I am Janx."

"Janx." Darri tilted her head back and forth a few times, then poked it out like a child trying to emphasize her words. "Go away, Janx."

"I can't."

"You will wish you had."

"Perhaps." Delight bounced through him. Most people deferred to him without noticing. *Women* who did not were particularly splendid but Darri's forthright counsel went well beyond a lack of deference. It virtually threw down a gauntlet, challenging him to try whatever foolishness he had in mind to pursue. Almost no one dared do that; almost no one was bold enough to consider herself equal to him, a worthy adversary. The last such woman had managed to drive him from New York, a city he'd called home for three decades; the last such man—or something like a man, at least—had lately proven himself a far less admirable opponent than Janx had imagined. With his retreat, Janx had thought himself unlikely to find such another rival for decades, perhaps even centuries.

But Darri gave him hope, and for a creature as old as Janx, hope was precious indeed. "But

I would far rather regret what I have done, than what I have not."

"Then you are not very smart," Darri said cheerfully, "but you have been warned."

He rather expected the mask to be harder to steal, after all that. But no: it was left where it belonged, a ceremonial piece at the heart of the gathering. There, visiting outsiders gave it uncomfortable due, and Darri's people treated it as more of an old friend, apparently capable of taking care of itself. Janx watched it well into the night, stars catching in its opal eyes, and listened for the particular silence that said all nearby humanity had taken sleep.

Once, a very long time ago, he would have changed form then and there, letting the concussive blast of shifting knock sleepers awake and send them staggering from their tents to catch a glimpse of his sinuous shape striving for the skies. That was in a time of legends, though, long before video cameras and corroborative evidence. Tonight, prosaically, he hefted the mask's weight onto one shoulder, and walked out of the camp into the desert, like any other thief.

He could not, of course, leave the country in the same way he'd entered. Not carrying a dreamwalker's mask half the height of a man, though the sheer outrageousness of bringing it through customs seemed almost worth inevitably losing it.

Almost. Chortling, Janx took to the sky, leaving behind the echoes of his transformation with a few wingbeats. Wisdom dictated he fly to the northern shore, and wait for nightfall again before crossing to Indonesia's southernmost islands. But the flight across the ocean would be wearying, and there was a dragon in the Northern Territory's capital. Better to not alert it to his presence by transforming too close to Darwin, and to rest somewhere he would certainly not be disturbed. Uluru would welcome him; it always had, red rock calling to red beast, and he could linger there as long as he needed to prepare for the unpleasant flight across the ocean.

Besides, the sun-baked stone was warm even at night, and the temptation to flatten amongst its broad smooth top and let distant satellite-viewers imagine they saw a dragon on the holy mountain was too great to resist. Playing to human rules all the time was exhaustively dull. Making a handful of scattered mortals wonder if they'd lost their minds made up for it in some small way.

Darri, quite impossibly, awaited him atop the sandstone mountain. He was no sooner settled comfortably in its red ridges, mask safely curled in his talons, than she was there, looking for all the world like a mother who'd caught her toddler misbehaving. "I told you not to take the mask, dragonlord."

Just that: no shock, no surprise, no wonder at his vast serpentine form, just a single scolding sentence. Astonishment flapped Janx's jaw, human words unwilling to scrape from a throat not meant to shape them. He transformed back to his mortal shape, barely disturbing Darri's thick curls, and knew he sounded exactly like the petulant, chastened child Darri was treating him as: "You can't possibly be here. And how do you know I'm—"

That, at least, was so self-evident he bit his tongue on finishing the question. Darri laughed anyway. "I know so much about you, and you hardly know we exist. Dangerous, dragonlord. Dangerous to think you Old Races are the only magic-users in this world."

"I know we aren't." An automatic, peevish response better suited to an infant of any race than a creature his uncountable age. Janx bared his teeth, submitting to a rare inhuman impulse, and saw Darri mark that they were too long, too white; that they were, by all mortal legends, vampire teeth, with canines far too sharp for human comfort. The vampires, though, had ordinary flat teeth, at least until they shifted to feed, and no one lived to speak of what they saw then.

Or they had, until their lord and master, Daisani, had betrayed them all, which in itself was what sent Janx to the Outback, hoping to find a new and worthy rival. Which was what put him here, now, facing a girl whose bright smile seemed suddenly laced with daggers. "There are witches," he grated. "I have met a few. Are you one?"

Darri mimed spitting, too elegant—or too aware of water's cost—to waste it in the actual action. "No. Maybe their cousin, because all human magic is related, just as all Old Races magic is. But no, dragonlord. The witches are born of secrets, and only the one who was made by learning God's most secret name might be a force of good. The rest are evil. Dreamwalkers are something else."

"Something which knows about the Old Races, when we know nothing of you," Janx whispered. "How do you know us?"

"How could we not? Your memories are collected and archived, kept tidy by your stone men, within the Dreaming."

"The—" Cold sluiced over Janx's arms. Cold *never* touched him, not like that; it was a gift of being what he was. But the repository of knowledge Darri spoke of went back beyond active memory, even beyond his own long remembrance. "You mean the gargoyle gestalt? The memory banks? You can access those?"

"Where do you think you are now, dragonlord?"

He straightened, affronted. "Uluru. Ayers Rock. This is no dreamtime."

"Is it not?" Darri tipped her chin back, gaze going to the stars, and Janx followed it automatically. Familiar band across the sky, the galaxy stretching out uninterrupted by usu-ally-pervasive human lights, distant stars fading in and out at the corners of his eyes.

It writhed, that milky strip across the sky. Writhed, pulled itself loose from its black background, and twisted to gaze down at him with eyes that were the hearts of stars.

Janx, in as human a thing he'd ever done, gasped and scattered backward, scrambling on hands and feet under the sound of Darri's laughter. The serpent in the sky coiled downward, heat raging into streaks of brilliance across the night before it faded away. Faded entirely: moonlight rose, eating the stars and turning the red stone around them to ghostly purple. Then the earth shifted beneath them, rising up into mountains more familiar to him: jagged, alpine, snow-capped. "Where are we?"

"This is how your stone men see the Dreaming," Darri murmured. "Each new memory adds to the mountains. But see how they are dying, dragonlord. See how the memories are fewer and farther between in collection than ever they were, and how wind and water and time wear away the tips, the very oldest memories of who and what your people are. This worries us, as you are living things of this earth, it is our duty to protect you."

"*You*. Protect *us*." Equilibrium briefly restored, Janx stared at Darri. "We are the *Old Races*, little girl. We are dragons and vampires, selkie and djinn, gargoyles and once, so much more. You're *human.* How could you be meant to protect *us*?"

"We were all souls in the Dreaming before we were given physical form. Humans were the last to be shaped, and in our creation accepted custodianship of all that had been made before. We lose so many, every day, and now the Dreaming fears losing you too."

"No." Janx passed a hand over his eyes, then flicked his fingers, throwing the action away. "We have made laws amongst ourselves recently, laws to change who and what we are, and those would be written by now in the gargoyle memories. You would know that, if you were genuinely conversant with the memories, and because you don't I think I can safely say this is a trick, nothing more. Dragons don't dream, my dear. This isn't what you say."

"Beings who do not dream," Darri said, drolly, "perhaps should not steal dreamwalker masks."

Cold washed him again, discomfiting *human* response. Janx's gaze snapped to the mask, almost innocuous under the blue-lit sky. Only its eyes were alive, opal drinking down the moon, dancing with stars that no longer shone above. "That sent me into the gestalt?"

"I sent you into the Dreaming." Darri no longer sounded young, but ancient and implacable. "I told you, dragonlord, that you should have gone away. You will not leave here unless I consider you fit and trustworthy enough to go. A dragon who does not dream," she said, more quietly but no more gently, "will not wake up on his own."

Anger knotted a place beneath Janx's breastbone, though he was careful to only let a smile show. He smiled easily, and knew it; it made him seem approachable and friendly, which made turning coat all the more delightful. "Then I had best learn as much as I can from the gestalt while I'm here, hadn't I? Surely there are ancient memories of my own people which might stand recovery." Or better yet, memories of the others, which could prove invaluable.

Darri tipped her head. "Be warned, dragonlord. No one takes anything from the Dreaming without leaving something behind. Are you very certain you have no memories you would rather not share?"

"The secret I have spent rather some centuries protecting has been outed," Janx said dryly. "I believe I have nothing to fear. But here, Dreamwalker." Dismayed amusement coursed through him: most humans took months, more often years, to earn a title from the Old Races, and he'd granted this girl one within minutes. Daisani would never forgive him.

Daisani, Janx reminded himself, was in no position to forgive anyone.

"A game," he said, more subdued by that recollection than he would have thought possible. "Let me search the archives for ancient histories."

"*An* ancient history," Darri said. "One in particular, dragonlord. What knowledge do you seek?"

"A history," he agreed in a mutter. "If I find it before any of my own so-precious memories slip loose, you'll release me and let me take the mask. If instead I add something to the gestalt, then I'll admit you've the better of me and return your mask with all due apologies, and a promise to never steal from the dreamers again."

"A fair bargain." Darri flashed her brilliant smile and spread her fingers wide. The landscape shifted, smoothing into plains again, then rippling into ocean-bound mountains which smoked and spat fire at the sky. "This is the land of your birth, is it not?"

"The ring of fire." He could feel the changes Darri wrought, but trying to make them himself was like trying to clench water. Distance should show him the ever-changing shape of the Pacific Ocean, but he couldn't force himself higher in the Dreaming, to take that longer view of the ocean's attendant volcanoes and fault lines. Those were the birthplace of his people, indeed: dragons came from the fires of the world, as the gargoyles came from the mountains, or the selkie from the seas. "Does your Dreaming contain all the knowledge that ever was, or only what we visitors bring to it?"

"All that ever was," Darri said, but turned a palm skyward. "All that could ever be comes from within us, dragonlord, and we come from within the Dreaming. It's one and the same. Can you take the dragon out of the man?"

Exasperation roiled through Janx, gratifying in its simplicity. "I hate philosophers."

Darri's laugh drowned him out. "If you seek an answer it will be here. Whether it can be found before you unearth or expose a secret of your own..."

"Aye, there's the rub." The impulse to take wing caught him, but the ability wasn't there. "How am I to find anything if it's your will that guides me?"

"Choose a quest, dragonlord. Once your goal is fixed in mind, you'll have a free hand to pursue it. But I won't let you pretend you're after one thing when it's another you want. What do you seek?"

"Dominance over my enemies and a hoard any emperor would envy," Janx said, disconcertingly truthful, and Darri smiled.

"I don't think you'll find that here."

"I might find the hoards my sleeping brethren have hidden." The idea lingered, shifting in his thoughts, until more softly he said, "I might find my brethren themselves. Do you know, I'm unsure of how many of us are left?"

"Then seek them." The phrase, almost ritualistic, released him skyward in a burst of displaced air and sweeping wings. It was *her* will, without question, which propelled him; in other circumstances that would distress him beyond reason, but there was little time now. Janx was not a creature of the Dreaming, nor of the gargoyle gestalt, and another chance to explore it would never be had.

It didn't behave like the world he knew: a few wingbeats brought him impossibly high, showing him the great ocean ringed by continents and peppered by mountains. His people wouldn't all be resting in the lands they'd been born of, but many would; they would find it comforting. He wished—and that was the best word he had for it—that the world would turn beneath him, spinning to show him the other places they might hide, and it did, a whirl that dizzied him. He could navigate here, then, this land controlled by his desires.

Amusement rippled through the Dreaming, rejecting the very thought. He wasn't a dreamer, wasn't built to connect to the memory that ran as deep as the earth's core here. The gargoyles were, and for a moment, through the very world's laughter, he felt what it might be to *be* connected. It made the gargoyles who they were, solid, reliable, and in Janx's opinion, frequently dull as stone.

Darri's voice, sounding very much like the humor of the Dreaming, murmured, "You're wasting time, dragonlord, and you might not know it, but you're leaving thoughts behind. See it this way: maybe it will help."

A handful of scales shed from his spine as she spoke, leaving cold patchy spots of skin. Janx yelped, painfully aware it was a child's sound, and brought his focus more sharply on the world below him. His kin numbered in the dozens, perhaps the hundreds: they could be found, if he had time and wit enough.

Begin with one he knew: his daughter, lying beneath Krakatoa's heated peak. He had left her only a few days ago, still admiring the gold sheen of her newly-adorned talons; she would remain there yet, and possibly for months longer, before any impulse to leave took her.

Oh, but she was a spark, barely visible. That was her youth, not yet four hundred years in age, and perhaps her human blood as well, diluting what strength she would have. But she *was* a spark, a pinpoint of light, and that, at least, told him what he might look for when searching out the others.

With that knowledge, pinpoints lit up all the world around, smears of light that were hardly more than promises. Dozens, even more, with some small handful of them clustered, which was no more likely than a gargoyle walking in daylight. Janx dove toward one of those clusters, wings folded, and gasped shock as wind ripped his scales away.

"Oh, Pompeii," Darri whispered. "London, and Chicago. So many cities burned and ashed, dragonlord. So many dreams lost to the Dreaming. So many women," she added, surprise in her voice. "And so many laws disparaged. Wars fought between the Old Races. Children bred outside them. How many more scales will fall away before I learn you've killed one of your own, dragonlord?"

Janx grated, "All of them," and hit the earth gracelessly, his wings in tatters and claws breaking rough and raw as he tumbled across the ground. "Search all you like, Dreamwalker. That's a crime you'll never uncover." The Pacific coast; *California*, for pity's sake. *A* dragon in San Francisco was likely, but an enclave lay beyond the bounds of reason. Perhaps if they all slept, tangled along the fault line and leeching heat as it rose from the bowels of the earth, but even so, the sparks of life he saw numbered five or more, and that was nearly impossible.

And there were so many; so many others, scattered around the globe. Not an uncountable number, except he lacked time. Each step forward shed more scales; each one brought another exclamation from Darri: names, places, events he had long since left behind, all coming raw as he worked his way forward.

So it was not these five in specific who were important, but all of them: the sum total number of surviving dragons. He spread his wings again, rising into the air a second time, but only a little, this time; only a little. The Dreaming was shaped by need, not by action, and he needed the numbers, some ghost of their locations, so he might later find and waken sleeping giants.

With closed eyes, with agonizing concentration, the world retreated, points of light turning again to guiding beacons. They were there, difficult to count, but coming clearer with every passing moment. One moment, more, and —

"Oh," Darri breathed. "One moment more, dragonlord, and I'll hold your dearest secret of all."

One moment more and *he* would know what he came for; would have the chance, finally, to number his people. To seek them out and wake the sleepers, to invite them back into a world so many had long since abandoned. To reach, for the first time in crumbling memory, for a future instead of mere grim survival.

And yet she was right, and he knew it. Scales were stripped from his body, and the fire gone from his belly. He was tender and naked to the elements, a snake of unimaginable size, but without even the weapons those lesser creatures might have. *Vulnerable.* That was a state his heart could manage, but not his body; only once in the past millennium had he found himself in physical danger, and even then whether he might have died was a question for debate.

He could, today. Here in the Dreaming, torn away from the physical world that dragons belonged to, he could be taken apart sinew by sinew, claw by claw, until all that was remained was a bleached skeleton on volcanic shores. Dragons knew, in the world, when one of their own died. They came to take the body, to return it to the fires it was born of; to burn it, so mankind would never know they existed at all.

No one in the Dreaming would burn his

bones. He did not move, save to turn his head back, not quite looking at Darri's near-distant form. "What do you know already?"

She all but sang the response. "It is the witch's secret, this one you carry so close. Perhaps it's the secret that would be her undoing, but certainly it's the one that would be yours. One step more, Janx. One step more, and I'll hold in my hands the knowledge of how to capture a dragon."

The memory of a Russian winter turned his stripped skin to ice, more literally than a dragon could like. Hoarfrost cracked and bit at unscaled skin, built feeble claws where he had lost his own, steamed from his throat where fire ought to have lived. The price, the price to bind a dragon was so rare, so dear, it could almost never be used against him, and the chance to return his people to the world so rich that for a fleeting moment, the one seemed acceptable recompense for the other.

For a moment. Only for a moment, because to find them in the Dreaming was to waken them to a world where they could be bound, and that would never do. Better to sleep until the earth burned, and rise up masters of a changed land, than to give into human magic the knowledge of how his people might be conquered.

Ancient, alone, angry, Janx stepped backward. Frost retreated, scales returned, and if it was Darri's will and not his own which permitted him to slip on his human form, he let nothing of that knowledge show in his expression as he sauntered back to her side. "Which witch is it, who discovered the secret of binding a dragon?"

Darri sat on the mask, the damnable troublesome mask, her smile a bright crease across her face. "Another step might have told me."

Janx dropped his chin to his chest, such a human action. That was the dreamwalker's influence, not his own body language of choice, but the chagrin inherent in the motion was unmistakable. "You bluffed."

"And you folded."

He couldn't remember the last time someone had played him so smoothly without herself faltering. He lifted his gaze again, rue and admiration in his smile. "The mask, my dear, is yours, and I foreswear any foolishness with your people in my very long and profitable future."

"Are you a man of your word, dragonlord?"

"Oddly enough, yes."

"Then waken." Her lips were against his forehead, warm and soft, but when he opened his eyes there were only stars above him, and no woman. No mask, either; his fingers flew for it without thought, and were left fondling sandstone and nothing more.

Fingers, when he ought to have been still a dragon, and therefore clawed. Nothing, not in time immemorial, had been able to force the change on him unwilling; nothing save a dreamer, and a witch.

Human magic, it seemed, was dangerous. Or human women were, though that was so obvious as to be beyond discussion. Janx tapped fingertips against the mountaintop, then, a slow grin sliding into place, got to his feet to judge the horizon's light, and sunrise's distance. There was so much to do, in this world. So many of his own people to find, so much of a new future to shape. And so many more games to play, now that he could be so wonderfully certain of finding worthy adversaries.

With a thunderous clap of wings, he went to meet the day.

THRENODY

A *THING* LAY AT THE BOTTOM of the hoard.

It smelled of power. It smelled of *human*, which little in her father's hoard did anymore; it had all been his too long for any mortal scent to remain. But the *thing* still smelled of human, and of power, and Kate had been swimming toward it for nearly a year now.

Not constantly, no, of course not: even Janx's hoard wasn't that large. But she had bathed in molten gold until it cooled and bedazzled her claws with jewels until they glittered, and when she was bored with that, she had nosed her way through texts and scrolls so old she couldn't begin to imagine the languages they were written in, much less read them. They smelled, of old dust and ancient paper and bitter inks, smelled so strongly she could catch the scent easily, even in her human form. That was the only shape she was allowed to come near them in: Janx had not saved them from Alexandria, Kate was informed, so that a careless spark could now set them alight. She had stared at him a moment before demanding to know if there were *any* notorious historical fires for which he was not responsible. He had declined to answer and sauntered off with a sniff, leaving Kate with the taste of dust and curiosity in her mouth.

It was with that flavor lingering that she first caught a hint of the human magic. She had followed it, lips peeled back, mouth open, inhaling like a cat and holding the scent in her throat. It faded: it always did, only to come again from a different angle, carried on some faint breeze made by changing temperatures in the caverns beneath a sleeping volcano. She circled and edged and dug and explored, often distracted by other treasures within the hoard and yet always returning to the hunt.

She found it in a space too small to be considered a cave. A fissure: hardly more than a crack in the wall, and far too small for a dragon to fit through. The scent was strong there: Kate thrust her face forward, nostrils flaring as she dragged in deep breaths of the stuff. Human magic smelled *human*, not the dry crispness of dragons or the old blood of the vampires, not the arid wind of the djinn or the fresh-broken stone scent of the gargoyles. It came closest, perhaps, to the salt-water odor of the selkies, but then, the selkies had been interbreeding with humans for generations. And even so, it had a little of all of those things, and more besides. There was a breath of ice and snow, of wet humid greenery, of fresh-tilled soil and sour milk. She could stand there and breathe its scent for days, weeks, months, and find new things with each breath; that was humanity, ever-changing, ever-adapting. That was half of her blood: perhaps that was why the scent nagged at and called to her. She shifted to human—the fissure would never allow her dragon shape to pass through—and pushed a shoulder into the breach before inhaling and squeezing forward.

Crushing a dragon, even one in human form, was nearly impossible: their mass remained, shifted a step out of alignment with the visible world but always there. The narrow passage still pressed in, until the only thought that kept her moving forward was that her father had fit through here at least once, and he was bigger than she.

She popped through the other side in a scrape of blood and skin, whistling with pain and resisting the urge to snap into dragon form and heal the injuries. The slickness would only help her get out again, prize in hand. In the darkness—because to human eyes, even half-human eyes, the dark was nearly complete—she knelt in the tiny room, hands extended, mouth open again to catch scents. Her sister clicked like a bat in the darkness to find her way; Kate had never had the knack of it, always trusting Ursula's guidance when they explored dark places together. Still, there wasn't enough space to become lost; the tantalizing thing sat in the center of the small cave and she could reach it from where she sat beside the fissure.

Her fingertips touched wire strings, first. Notes rippled, unexpectedly pure in the darkness. That, Kate thought, was absurd: this thing had been in the heart of Janx's lair for centuries, at the least. No instrument could hold its tune that long.

No instrument could keep its strings that long, for that matter. Her fingers danced gently upward and outward, finding the shape of the thing. A harp; not a harp. A lyre. They had still been popular when she was a child, four centuries earlier, though they had since fallen out of favor. Almost no one would know how to play one.

Bemused, in darkness, Kate drew the instrument into her lap and pulled a few more notes from it, relying on ancient memory to guide her fingers where they needed to be. Eight strings: an octave, no more. The body of the instrument was wood or stone; she thought stone, because wood should have warped or disintegrated in the years it had spent here. But then, the strings should have rusted away too, even in the dry constant temperatures of the hoard caves, and the thing *did* smell of magic.

She was better with it than she expected, after not playing for centuries. Old songs came back to her fingertips, finding depth and resonance in the notes. They reverberated off narrow walls, filling the chamber with music even after she stopped. When the sound finally faded, she turned to the fissure, preparing to leave.

An enormous green eye stared at her from the fissure's other side. Kate shrieked in surprise, then fell into laughter as Janx slammed from dragon to human. He carried no torch, but a glow of fire radiated on his side of the crack regardless, as if his very being brought forth the light. Which it did; Kate had not, and might not ever, master that trick. Still laughing, she slipped the lyre along the bottom of the crack and followed after, nudging it with her foot until Janx, exasperated, reached in and took it so she could scrape her way out again. Rubbing her chest, she muttered, "I don't know how you fit through that," before changing swiftly to dragon form and back again to ease the sting of the wounds.

"I didn't," Janx said beneath the explosions of air. Kate paused in rubbing her chest and his eyebrows darted upward. "I pushed it in with a stick, Katherine. I had no intention of taking it out again, and even if I had, I would have slid a wing-tip in to draw it out. Why abrade my tender flesh when it wasn't necessary? I admire your dedication, though," he said with solemn mockery. "Perhaps you should have considered *not* playing it, though, if you were planning on stealing it from me." The mockery left his voice, leaving a growl in its place. Not a wholly convincing one; children were rare and precious to the Old Races, and Janx would probably not destroy his own daughter over an artifact.

Probably, Kate thought, and gazed at the lyre now in his hands. "I didn't mean to steal it."

"No? You've spent half a year and more working your way here out of happenstance? You just went to a great deal of trouble to squeeze yourself into a crack because you had no interest at all in the thing hidden inside? You took it out because you only wanted to see it in the light?" Thunder grew in Janx's voice, until dust began to shift and fall from the cavern roof.

"I took it out because it called to me. It's been bothering me almost since I arrived. And if I was going to steal something I certainly wouldn't do it while you were *here*."

As quickly as it had come, Janx's fiery offense faded. "That, I trust, is true. Interesting, that it called to you. I can't play it."

Kate's eyebrows rose dubiously. "I think I would have guessed you could play any instrument in the world."

"I can play *a* lyre. I can't play *this* lyre." He ran his fingers over the wires in demonstration. No sound emerged, and a trick of the light made Kate think the strings themselves tried to squirm away from his touch. "It's a human instrument."

"But I'm—"

"Half human. Enough to draw its song out, it seems. Do you know whose this was?"

"No, I—" And then she did, and her breath caught.

"Long ago," Janx said, softly now, "was born a bard. His voice was the sweetest ever known, his songs the most poignant. He never struck a false note, and the gods themselves sought him out to hear him play."

"The gods...?"

"Gods of fire and of speed, gods of stone and of wind. Gods of war and beauty and song, and of all of these, he was naturally most drawn to the song. But you know this story, Kate; tell me how it goes."

"He wooed Eurydice," Kate whispered. Her hands ached to hold the lyre now, knowing whose it was. Whose it had been. "And then sang her back from the Underworld when she was unfairly taken from him, but he lost her again forever when he looked back to make sure she followed. And he never stopped lamenting her loss."

"That," Janx said, and his smile was bitter, "is the human way of telling the tale. Who were the gods, Kate? Who do you suppose were the creatures of magic and might to whom the humans looked?"

"They were imaginary," Kate said, then, as quickly as before, caught his meaning. "Oh no. Oh, don't tell me..."

Janx shrugged a lazy shoulder. "Did you suppose it was only coincidence that they have gone more and more toward believing in only

one god, or none at all? Why should they continue to believe, when those they worshiped
withdrew? We had to." He cast away regret
with a fluid gesture. "We had to, because they
were beginning to develop the weaponry to
kill us, and gods cannot allow themselves to
die so ignominiously, but there was a time,
Kate, when we walked among them and were
their highest powers. And of all of us, who had
the gift of song?"

"The siryns? If the legends are true."

"They are, in that regard. Come." Janx
turned swiftly, stalking away. "This is not a
story to be told standing still. Bring the lyre,
since it wanted you so badly, and listen as we
walk. They didn't—then—lure sailors to their
deaths. They sang for them, and I'm sure a
careless ship or two foundered on the rocks as
a result, but they were hardly ruthless killers.
And Orpheus didn't happen on them by
chance. They were known to have a fondness
for Lanzarote—"

Kate breathed, "Who doesn't?" and laughed
at the reproving glance Janx bestowed on her.
"I'm sorry," she said with no more genuine
contriteness than she would expect of him. "Do
go on."

"So he went there looking for them," Janx
said sourly. "And he found them. Kate, if
you're going to be difficult I won't tell you this
story at all."

"Perhaps the lyre will."

Janx gave her a second look, this one sharper. "I wouldn't believe whatever tales it tells. It's meant to make you weep, not reflect history."

"History often makes me weep," said Kate, who had lived enough of it to know. Not so much as her father, perhaps, but enough, and she had been, in her way, closer to humanity for all of her life than he could ever be.

"There is that." Janx fell silent for a little while as they walked to the lyre's accompaniment: notes trembled when they crossed uneven ground, though Kate's footstep was as light as any could be. "He came to listen. That's what he told her, when the ships landed. That he'd only come to listen. To hear the music of the gods, and learn from it if he could. And she let him stay, to the doom of them all."

"She?" Kate barely asked the question, half afraid Janx was no longer talking to her at all, half afraid that if he remembered her, he would choose not to share the story after all.

"Eurydice." Janx's nose wrinkled as he spoke the name. "Who was first known to mortals as Inanna, and then Persephone, and a dozen names more around the world. But to the Old Races she was Ninanak, the siryn queen, whose voice was the purest thing ever born of this earth. She sang for him, and he for her, until she loved him for the sweetness of her voice. She learned all of his mortal songs and he captured an echo of her own, which was all the more that he could manage. She felt sorry for him, and so sat with him to craft an instrument. As he shaped it, she sang, so that it would know nothing but purity of music in its making. It would be the greatest instrument ever made, unable to strike a sour note, able to convey depth and power far beyond its humble shape. And when it was done, Ninanak sang for Orpheus and he matched her song note for note. Then he played it back for her, and when he was done she opened her mouth to sing again and only silence came forth. She had given him everything. Everything.

"And he would not give it back.

"The siryns did drown the sailors, then. All of them save Orpheus, whom Ninanak wouldn't allow them to harm. She took human form and went with him instead, perhaps hoping he would return her voice, perhaps simply wishing to be near the music. She never spoke again, so it's hard to know. In time, though, it became such that she could no longer bear to hear the music she couldn't make, and so she ran to the underworld, just as the stories say. And who do you think was King of the Underworld, Katherine?"

Kate turned to him with a question in her eyes, on her lips, and exasperation flitted across Janx's changeable expression. "No, not me. Don't be silly. I may keep my treasures beneath the earth, but I'm at my most magnificent in the sun. No, it was the other one. Your sister's father."

Daisani. Kate didn't so much as breathe the name, only nodded. It had been over a year since New York and her father had yet to forgive Eliseo Daisani for the discovery that he'd betrayed his own people decades earlier. She knew that in lives as long as theirs—even in a life merely as long as *hers*—a year was nothing, and yet it surprised her that they hadn't reconciled. Daisani, loathe as Janx might be to admit it, had been right...but if he could betray his own people, it was possible, perhaps, that he might someday betray Janx as well, and that, Kate thought, was the wound that cut. Not that they hadn't spent aeons doing just that, as it was part of their game—but that was what it was, or had been: a game. Daisani's choice to betray his own kind had somehow moved the game into deadlier stakes, and Janx had yet to let that action go. He would: their camaraderie was greater by far than their differences. In the end they would always be there for one another.

Unless, of course, they were not, and that seemed to be a possibility too unpalatable for Janx to face. Kate shook off the worry; they had gotten on forever without her interference and would no doubt carry on that way. "What happened?"

"She went to him," Janx muttered. "She ran from her enslaver and went into the underworld, and she made it clear she would rather die than go back to Orpheus."

"Oh my God," Kate said faintly. "Did Daisani kill her?"

"*What?* No!" Genuine offense sent Janx's voice unexpectedly high. "That's against our rules!"

Katherine Hopkins, proscribed daughter of a dragon and a human, stood in front of her immortal father, looked down at herself, up at him again, and lifted her eyebrows in incredulous challenge.

"Oh, stop that. I didn't know about you, it doesn't count."

"Really." Kate's own voice went flat. "The year you spent as my mother's, that doesn't count? Because that was against the rules too, Janx."

A little silence, a little stillness, filled the room, until Janx finally said, so softly as to be dangerous, "This is not my story that I am standing here telling you now. This is not your mother's story. Do not test me on the matter of Sarah Hopkins, Kate. Not now. Not ever. If you are wise, you will never test either of us on the matter."

"Did you love her?" It was not the time, it was not the story, but the question spilled out of her, and Janx turned his head to look at her as though he had never seen her before. Or, perhaps, Kate thought, as though he saw someone else entirely within her.

"Better than Orpheus ever loved Ninanak," Janx said, again softly. "Better than you will ever know. And no. Your sister's father did not kill Ninanak. He constrained her in a circle of blood she could not cross, and when Orpheus looked back it was to see her on her knees, screaming silently for the song she could never again sing. He might have gone back for her again, but no living creature crosses twice into Hades' realm and survives. The king of Hell waited, hoping and praying, if we can be said to pray, that Orpheus would turn back a second time. If he could have slain Orpheus, there might have been a way to restore Ninanak's voice."

"But why wouldn't Ninanak let him kill Orpheus in the first place?"

Janx's mouth twisted. "She loved him, or she had once, and he still had the most beautiful voice of any mortal who ever lived, and she was the queen of song. She could not bear for his voice to be lost, even at the cost of her own. There are reasons that we had those strictures in place, Katherine. Good reasons. Not that, in the end, the Negotiator was wrong, but...we Old Races paid heavily, time and again, for dallying with humans. None more heavily than the siryns, because in the end it turned out that they couldn't breed, without Ninanak's song. By the time they realized, Orpheus was long dead and could no longer release Ninanak's voice even if he wanted to. I've had the lyre here ever since. The last person to make music on that was Orpheus, Katherine, and now it answers to your touch. I think you should be honored."

"I'm holding the voice of a ghost." Kate shuddered. "I don't know if that's honorable at all. What happened to Ninanak?"

"She stayed in the underworld until Orpheus died, always hoping he would return her voice. After that..." Janx shrugged. "I suppose she died too. Your sister's father might know otherwise, but I doubt she lived long after that. Even we can die of grief, if we try hard enough. Of all the men who have told her story again through the years, I've often thought that Anderson came closest to its truth."

Kate couldn't help glancing at her feet. "It doesn't feel like knives to walk in human form."

"Find a little poetry in your soul, child. What is the loss of a voice like that, but knives in the soul? Keep the lyre safe, Katherine. It's precious to me."

"I will." Kate hesitated, arms curled around the instrument. "Thank you."

"For giving up an item from my hoard? You're welcome." Janx's eyes glinted. "Don't imagine it's likely to happen again."

"I wouldn't have imagined it was likely to happen once. But I meant for the story, too. Will it bother you if I play it?"

"Play the story?" Janx said lightly. "Are you a child now, to act all the parts of the play? No," he said, at her exasperated glance. "It won't bother me. I might like to hear her voice again, in its songs."

"I don't know those songs."

"The lyre does." Janx left her then, in the too-fluid way that the Old Races had. He was much too large to simply disappear, but she, who could do nearly the same thing, was still left smiling in bemusement at the space where her father had been.

She did not, despite the invitation, begin to play again. Not then, anyway: less-than-idle footsteps took her back through Janx's hoard, her prize wrapped in her arms and its song lulling the hoard's glimmering appeal into insignificance. It wanted — *she* wanted — to go to the sea, through miles of treasure and more miles still of twisting cavernous tunnels. Away from the heart of the hoard, away from the belly of the volcano that warmed it, the air grew more temperate, until for a long time it was neutrally cool: the temperature of the underground world. She went up, blind certainty guiding her feet, until she could smell salt water. The lyre sang then, a tremble that had nothing to do with her touch. Kate was running by the time she burst free of the lair, and the warm lash of sea salt sat heavily in her lungs as she drew ragged breaths.

The wind itself played the lyre, not tunelessly, for the thing could never be out of tune, but aimlessly, as if searching for a song. Kate found stones only just high enough to avoid holding tidal pools and sat on one, her toes stretched toward the water. The sky above was molten grey, thick and heavy with rain, and turned in the distance to a blur of ocean, the line between them indistinguishable. There were other islands out there, thousands of them not so far away, but with the equatorial waters turned dark from the oncoming storm, she might have sat alone in the single inhabited place on the planet.

A lament came to her fingertips, old and mostly forgotten. It had been composed by an Irish bard called Ruaidrhí, when she was young; until then she would have said she'd forgotten it. But laments were for those who might be forgotten, too, and so when that one ended it became another, a piece by a Polish poet who had died before Kate was born. Kochanowski: that had been his name, and his poem had been for a lost daughter. She had been Ursula, like Kate's sister; Kate's Ursula hated that Kate had memorized the lyric, and put it to music. It was made up of nineteen stanzas, and Kate's fingertips ached long before it ended.

She might have edged a little into her dragon form, callousing her hands with tough scales, but she was afraid she would lose the lyre's song if she did. She would heal quickly anyway: the Old Races almost always did. When she might have stopped for her own sake, the lyre whispered music to her instead, and the notes she pulled from its strings were poignantly unfamiliar. A new lament, or more truly, an ancient one: a song given to Orpheus by Ninanak, and captured for eternity in the lyre.

It carried the howling of a storm in it, the relentless wail of wind over water. It held the sun, rising red over the broken bones of a ship on a still sea. It had the hiss of rain approaching from the distance, a sound so vivid Kate could see it with her eyes closed: flat seas and oncoming clouds, the leading edge of rain a wedge of darkness in the sky. No wonder ships had stopped sailing to listen to the siryns' songs; the lament told the story of the sea, and of all the things lost in it. Sailors would find their loved ones in this music, and no few would be drawn to join them. Kate's fingers bled as she made the music, but it had been aeons: surely a lost people deserved to have a little blood shed in their memory.

Other songs lay beneath the lament, but those mournful strains came back to her time and again, binding one melody to another, and making all of Ninanak's stolen voice part of the same sorrowful tune. Kate played for hours, never opening her eyes, not until a shaft of sunlight turned the darkness behind her lids to red. She blinked then, scattering a crimson sunset across the horizon: only there did the clouds break, just enough to set fire to the sea and sky. Grimacing, she took her hands from the strings and flexed her fingers, finally allowing a hint of transformation to ease the burst and bloody blisters. Janx couldn't do that: no full-blooded Old Race could. Shifting for them was all or nothing, but Kate and her sister Ursula could linger in any half-state of transformation that they wished. So they were clawed, those fingers, delicately serpentine and scaled above almost-human palms, when Kate realized that in taking her gaze from the horizon to her hands, she had seen something in between.

They were there in the water: all she had to do was change her point of focus. The low stones she'd settled on were more deeply immersed now, thanks to the changing tides, and the ocean licked her toes. They could touch her if they wanted to, touch her without even breaking the water's surface. They didn't, though: they only hovered in the shifting sea, their hair inking the surface like seaweed and their black eyes unblinking as they looked up at her. Half a dozen of them, no more, and when they knew she'd seen them, they darted into the depths as one, disappearing between one breath and the next.

"Wait!" Kate slid off the stones, plunging hip-deep into shockingly cold water, and gave a cat-like hiss of disgust. Once upon a time the dragons' sea-born cousins, the krakens, had swam the oceans, but dragons themselves did not like to get wet. Still, there were times that it was worth it, and chasing siryns into the sea seemed as worthy a cause as any. She held herself still, though, once she'd dropped in: she wasn't a strong swimmer, and most fish scattered if chased. Siryns might do the same. "Wait," she said, more softly, doubting they could hear her. "Come back."

The sun fell past the horizon before they did, and with clouds blocking starlight, it was only her Old blood that let her see them return at all. One surfaced and sank again with a chitter of undersea noise that reminded Kate of Ursula's blind-sight clicking. Another rose and dove, speaking again: their conversation bounced off Kate's skin, tickling her. Then at once all of them rose: five women whose slick hair lay against almost-earless heads. Their eyes were large and black above high cheekbones and small chins, making them more elfin than human, save for the ears.

One shimmied closer, her approach reminding Kate of dolphins tail-walking. Up close she was bigger than Kate had expected: half again Kate's height, with broad shoulders that put a large body into proportion. She stayed far enough away to remain in deeper water, surging up and down with idle flicks of her tail; when she rose, Kate saw the sleek but not slender lines of her torso, and strong arms whose power was in no way compromised by the layer of insulating fat that packed them. She looked as though she could effortlessly tear a human into pieces, and Kate knew a moment's gratitude that *she* wasn't human.

The siryn spoke suddenly, a cadence of words so unfamiliar and well known all at once that Kate laughed in surprise. "What?"

Offense flew across the siryn's face. She breached, diving backward into the water and soaking Kate with a flick of her massive tail. The others all dived as well, slapping the water with their tails in rejection. Kate, alarmed, called, "Wait!" and then, shaping her tongue to an older way of speaking, repeated the word one more time.

The siryn surfaced again, hesitantly. Kate had gotten a glimpse of her whole body with that breach, and had been wrong: she was *twice* Kate's own size, with flukes like a dolphin's. If she and her pod wanted to be away from Kate, Kate would never catch them in the water, or risk flying low enough to track them in dragon form. Kate spoke hastily, tripping over her words. "My accent is bad. I'm sorry. I haven't spoken this language since I was a child."

Four hundred years: it had been four centuries since the siryns were seen regularly, and two hundred years since the last ones had been seen at all. Their knowledge of human language was archaic, and Kate hadn't begun to learn other tongues than English until she was nearly a hundred years old herself. They were lucky they could communicate at all: she certainly couldn't emulate the clicks and whistles she'd just heard echoing under the water, and much to her father's disgust, she had only the barest grasp of the dragon tongue. "My name is Katherine, and my father is Janx."

One by one the other siryns came to the surface again, whistling at each other. One swam closer to Kate, then rolled, a shiver rippling down her body as she did.

Bioluminescence bloomed from her temples to her tail in orange and blue spirals that lit the water around her. Kate gasped and clapped one hand to her mouth, gazing at her in astonishment. "Thou'rt lovely, lady."

The siryn who had first spoken gave the glowing one a look of exasperation that transcended species, but the single phrase of admiration Kate had uttered encouraged the others to spin and bring their own light to the darkness as well. The leader was the last to concede, and her colors glowed more deeply than the others', as if she could express disapproval through light as well as sound. Kate, still speaking through her fingers, whispered, "They ne'er told tales of this, my ladies. What a crime, that thy secrets should go untold."

"Nought else keeps us alive, save that they go untold. I am Mymyrat, and your sire is known to us. How came you by that lyre?"

"It was in his hoard. I—"

"How canst thou *play* it?"

Kate glanced at the instrument, tucked safe against her chest. In the siryns' luminescence it had depth of color unlike anything she'd imagined: it *was* a thing of magic, awakening to not just her half blood, but the very presence of the people it had come from. "My mother is human."

"So was mine," Mymyrat spat. "It does not lend me the power to call songs from those wires."

"Really?" Kate looked up, eyebrows drawn down in surprise. "Your mother? I thought siryns were like the harpies, mostly women...."

Exasperation slid across Mymyrat's face again as one of the others laughed. "Mine father, then, if you must have the truth, but—" She stopped herself, and Kate fought down a laugh.

"But that lacked dramatic impact? Sorry." Laughter won after all, or at least, a smile did: she smiled at the siryn with sudden deep affection. "Accept my apologies, I prithee. I would have spoken as you did, for the impact, mine own self." More quietly, she said, "Can none of you play it, then?"

"We tried. All of us who were left, tried, in hopes that we might crown a new queen and survive another long night beneath the ocean's waves, but the lyre is as silent for us as it left Ninanak. Why you, a child of flame and sky and man, should be able to bring forth its voice—"

"Mayhap that's why. All the things you are, I am the opposite, save for the blood of man."

"And that is wild," said the siryn who had laughed. Her voice was light and sweet, a soprano's in comparison to Mymyrat's deep alto. She spoke again when Kate looked her way. "The blood of man is wild. It frees us, but only for a price. Mayhap thou canst as well."

"Free you? For a *price*? I wouldn't. Not for a price," Kate amended as Mymyrat's face darkened. "If I could, I would. Of course I would. There aren't that ma—" A memory of her sister came to her, all at once: Ursula's anger at learning about Daisani's betrayal of the vampires. Ursula's determination to right that wrong had been clear. She hadn't said so, but Kate had known where she was going, when she left the wreckage in New York. There were so few of the Old Races left: to condemn any of them, even wisely, to eternity, went against Ursula's soul. Kate—whose own people had not been betrayed—had not been certain her sister was in the right. And yet to see herself now, standing before a handful of siryns and about to make promises to them, it seemed that in her core, she agreed with Ursula after all.

Their world had been simpler before The Negotiator had entered it, Kate thought ruefully, and finished the promise she had begun: "If I can help somehow, I will. There aren't that many of the Old Races left to begin with. I wouldn't stand by and let you come to harm— or even simply waste away—if I can stop that from happening." She had fallen entirely out of the Elizabethan cadences and word choices by the end of her speech, but the phrasing of that era was, in the end, close enough to modern: after casting glances between themselves, the siryns nodded their understanding. More, their luminescence brightened, unquestionably reacting to their emotions. Mymyrat's remained the darkest, the most tamped-down, as if she was the least willing to commit to hope. She was old, Kate thought: old enough to remember

Ninanak as a living queen, and bound by the caution of experience.

"Come with us. We will bring you where you must go, to be of use to us."

"Come *with* you? Are you nuts?" Kate trusted her sentiment, if not her words, were clear enough, but reached for how she might have said them as a child. "Art thou mad? I am, as you said, a creature of air and fire. I will not go into the sea. I cannot!"

Mymyrat squealed with enough force that Kate flinched back, struggling to cover her ears without dropping the lyre. The sound lodged itself in her bones, rattling her, and the series of furious clicks that followed left Kate's chest feeling bruised and airless. She had thought the siryn could tear a human apart, but they wouldn't have to resort to physical attacks. Their voices could kill men.

Which was just as the legends had always said. Kate gave a shuddering laugh and crawled painfully from the hip-deep water that she'd stood in. "Were I human, thou wouldst have rendered me senseless and of no use to thee at all. Mind thy voice, Mymyrat, and tell me whence I am required, and why."

Anger creased the siryn's alien features, and it was the soprano who finally responded. "The island men call Crete, there to return our voices, lady dragon. Play the lyre on the southern shore, and those who can will come to thee."

#

Those who could were *waiting* for her. Dozens of them, diving and surfacing again, watching a dimple in the southern shore in anticipation. Kate saw them as shadows in the water from the cliffs above. Sailors had been told for centuries now that they were seeing dolphins or manatees in the water, not women who were also half fish, but seeing them now, there could be no mistaking their forms for other than what they were. Even from dozens of feet above them, they were clearly female, and clearly—well, not fish; they were mammalian, but they were no more manatees than Janx was.

Kate, imagining her father's expression at being likened to one of the mellow warm-water beasties, grinned, then leapt lightly from the cliff to the rocks below. She landed easily and spat as salt water, kicking against rough rock, sprayed her. It was no cove there, no quiet safe harbor; if it had been, neither she nor the siryns would have dared to meet there. Humans could scale the cliff, or dive from it, if they were enthusiast enough, but there were innumerable easier and more pleasant places to explore. Bits of sand and smooth stone were occasionally revealed by the shifting waves. Kate took the highest of them and sat down cross-legged, holding the lyre in her lap. It, she suspected, would be less offended at getting wet than she was.

The first notes sang true and called the siryns to the surface. Kate glanced skyward at the afternoon sun, and for the first time thought she should have waited until nightfall: human surveillance was ubiquitous now, with their satellites and drones. Too late now, but the Old Races would need a magic to hide them from that kind of observation, if they were to survive long enough to merge with the modern world. "Mymyrat asked me to come," she said, then wondered if she ought to speak Greek, and a Greek of four hundred years ago besides. But she no more had the skill for that than she did for swimming, so she shrugged and hoped the music might say it for her.

Besides, they'd known she was coming: perhaps Mymyrat had somehow sent word ahead. Whales could send songs all over the world. Siryns no doubt could as well, if there were enough of them. So she looked for a song of greeting in the lyre, and found one. A rush of sorrow-filled joy rippled through the gathered mermaids, and for the length of the piece none of them moved. Then two came forward and left the water, shedding their Old forms for human ones.

They were still tall, as humans, and retained the powerful builds of born swimmers: broad shoulders, tapered hips, strong thighs. One worked her mouth as if becoming accustomed to it, which she probably was: humans had simple flat teeth, compared to the more dolphin-like sharp teeth the siryns had. "I am Kekeal. I haven't worn this form in some eighty thousand tides," she said carefully. "Forgive me if I am...awkward with it."

Eighty thousand tides. Kate glanced skyward again, this time at a moon she couldn't see. Eighty thousand tides, at two a day, was close to sixty years. The human world had changed considerably since Kekeal had gone into it, but not so much as it had since Mymyrat had been part of it. She looked back at Kekeal, who waited for her response with untested patience. "You'll be fine. My name is Kate, and Myrmyrat sent me. I have Ninanak's lyre from the dragon Janx's hoard, and...I'm meant to play it for you."

At the queen's name, Kekeal glanced at the other siryn who had emerged with her. She was smaller than Kekeal by the length of a hand or more, though she still stood inches taller than Kate, and her hair, drying swiftly in the sunlight, turned the color of amber. Kekeal's was darker, though still in the same hue; together with Kate's own red hair, they ranged from embers to flame. "You are Janx's daughter?" Kekeal asked. "The half-blood? This is how you can play the lyre?"

"It is not enough," the other siryn said before Kate could do more than nod. "Blood tells all. She must be of *his* blood, or the lyre would not speak to her."

"His—*Orpheus*'s?" Kate grimaced at the second siryn's nod. "If he had children, I suppose I could be. It's too far back to track, but something like every other human male is descended from Genghis Khan, and that's only a thousand years ago. Granted, Khan *did* put an unusual amount of effort into trying to impregna—" She broke off at the siryns' uncomprehending and uncaring expressions, and returned to what matterd to them: "You're certain Orpheus had children?"

"We are."

"Then he could be one of my forefathers. But if it takes his bloodline and an Old bloodline to play the lyre, why didn't you—"

"It was not enough. *They* had children, Ninanak and the betrayer, but not one of those children could play the lyre either. So it went into Janx's hands, for safe-keeping. And now all these centuries later, it is *his* child who can play it?" Suppressed rage glittered in the other siryn's eyes, and Kate again thought that if she was human, she would be wise to fear these creatures.

But she was not human, and she had come halfway around the world on a moment's notice to offer her help. No more than any other being did she care to be met with fury for such a gesture. She lacked Janx's age and size: she could not bring the strength of her presence into the mortal world with such authority as he had. But she was still dragon, and four centuries in age:

she surrounded herself with that, and felt its weight suddenly change the air around them. Half a breath more and she would change, but she didn't need to change. She only needed to remind this raging sea-creature that she, too, was to be reckoned with, and if there was a taste of flame in her next words, so be it. "Aye, it is the dragon's child who can play it, and if the blood says it must be so, then it is the bard's grandchild, too, and if I have the strength to play it, sea-dweller, then perhaps I have the strength to destroy it, too."

Her hands were not—not *quite*—clawed as she clenched them around the lyre, but her dragon strength was in them, and the enchanted wood creaked within them. It had survived centuries; the whim of a dragon should not take it from the world, but neither should the help of a dragon be lightly cast aside.

"*No!*" Kekeal thrust a hand out, not quite catching Kate's arm, though the wish to do so was clear. "No, please, do not. Forgive Inhihine; she feels the inability to play that lyre more deeply than any of us, and it hurts her to see that someone else can fulfill the destiny she could not."

"That she couldn't?" Kate's hands slowly relaxed around the lyre, releasing the strain in its ancient fibers as she gazed at Inhihine. "You're their daughter. Orpheus and Ninanak. You're the child who couldn't play the instrument that stole her voice."

Inhihine turned her face away, answer enough. Kate put the lyre down, not entirely trusting herself with it at the moment, and spoke again when she had gathered herself. "Then you are their hope, aren't you. If I can release the songs back to you, the siryns can breed again. Without you — without me — there is no hope for your people." She breathed a laugh. "Cousin."

"I am the last of their children," Inhihine whispered. "Two sisters and a brother, all long dead of despair. I cannot allow myself to die and take the last hope from my people, but neither is this living, dragon's daughter. *Cousin,*" she echoed, but the word had poison in it. "Will you play for me? For all of us?"

Kate sank back to the stones, drawing the lyre into her lap once more, and when she answered, it was a whisper, too: "Of course I will."

A song waited in the lyre: a song of comfort and gentleness. A lullaby, the sort a mother might once have sung for her daughter. Inhihine wept; Kate knew that without looking, and still played without surcease. From lullaby to lament, the music grew, and from time to time Kate opened her eyes to look at the strings in surprise: still only an octave, but they carried richness and depth beyond their ken. Different voices were plucked from the wires, until the siryns in the sea answered with their own music, sometimes broken and uncertain, other times strong and proud.

They were none of them human, and a spell had been cast long ago: the need for sleep fell away in the face of those truths, and Kate played on through sunset and moonrise, through the dark of night and the rising dawn. No mortal came to disturb them, and the music went on, every song the lyre had ever known, the voice of Ninanak, the siryn queen, released into ever-changing days. Clouds gathered and rain fell, then cleared away again; it had taken untold hours to create the lyre and pour Ninanak's music into it; to unwind that magic took at least as long again.

She didn't know it was the last song the lyre held, not until the thing turned to dust under her fingertips. Her hands fell together in a useless clutch, trying to catch the fragments whisking away on the wind before she lifted her gaze in weary, sharp hope to meet Inhihine's eyes. Ninanak's heir met her gaze for a moment, then turned swiftly to her people and opened her mouth to sing.

The sound that emerged was pure: sweet and true and without flaw, and — Kate knew it from the first note — not the stuff of the lyre.

Inhihine knew it too. Within a few measures she faltered, and fell to her knees with a cry of despair. Kate grasped again at the particles of dust, already long-since torn away by the wind, then let her hands drop as she looked helplessly from Inhihine to Kekeal, and finally to the gathering of siryns who had waited so long and so patiently. One by one they sank beneath the water, but not to disappear: strains of music, like whale song given half-human voice, began to shift through the changing waves. Harmonies grew, expanded and fell into discord before finding their way again, and the song they sang was the first that had come to Kate's fingertips when she'd played the lyre on Janx's lonely island. It had been nameless then, that piece, but now she knew it for what it was: an elegy for a lost queen and the end of hope. Tears did not come easily to dragons: they were water, and anathema to the fire, but Kate wept into her hands as she listened to the last song of a people. She wept that a man had betrayed them so many centuries ago, and for the twisting of stories that had made Ninanak's truth into a myth, and most of all, that she herself had failed them, here at the end of the tale. There was a humming at the base of her skull, a buzz of building regret, and she spoke to shake it off, even though they had not yet finished singing. "What will you do?"

"Dive too deep to breathe, perhaps." Inhihine broke off to respond listlessly, all the strength of her song washing away in the spoken word. "All of us together, at once, and in the toothed whales' hunting grounds, so our bodies might offer sustenance back to the sea.

Better that than to rise bloated and be found by men. You play well. Will you take our story to the gargoyles, and sing it for them so our memories are not lost even to the Old Races?"

"I don't play that well. Not without the lyre." Kate clenched her teeth, swallowing against the ringing in her ears. Even other immortals weren't meant to stand at the heart of a siryn lament. It shook the stones under her feet, too, endless vibrations sung by inhuman voices. "But yes. Of course I will. I'll give them everything I can remember of your songs, and I'll make sure Ninanak's story is remembered. Inhihine, cousin, I'm sorry, but I don't think I can stay any longer. I'd like to hear the end of your song, but..." She touched her nose, which tickled, and came away with a streak of blood.

Inhihine lost her listless tone. "Your ears— and that is not—"

Kate swiped, then scrubbed, at her ear, caught between alarm and astonishment as her fingers turned red as Janx's scales. "It's not what?"

"It's not our song!"

The cliff wall behind them dissolved into fragmented stone. Sound burst forth, such sound as to knock Kate from her feet. She knew an instant's disbelief: *nothing* could un-foot a dragon; even a gargoyle at full strength could no more move a mountain. Beneath disbelief, instinct warred with caution: they had gone undisturbed for days, but surveillance still rode the skies, and a dragon's transformation was vastly larger than a gathering of siryns. The sea reached up to claim her before she had decided, and a thrill of genuine fear turned her guts to ice.

She landed, astonishingly, in the unfaltering hands of siryns. Dozens of them, all breaking off their song to leap upward and catch her above the waves, and to catch a dragon's mass, even in mortal form, was no small thing. Kate gasped, almost laughing, then did laugh as she was cast forward again, returned to the rocks she'd been thrown from.

A woman stood there now. Another woman, slighter than Inhihine or Kekeal, both of whom were also dragging themselves from the sea. She was still more than Kate's height, and her hair, cropped short around large dark eyes, gave her a sense of fragility that was undone by the echoing strains of power she had unleashed. Her lips were still parted, though she no longer sang: the ache in Kate's ears faded, though blood still itched them. She examined Kate briefly and as quickly dismissed her, seeking out the siryns instead.

They were coming from the water now, not just Inhihine and Kekeal, but all of them. Kate stepped back, and back again, edging between siryns until she'd half-climbed what remained of the cliff wall, far out of the way as a new song began. They crooned this time, soft incredulous joy that lifted the hairs on Kate's arms without driving pain into her marrow. Dragons might not cry: siryns did, with tears so salty Kate could taste them on the air. It was theirs, and not her own: that would be the story she told, when she bore witness.

Crete, entrance to the Underworld. Where else would the King of Hell reside but in the sacred caverns there; where else would he draw his circle of blood and imprison the siryn queen; where else would she wait, but near to where her people had once thrived in the plentiful seas, in hopes of her voice someday returning to her. She sang now, murmurs of healing music that washed over the women crowding her, and Kate could hear the lyre in her voice.

She would ask, soon. She would wonder what a dragon's child was doing at the heart of her restoration. The question would take her from her people, even if only for a little while, and that — that was a thing that did not need to be done. Not now; not when they had always in front of them, awaiting discovery.

Quickly, quietly, while the joy of reunion captured them all, Kate climbed the ruined cliff wall and swung over its lip, then took a moment to glance back down at the gathering below. Colorful heads, all bowed together, bodies pressed close in a multi-hued bloom against the rocks. A song that sobbed with joy, in time to the surf rushing over the stones, and the sunset casting gold across it all.

This. This was such a jewel in a dragon's hoard as could not be equaled. Kate tucked that gem into her heart, cast a glance toward the setting sun, and smiled. There was new hope in the world, new magic waiting to be born. Humans were going to have to get used to it.

A moment later, a dragon winged its way west, into the sunset, into the world.

CHOICES

WHAT GOT COLE WAS THE RAPTURE in Cameron's eyes when she learned about them. It hadn't been a *smart* reaction, nobody would think it was smart. Not even Cam, if she had to admit it, but mostly she wouldn't. Mostly it was just this unabrogated *joy*, this wide-eyed wonder at discovering the world had been hiding something huge under their noses all along. Gargoyles, for crying out loud. Vampires. Eliseo freaking Daisani, the biggest mogul in New York, was a *vampire*. And it got worse, because according to homicide detective Tony Pulcella, it wasn't just Daisani. Janx, the underworld kingpin, he was a dragon, and when Margrit was pressed about it she said something about an old rivalry between the two of them. Between Janx and Daisani, not Tony, though apparently Tony was in it up to his eyeballs too. Margrit had made some kind of bad trade with Janx for Tony's life, or that was what Cole had surmised, anyway. It wasn't that he hadn't listened when they'd sat down in the aftermath to talk about it all. It was that the rest of them, Cam, Margrit, even Tony, were in love with the *idea* of the Old Races, even after the Old Races had been trying to kill them.

Cole smashed twelve pounds of dough with his fists, then put floury hands on the edge of the counter and lowered his head with a sigh. There were good sides and bad sides to being a pastry chef—the early mornings sucked, but having afternoons off was a plus—but one of the definite up sides was taking aggression out on unsuspecting bread dough. Mostly he used the giant mixers, to save his wrists and shoulders, but some mornings having something to hit was the only way to get through the day.

The problem was knowing. He couldn't *un*know it, he couldn't erase the memory of Alban's transformation from a big man into a massive gargoyle, he couldn't forget how Margrit had staggered home at dawn a week earlier, covered with greasy smoke residue and with a fiery light in her eyes. He couldn't go back to how things had been three months earlier, before any of them knew about the Old Races.

And that was why Margrit, last night, had looked both hopeful and apologetic when she sat down across from him in their apartment and had said, "I have a job lined up for you," in a more cautious voice than usual.

He'd been watching the news. He'd glanced at Margrit, then sat up in the couch and turned the TV off while giving her a fish-eye. "And why is it you think I'm not going to like it?"

"Because it's for Kaimana Kaaiai."

Cole collapsed back into the sofa, eyes closed. Kaimana Kaaiai, leader of the disproportionately large selkie contingent of the Old Races. If he hadn't been an *alien*, Cole would probably like him: big dude, mellow, concerned for his people. Rich, too, rich enough to buy out Eliseo Daisani's empire when Margrit yanked the building blocks out from under it. "Yeah, you're right, I don't like it. Grit, look, it's your life, you got that through to me, but I don't want—"

"He's offering three times your normal rates."

Cole's eyes popped open and he sat up like a marionette, like somebody else was manipulating his strings. "Three *times? Why?*"

Margrit sank into the easy chair, plucking at its threadbare arms. "Because they're celebrating their victory, and they want to be able to be themselves. It's a very private party."

"You mean there's going to be a big water slide and people are going to dump the formal wear for seal skins and go swimming? What am I supposed to provide for catering, a truckload of raw fish?"

"A water feature, anyway. Probably a water *slide* would be for otters, not seals. I don't know."

"Please don't tell me there are otter Old Races."

"There used to be otter ones," Margrit said brightly. "Yeti and siryns and sea ser—" It took about that long for Cole to realize she was making a play on *other*, rather than telling him there had been otter Old Races. He scowled and her false brightness faded. "I wish they didn't bug you so much, Cole. They're not our enemies."

"*They killed you.*"

Margrit put a hand to her throat, swallowing convulsively. "They saved me, too."

"Eliseo goddamned Daisani did not give you healing blood to save you from getting your throat cut. He did it on a whim, and the fact that it later saved your life is pure coincidence. The djinn didn't cut your throat accidentally, Margrit. You were murdered."

"I got better." Margrit shifted her shoulders uncomfortably, then sighed. "Look, Cole, obviously you don't have to say yes. But you already know about them, so I told Kaimana I'd ask. They don't often get a chance to ask outsiders for something and still be themselves."

"Are you trying to guilt trip me into cooking for them? Because it's not—"

"No." Margrit blinked, then leaned out of her slump, elbows on her knees and hands spread wide in supplication. Good lawyer body language, Cole figured: it was supposed to make her seem open and reliable, somebody he would want to join forces with. He'd known her way too long for it to work on that level, but he'd also known her long enough to recognize that she wasn't playing him: she'd unconsciously incorporated that kind of body language years ago. So he could be pretty sure she meant it when she said, "No," again. "No, I'm just stating the facts, Cole. From Kaimana's point of view it would be a huge advantage to have you cater for their party, even if you don't like them, and he's willing to pay for it. He'll hire somebody else if you don't want to do it, but I said I'd at least ask."

Cole got up, impatient for action while they talked. Cooking was most soothing, but there were dishes to do, which was good enough. Margrit followed him into the kitchen, picking up a dishtowel to dry plates as he handed them to her. "They're dangerous, Grit."

"Anybody can be dangerous. We've had this discussion before, Cole. I'm part of their world now, way deeper than I ever thought I'd be. I not only won't turn away, but realistically I can't."

"And you want me to get more involved."

"It's one party."

He gave her a look that she accepted with a twist of her mouth and a downward glance. "Yeah, all right, it's hardly ever just one anything with the Old Races. So I'll tell him no?"

Cole sighed. "Tell him yes."

"*Really?*" Margrit clapped her hands together, then fumbled the plate and towel she'd been holding, finally catching them with a laugh. "Really, Cole?"

"Three times my usual rate will get me a little more than halfway to the start-up capital I need to start my own place, so yeah. Really. And then practice balancing plates, because I'm going to need staff and you, Tony and Cam are my Old-Races-savvy short list."

Because they couldn't un-know any of it either, but the memory of Margrit's delight last night had made it clear, as always, that she didn't *want* to forget that the Old Races existed. And the truth was that once anybody knew, the Old Races became an indelible part of their lives. Cole punched the bread dough again, then broke it into loaves, rolling, tucking, shaping it into artisan circles. This was the bread and butter, almost literally, of the Fifth Street Bakery, but they made increasingly elegant goodies as well, from cookies up through extravagant wedding cakes that had been featured on *Best Of* and competition baking shows. The bakery had an associated restaurant that catered to enormous events, so there was almost always something new to do, no time to get bored. Cole worked with five other bakers, each of them changing stations every day of the week so they could keep up to speed on every element of the bakery's offerings. Beating down bread was satisfying, but it was the more delicate creations of extraordinary pastries that Cole loved. At a restaurant of his own, bread could be left to the bakers' assistants and second-tier pastry chefs. The most dramatic pieces would be ones he created.

A dessert and coffee house in the theatre district, that was the goal. Not on Broadway: too expensive and too much competition. Probably out in Trenton, where Cam's family was from, and where neither real estate nor coffee houses were at quite the premium of New York. It was still an expensive proposition, and saving for the start-up costs while paying off student loans had been slow going. That was the only reason to take the Kaaiai job. Cole tucked the last of the dough leaves that topped the bread, marking them as the bakery's house loaves, and set them aside for the second rise. Later he would slide them into ovens so enormous they were easily mistaken for walls, but for the moment he had quick breads to mix up, then a break that would re-mind him that even the city's sweltering summer mornings were a breath of fresh air compared to the heat-wave-ridden kitchens.

Half an hour later a text message rattled the phone in his pocket. He didn't need to check it: Cam always texted to say she was stopping by, on mornings when her schedule let her. He came out, floury, red-faced and sweating, and couldn't help laughing as Cam jogged up the block, her blonde braid bouncing around her shoulders. She'd been at work for two hours and had just run ten long blocks from the gym, but her cheeks were barely flushed and she'd hardly broken a sweat. At 6am, there were enough people on the street for Cole to catch envying or appreciative glances Cameron's way, and a grin burst out of him. She was two inches taller than he was and an Amazon god-dess to his Pillsbury Dough Boy, though with a personal trainer for a fiancée he wasn't all that soft. She swooped in for a kiss, trying not to get flour on her workout clothes, but he grabbed her and spun her in a laughing circle.

She staggered when he put her down, and brushed flour off her shirt. "You look like my last client. He was the same color you are right now." She gave him a quick critical look that had no malice in it at all, then smiled. "Except you're in much better shape than he is. This one's a new guy, maybe forty pounds overweight, and coming in fast on his fortieth birthday. Running marathons is the new Ferrari, you know. Are you really going to cater for a selkie party?"

Cole lifted his eyebrows. "I guess you talked to Margrit this morning."

"You know how she's up all night anymore. It's weird." Cam gave a cheerful shiver. "Sometimes I wish it'd been me who got to drink vampire blood and the rest of the time I'm glad it's not. Anyway, yeah, she said we had to break out our tuxedos because you figured we'd be your catering staff. You remember what happened last time you handed me a bottle of wine, right?"

"I've never seen anyone break a bottle that completely," Cole admitted. "I still don't know how you did it. People have harder times shattering bottles on ship prows than you did on, I don't even know what."

"It was the *table*," Cam insisted, which she'd been doing all along. "I don't know, I just turned around and it was *there* and it *broke*—"

"—at about a thousand miles an hour, all

over the white shag carpet—"

"Well, I *told* you not to give it to me! And you think *I* should be helping cater a posh party?"

"Who else am I going to hire?" Cole slumped against the bakery wall, the energy that had a-wakened with Cameron's arrival draining away. "Grit says they want me in the first place so they can let their hair down, so they sure don't want a bunch of random catering staff cluttering up the place and harshing their groove."

Cameron pushed her mouth into duck lips. "I kind of think of them as people who harsh other peoples' grooves, not people who get their grooves harshed. Although I guess Kaimana is kind of mellow, so maybe he can be harshed. If I spill on anybody I'm going to tell them to take it up with the management." She put a finger against the middle of Cole's chest. "That's you, in case you were wondering."

"Yeah? I got an upgrade, huh?"

"Only for catering jobs. Otherwise I'm still the boss of you. No," Cam added in the same breath, "not really. Not up for bosses and underlings here. Partnerships. Otherwise, blick."

"Blick," Cole echoed. "That's your summary of an unequal relationship?"

"If you want a wordsmith you should be marrying a writer, not a physical therapist. One will write you a beautiful eulogy, the other will keep you in shape so you don't need the eulogy for a really long time. Take your pick."

"I choose you, Pika—"

Cameron put her fingers over his mouth and made her eyes very large. "Don't even. Because then I'm going to get to pick a Poké-mon for you, and you don't want me to do that. I've spent way too many hours with the TV show blaring in my ear at the gym and I know them *all*."

Cole wrapped his hand around her fingers and kissed her knuckles. "Okay. Not going there. I'll never understand why you have cartoons on at the gym, but—"

"They're more invigorating than the news or reality shows. Cartoons and sitcoms engage people and we want them engaged. Anyway, this catering thing, Cole. Are you sure about it?"

"And this is why I love you. This and your amazing legs." He pulled Cameron close again and she didn't object, though he knew he was getting flour all over her clothes. "It's a lot of money. And really, it's a catering job. What can go wrong besides the kitchen catching on fire and the guests being allergic to shellfish? But no, I'm not sure. I don't want any part of them, Cam."

Cam, muffled, asked, "So why'd you say yes?" into his shoulder, and Cole blew a hot breath over her shoulder in turn.

"Because Margrit's crazy for Alban, and she's one of our best friends. I've either gotta suck it up or never see her again, so I'm trying to suck it up. So this is kind of a peace offering, I guess."

"And this is why *I* love *you*. Are you sure you don't have to turn in your man card for displaying this level of sensitivity?" Cam leaned out of his arms to see his expression, which went dry enough to make her smile.

"I make up for it by being a lead baker. Chefing is all about the hierarchy and alpha dog thing."

"Silly me, I thought it was all about the food." Cameron scooted a few inches away to bend double, stretching her hamstrings by putting her palms against the sidewalk. "When's the party?"

Cole tipped his head, admiring the view. Cam gave him a wink that said she knew he was, but also rolled her hand, asking for a response. "Next Friday. Ten days, not three days. Are you working?"

"Nah, it's summertime, so my Friday clients are all canceling or moving their sessions back a few hours. Nobody wants to meet with a PT when they could be out showing off the body they've worked so hard to achieve." She wiggled her hips, emphasizing the body she'd worked hard to achieve, then craned her neck to look up at him. "Are you going to get Alban to help cater?"

"I'm trying really hard to figure out a way not to, but there's gonna be like two hundred people at this thing, maybe more. I'm going to have to hire every non-selkie Old Race...person...we know. What's that other gargoyle's name?"

"Biali?" Cameron straightened with a laugh and turned to plant her hands against the wall, leaning to stretch her calves as well. "I don't think he'd agree. Margrit says he's a grump."

"Too bad she chased Eliseo Daisani out of town. He's fast, right? I'd only need one waiter if they were fast."

"Can you really imagine *Eliseo Daisani* waiting tables?" Cam stopped stretching to make helpless gestures, somehow encompassing Daisani's small size and deadly charm with them. "It'd be like asking…"

"Eliseo Daisani to wait tables," Cole finished dryly.

Cameron laughed and nodded, then stood bolt upright. "Oh! Oh, but know who could help? Margrit's Mom and Dad. Her Mom, anyway. And Grace!"

"You want me to invite Margrit's *mother* to come sling booze for selkies?" It was Cole's turn to make useless hand motions, trying to describe Rebecca Knight's slender elegance and cool reserve without words. "That's almost as bizarre as asking Mr. Daisani. And Grace, Grace is like a superhero, Cam, she doesn't do normal stuff. She lurks."

"See, now I totally want her to come lurk at Kaimana. C'mon, who else are you going to get? I'll go with Margrit and we'll ask her mom and Grace and maybe she'll ask Biali. They had some big moment together when all this stuff went bad, so maybe he'll say yes."

Cole closed his eyes and lifted his eyebrows, knowing he hardly wanted to know: "She had a moment with *another* gargoyle? Why do I not know this? Why do *you* know it? And what happened?"

"I don't even know as much as I want to," Cam said with a degree of petulance. "She gets all coy about things, like we don't already know they exist. But she went to the mat for him on something—"

"That's why she's being coy," Cole said, more to the street than Cameron. "Look how thrilled she was with the Luka Johnson case, but she talked about it like it was everybody else's effort, not hers, that got Johnson's clemency granted. If she helped Biali out with something you're never going to get the details from her."

Cam exhaled a raspberry. "Yeah, I guess so. Still, I want to know. Maybe Alban knows. Anyway, so even if he's a grump they're bros, or something. She can ask him, at least. Is six people enough to cater?"

"Not even close, but it'll have to do."

Cam leaned in to kiss his cheek. "I'll make it happen."

Poor Cole looked like he'd rather suck lemons than agree to her making it happen, but since he was at work and she had three hours until her next training session, Cameron bounced off down the street with a wave and a grin, then dialed Margrit and snorted when her voice mail picked up. "C'mon, it's seven thirty, I know even your workaholic self isn't at work yet, and you can't pretend you're sleeping, either, Ms 3-Hours-A-Night-Chick. Look, give me a call, will you? I want to go talk to Grace but I don't know how to find her. It's for Kaimana's party, so you have to help. I'm, oh hey, I know, maybe the speakeasy. I'm going to the speakeasy, I'll see you there, huh? Hurry up, I've got a client at ten." She ran down a set of subway stairs as she hung up, catching the next train downtown, and nearly had a heart attack when Margrit stepped in front of her at the top of the stairs going back up. "Holy crap, I didn't think you'd be that fast!"

"I was out for a run. I just changed directions to meet you here. Hi." Margrit flashed a bright smile, then gestured at Cam's workout clothes. "You want to run down there, or should we meander?"

"Run. I've only done six miles."

"'Only.'" But Cameron smiled and chased Margrit through the streets, aware that Grit, who was much shorter, could have outrun her six days of the week even before she got a metabolic boost from Eliseo Daisani's blood, and was now holding back so she didn't leave Cam in her dust. It only upped the challenge as far as Cam was concerned, and she was hot on Margrit's heels as they finally skidded down another set of subway stairs and burst through a small crowd of tourists who were gathering to see the speakeasy. Cam tipped her wrist up, checking her watch, then turned to Margrit and made a face. "We're way early. It's only ten after eight and it doesn't even open until nine. I didn't know that. "

"I don't think it's going to be a problem." Margrit nodded at the speakeasy doors, which were propped open and revealed a sliver of the space within.

Italian marble floors gleamed with art deco black and gold squares, half-hidden by thick, richly colored rugs that didn't look like they'd ever been crushed beneath the weight of bodies. Armchairs and chaise lounges had left their impressions on the rugs: Cameron had seen that in the brief time the speakeasy had been in disarray while all the items were cataloged and examined. A chess game that had sat unfinished for nearly a century still remained with its last plays set up, the pieces given a soft colorful glow from the abstract stained glass windows that had been set into the curved walls. There were lights behind those glasses, illuminating what sunlight couldn't, this deep underground. Even with only being able to see a fraction of the windows, Cam got a shiver. She was one of very few people who had seen them as they were meant to be: overlaid, so that their abstract colors built an actual image. Five Old Races were represented there, the five remaining magical people in a world that had long since dismissed magic as real. Dragons and djinn, vampires, selkies, and gargoyles. Cameron shivered again, then blinked as a woman came into view within the speakeasy, stepping over the heavy red velvet ropes that had been erected to keep tourists off the rugs and furniture.

She was nearly as tall as Cameron, though curvier and far more dramatically dressed: even in the heat of summer she wore leather. Black leather, even. Leather pants, a leather coat, heavy-duty boots and Cameron was pretty certain the 'shirt' beneath Grace's coat was a corset, though not a tight-laced one. Just enough to give her some extra va-va-voom shape, not that Cam thought she needed much help in that department. And Cameron, who was naturally blonde even as an adult, couldn't hold a candle to Grace's white-blonde hair, which she wore in a close-cropped pixie cut. The effect was striking, making her so pale that she could be a ghost.

Except ghosts didn't seem like they'd be inclined to stand leading with the hips, or to glower suspiciously at chess boards set up in an eternally paused game. She looked away from the board as Margrit called her name, then sauntered to the door as Margrit and Cam approached the guard who stood at the door. "They're with me, love, let 'em in."

The guard looked between the three women and sighed. "Ms. O'Malley, I know you found this place and you're supposed to have the run of it for coming in and out, but the Mayor didn't say anything about bringing friends in too."

"These aren't friends, this is Margrit bleeding Knight." Grace waited a breath, expecting the guard to recognize Margrit's name, then looked exasperated. "All right, then, call the Mayor, if you want."

The guard, looking put-upon, waved Margrit and Cameron past. Grace, satisfied, patted his cheek and minced away, her booted footsteps so light they couldn't be heard on the tiled floors. She stepped over one of the velvet rope barriers and gestured Cameron and Margrit to join her in one of the plush speakeasy chairs. Cam cast a guilty look at the guard, who looked even more put-upon, then shuffled outside and closed the door behind him.

Margrit's eyebrows shot up as she joined Grace. "How'd you manage *that*? This is a public facility now, ever since you took it away from Vanessa."

Grace smiled. "I tell the lads here that the Mayor's given me dispensation. None of 'em dares to call the private number I give 'em to verify it, so I get what I want."

"Would it actually go through to the Mayor?"

"That's for Grace to know. What's this about, Knight?"

Cameron stepped over the barriers, still feeling guilty, and couldn't quite make herself sit in one of the antique chairs. "It's actually me who wanted to talk to you. Cole sort of needs your help."

"Cole. The pretty one with the bad attitude?" Grace's smile turned bright and wicked as offense altered Cameron's expression. "He has, though. Neck deep in Old Races and hating it all. What's he want with the likes of Grace O'Malley?"

"He's catering a selkie party," Cameron blurted. "We need your help as, um, waitstaff."

Grace's pale eyebrows rose and she looked at Margrit. "You called me downtown for this?"

"I didn't know what she wanted!"

"Oh, come on." Cam sat down abruptly after all, right on the edge of an over-stuffed seat. "Please? We can pay you and everything—"

"Grace doesn't need cash, love." The vigilante pursed her lips. "Well, no, that's not true, but never mind that. I trade in favors. I do this for you, you owe me one."

It sounded straight out of a noir movie, which was as silly as it was exciting. Cameron swallowed a lump of suddenly nervous excitement and slid a glance at Margrit, who twitched one shoulder, saying *it's up to you* as clearly as if she'd spoken aloud. Cam arched an eyebrow back: *would you?* The corner of Margrit's mouth quirked before she dropped her chin in an almost-imperceptible nod. Cam nodded more visibly, then looked back at Grace and nodded again, though her heartbeat had sped up like she'd been working out. "Okay."

The others—the Old Races—they could hear heartbeats and caught breath. Grace was only human, even if she was as tangled up in the Old Races as Margrit was. At least, Cam *thought* Grace was only human, but the way she tilted her head and smiled a little suggested she heard Cam's crazy heartbeat just as well as Eliseo Daisani could. Cam swallowed hard again and gave Margrit another nervous look, but she didn't seem bothered. That was the thing, and Cam knew it: *she* thought the Old Races were amazing, romantic, magic, wonderful, a dream come true, but they'd become a lot more *real* than that, somehow, to Margrit. They'd become the shape of the world, not just for now but always. They made Cameron's heart beat faster, but they centered Margrit, calming her, giving her a focus for the rest of her life.

And it was going to be a long, long life, too, because she'd taken two sips of a vampire's blood, and she might be immortal now. She would be going to Cameron's funeral someday, and maybe to Cam's kids' funerals, too.

It was always warm in the subways, usually stifling hot in the summer, and the speakeasy's buried location gave it that same humid blowing heat, but that didn't stop a cold chill from springing up on Cameron's arms. Right up until that very moment she'd been thinking there were three human women sitting together in the protection of the quiet curved speakeasy walls, but that wasn't true at all. Maybe there was only one human girl here, and it was herself.

Grace O'Malley, who ran underground shelters for homeless kids, who got herself into trouble with the law regularly over it, who the whole city knew as a vigilante or a superhero, depending on how much they liked her, caught the faint change of expression Cameron felt slide over her own face. Margrit didn't: Margrit was looking at Grace. But Grace saw it, the little shock of realization and the follow-up blade of loneliness that stabbed Cameron, and Grace's own expression changed. Softened, when Grace wasn't someone Cam thought of as soft.

"It doesn't get easier, love," Grace said, "and you don't get used to it. You just live with it."

Cam pressed her lips together, then nodded. Margrit's eyebrows crinkled with curiosity, but neither Cam nor Grace explained. Grace, Cam thought, wouldn't, and she didn't feel she could. Margrit was on the other side of things now, on the side that was going to continue on and not get left behind. Or that would leave everything behind, depending on how you looked at it. And that was what Cam hadn't even been asking about, what Grace had instinctively understood: how do you live with everyone around you changing, dying, moving on, when you stayed the same, and how did you deal with being the one left behind. It only made sense that it didn't get easier and you couldn't get used to it. Living with it sounded hard too, but there was nothing else to do.

Except, it seemed, trade favors with strangers who lived beneath city streets, and cater parties for the rich and unusual. Cam's melancholy fell away into a quiet laugh and she nodded again. "So we'll owe you one. I'm good for it."

"You'd best be, love. Grace calls her favors in."

Cam's smile swallowed itself whole as a nervous gulp, and they left the speakeasy before it was even supposed to be open.

He should have known they would hold the party in the Daisani Building—no one had yet renamed it the Kaimana Building, and Cole wondered if they would. But he certainly should have known they would hold the party in the enormous, building-wide ballroom that had been used for the last gathering of the Old Races, at a ball hosted by Eliseo Daisani himself. The space could be broken up into smaller, more intimate rooms than had been displayed during Daisani's ball. There had been hundreds, maybe a thousand, people there; by comparison Kaimana's party was small and sedate. The largest room was enough to hold everyone, without giving up the visual dominance provided by two sweeping staircases and an overlooking balcony. Cole had retreated up there to see what kind of impression the long food tables made from above. Satisfying, he thought: the colors were beautiful, running through a rainbow hue that started with dark red Alaskan king salmon and ended with a purple Hawaiian sweet potato, all of it splashed along white platters held in place by long troughs of ice. Rapidly melting ice, because he'd used salt water to make it, as a nod to the selkies' home waters, so it would have to be replaced at least once and probably twice during the evening. But it worked as a visual presentation, and he already knew it tasted good. That was what mattered. As for the rest of it, the room and the people here, well, during Daisani's ball, the light had been artificially soft and gold, glittering through crystal shards and chandeliers.

Kaimana, though, was taking full advantage of the late summer sunsets, and had thrown back every cover or curtain that fell over the floor-to-ceiling windows. The effect was similar to Daisani's party: red and gold light pouring in, shattering rainbows from the dangling crystal, but there was a sense of openness and embracing the world that had not been part of Daisani's ball. That, Cole, thought, had been deliberately insular, whereas Kaimana was effectively announcing his people's presence to the world. Not quite literally, since it was a selkies-only gig, but pretty close.

The blond waitstaff—Alban, Cameron, Grace, and a sullen, short gargoyle named Biali—stood out among the dark-haired selkies. Margrit and her parents blended in better, though her father's hair was steely grey these days instead of black, and even though they, like the other four, were wearing white at what was otherwise a black-tie affair. Cole preferred it that way, marking out the staff from the guests in as visible a manner as possible, but normally he didn't have to find white tuxedos for such a range of body shapes. Margrit and Biali were the shortest, but Margrit was petite and curvy and Biali was built like a brick. His shoulders were nearly as wide as Cole's arm was long. On the other end of the spectrum were Alban, and Margrit's father, Thomas, a big man dwarfed by Alban's two-plus meters of height. The women in between were all tall for their respective generations. Even in New York, the catering supply shop he usually rented his staff's formal wear from had given him an odd look when he'd brought in the measurements. And then, even knowing who he was clothing hadn't prepared him for the sheer visual shock of the four blonds in their white tuxes. There was absolutely no doubt that every single guest at the party had noticed their waitstaff and knew half of them were Old Races, and half were extraordinary humans.

At least the food was normal.

"On the contrary, I'd say it's superlative."

A deep jovial voice rumbled from a few feet behind Cole, making him startle. He glanced back, then rubbed a hand over his forehead as Kaimana Kaaiai joined him on the balcony. "I'm sorry. I didn't realize I'd said that out loud. I'm glad you like it."

"It's excellent. Clever, too." Kaimana spoke with a faint Hawaiian accent, a lilt that made him instantly approachable, likeable: the politician next door. "I was unsure, as Margrit had indicated you're a baker by preference."

"I specialized in baking once I left chef school," Cole agreed, "but everybody learns all the basics. And even if I prefer baking, the challenge of a making a seafood spread this size was...fun," he admitted reluctantly. For a moment they both studied the long tables of food again, watching men and women stop to select tidbits as the waitstaff circulated with platters of champagne and treats.

"It didn't have to be seafood," Kaimana said eventually. "We eat all sorts of things, just like anyone else."

"I know. Or at least I assumed. But this way presented a challenge, and I could be fairly certain of having something that would suit everyone this way. Thank you for hiring me." The words didn't quite stick in his throat, not with the check having already cleared, but Cole felt awkward anyway.

"You're quite welcome. I suspect you could have an entire career catering to our rather select groups, if you were inclined."

"Yeah." Cole leaned on the railing, looking at the crowd below and trying not to let his voice or expression pull too far out of politeness. "I imagine I could."

Kaimana chuckled, a deep rolling sound that all but wobbled the air. "But you won't, because you don't like us."

Cole gave him a sideways glance, a little surprised at the blatant honesty. "I don't, but I'm stuck with you anyway, so maybe I should profit from it."

"We're not so bad, you know."

If he had hackles, Cole was certain they would rise. "I know. I get it, I do get it. Mostly you're just people. It's just that several of you are people who have specifically tried to kill my friends, and the rest of you make me…"

"Wish to defend your territory," Kaimana said when Cole faltered. "You perceive us as threats on an instinctive level, and you are rightfully afraid that we are stronger and more dangerous than you are. Your impulse is to challenge us, particularly the males, and that is at war with your intellect, which tells you that in unarmed combat you would be easily defeated."

"Thank you," Cole said dryly. "That makes me feel a lot better."

"Your people's lack of physical capability in comparison to ours has hardly stopped you from becoming the dominant species," Kaimana said just as dryly, and then less dryly, "and the savior of ours. We will not continue to exist without the tacit, and perhaps eventual outright, support of people like the Negotiator and her friends. I would not ask you to like us, Cole Grierson, but I will thank you for the honor you do us by keeping our secrets when you understand that it may be against your best personal interests to do so."

"It's not, really." Cole gripped the railing like doing so would make speaking easier. "Mostly it's not. We're not competing for the same resources, not generally. And I'm not deep enough into your world for Cameron or myself to be endangered from it. In some ways it's in my best personal interests to get along with you." He released the railing enough to gesture at the catered tables below. "You hire me at outrageous prices to feed your party, for example. So it's not really against my interests to be…friendly."

"Except for when it is. Except for when my kind—all of us in general, not necessarily the selkies in particular—move against your friends, because they *are* that deep in my world. Except for when you become collateral damage or an inviting target because of those friends and their connections. So your willingness to try—forgive me for reading too much into it, but it gives me hope for all of our futures."

Cole took a breath to laugh, and another voice snarled, "You read *far* too much into it," before the world fell apart into pain and dissolution.

Cameron was watching when it happened. Standing down there on the floor looking over the heads of short selkies—because even Kaimana, who came across as a big man, wasn't *taller* than she was, just broader—and specifically looking up at the balcony where

Cole and Kaimana were talking. Cole looked more relaxed than he had in a week, though he had quite a grip on the balcony rail where he was leaning. Still, the banquet was going off well, the fact that it was for selkies no longer seemed to be bothering him as much, and his waitstaff all looked freaking magnificent in their white tuxedos. The only thing that could've made them more awesome would have been getting Margrit and her mother to bleach their hair blonde—Grit's dad had enough grey in his hair to be almost as light-headed, if not bright-headed, as Cam and the three platinum blonds—but Cameron didn't think there was enough tea in China to get Rebecca Knight to bleach her hair. They made a great looking waitstaff anyway, and Cam was grinning up at Cole, waiting for him to notice her, when he vanished.

It looked like a special effect, something straight out of the movies. For half a second she had an afterimage burned into her eyes, an impression of a man grabbing Cole from behind before they disappeared. Not even *poof*, more like fog blown away by the wind: there one instant, gone the next. Her breath froze in her throat, undecided as to whether it should be a laugh or a shriek.

Before she could make up her mind, Cole reappeared thirty feet above them, in mid-air over the gathered selkies, and fell.

Alban appeared out of nowhere, slamming

his massive gargoyle form into the air with a leap that took him halfway across the ballroom. He caught Cole far more gently than could be expected, given the velocity they were both traveling at, and landed in the middle of the ballroom with a floor-rattling thud.

Cameron screamed, only finally catching up to the speed at which it had all happened. Cole, wide-eyed and pale, rolled out of Alban's arms but grabbed the huge gargoyle's shoulder, steadying himself. Biali, like Alban, had instantly shed his human form and leapt upward, broad white wings battering the air to keep him aloft, but he had no visible enemy to attack. Even Kaimana had barely registered more than shock, though something disturbing was happening to Margrit, whose fingers curved wide and whose jaw fell open a little, like she might use tooth and nail as weapons.

Of all of them, Rebecca Knight was the only one who looked calm or in control. She wasn't, she *couldn't* be, but there was no outward hint of perturbance on her regal features. It was she who said the word aloud, a word Cameron hadn't even had time to think of yet: "Djinn."

It echoed around the ballroom somehow, a crisp clear utterance that went far beyond the range her voice should have had. That was probably panic setting in, blowing things out of proportion, but it also seemed completely in character for Margrit's unflappable mother. If Rebecca had then taken guns from beneath her white tuxedo and begun shooting down the enemy with Matrix-style calm, Cameron wouldn't have been surprised. Rebecca *didn't*, but it would have seemed like a perfectly reasonable thing for her to do.

Instead Margrit arrived at Cole's side, not inhumanly fast, but pretty damned fast, and the undercurrent of her concern swept toward Cam as much as it was directed at Cole. She asked him something and he shook his head, lips shaping the words, "Fine, I'm fine."

Margrit gave a sharp nod and this time her voice carried, if not as loudly as her mother's had: "Good. Get out of here. Both of you. All of you."

All of you. The humans. Cameron and Cole, Rebecca and Thomas. Margrit clearly intended to stay for the fight along with the rest—the rest? —of the Old Races. For a fleeting instant Cam considered not retreating: she was tall, strong, physically as fit as most normal humans could expect to be, and Margrit was her friend.

A djinn materialized a few yards away, seized a selkie, and disappeared again as quickly as he had arrived. When he reappeared a second time, it was with the selkie woman thrust forward, so that she materialized *around* the back of a chair, her innards bisected by its presence. Cameron gagged, hot tears of horror and disgust burning her eyes. The room suddenly seemed full of enemies, too many people to decide which way to go, so she went forward, toward Cole and Margrit and Alban.

Hot hands closed on Cameron's shoulders and the world faded around her. She shrieked again, clawing at the nothingness that was trying to claim her. It hurt on every level, like her skin was being abraded, like her hair was being pulled out a few strands at a time, like her eyes were being pressed relentlessly into her skull, until each individual part of her was stretched and scoured and ready for removal.

Grace O'Malley thrust a hand through Cameron's throat and clenched her fist around something behind Cameron. Cam *felt* it happening, felt the play of muscle and the strength in the vigilante's grip. She couldn't swallow around the other woman's strength, but for an instant she caught a glimpse of wry apology in Grace's expression. Then Grace yanked, and a djinn passed through Cameron and came out the other side, caught in Grace's deadly grip.

Cam's cells snapped and stretched and slapped back together, returning to normalcy with a bone-deep, skin-twisting pain. She staggered and caught herself on a nearby selkie, but he was focused on the djinn in Grace's hands.

The djinn himself was pale with shock, fingers clawed around Grace's wrist. Cameron could see he was trying to dissipate, but whatever magic had let Grace reach through Cam wouldn't let the djinn fade away. She tightened her fist, an inexorable slow squeeze that her long-fingered hands shouldn't have been able to maintain, and after long seconds that grip snapped his neck, as if she was a strongman playing with dolls. He collapsed onto the floor, boneless, lifeless, and Grace shook her fingers as if loosening a cramp. Then she met Cameron's eyes again, a pained expression sliding across her face. "Grace's secrets are coming unraveled at last. Get down, girl, and stay safe."

Cameron nodded wildly, then ran for the gathering of her friends. Biali had landed with them by the time she arrived, making a small core of non-selkie compatriots near the center of the ballroom. Cole grabbed her into his arms, wheezing relief, and she buried her face in his shoulder for a few seconds before steeling her gut and putting her back to the middle of the circle. Like they could protect each other's backs that way, against an enemy that apparated at will. Still, it was better than nothing, and then Grace stalked up and insinuated herself into the middle of the circle, which after her display meant maybe the djinn weren't going to go for the humans after all.

They weren't *there* for the humans anyway. Whether grabbing Cole had been opportunity or distraction, it was the selkies they'd come to make war on. Cole, shoulder to shoulder with Cam, whispered, "What the hell," even though Cam was reasonably certain he knew the answer already.

Margrit said it aloud anyway: "Revenge." The stories she had told them in the aftermath of the dockland fires were more than enough to illuminate the list of what required avenging: djinn bound to corporeal form by salt water and killed in the battles between the Old Races. The selkies' complete sweep of Eliseo Daisani's fallen empire, now controlled by and benefiting them. The selkies were already the most populous of the remaining Old Races, and with Daisani's empire in their pocket they were suddenly significant in the human world too. So were the djinn, but they had taken the underbelly empire, Janx's crimelord territories, and it was an uglier, darker place to be. If they could wipe out the selkie here — if they could destroy Kaimana Kaa-iai in particular — they would be well-positioned to take over Daisani's empire as well, holding both sides of the gameboard in their hands. There was age-old bad blood between the selkies and the djinn as well: they were natural enemies, the salt-water-born selkie anathema to the desert-bound djinn. They had all the reasons in the world to fight.

And they were nearly impossible to stop. They had to become physical to hit the selkies, but they could wisp away again in less than a blink, and once they had their hands on someone they could take them into the ether. The selkies were strong — Cameron flinched back as a small, young woman ripped a chair apart with her bare hands to provide herself with a weapon—but they couldn't dissipate. Once they were made incorporeal—

A djinn seized the young woman and misted away with her. A few seconds later they reappeared again, but this time it was the djinn screaming: the girl had shoved her chair leg backward, into the djinn's chest, and when he solidified it had pierced him through. It was as horrible as the first woman's execution, and yet somehow this time Cam had to force back a shout of approval. The selkie just seemed too vulnerable in comparison to the untouchable djinn. Without salt water—or vampire's blood, for heaven's sake—there was no way to stop them.

Salt water.

Cameron's gaze snapped to the buffet tables, to the long troughs of ice that kept the food on the tables cool. Cole had used salt water for the ice, even though it took much longer to freeze and melted faster. It had been keeping in the theme, and that had been worth it. "Margrit—"

Half a dozen djinn came out of nowhere, grabbing for Alban. His wings snapped out, knocking their circle askew. Biali leapt over his head and landed on one djinn, flattening him even as his huge stone fists smashed at two more. Margrit, who was faster than she should be, ducked under Biali's wings and bashed another djinn in the nose. Of the others, only Grace kept her feet under the buffeting power of the gargoyles' wings. Cameron was knocked aside, then gasped as more djinn appeared above her, around her, everywhere, and she finally realized that it wasn't only Grace at the center of their protective circle: Kaimana was there too, his own meaty fists lashing out damage but risking far too much of himself.

Cameron reached below the djinn, searching for Cole's hand, and latched on hard when she found it. He gave her a wild-eyed look as she dragged him forward, scrambling between djinn determined to reach the selkie leader. They *could not* pass Grace, who was everywhere at once, doing the bone-shakingly awful thing she'd done to the first djinn, but there were so many of them that she would falter soon, and it would be over.

Cole blurted, "Grit said run—!" as Cam hauled him forward, but she shook her head and got her feet under her, pulling Cole upright as she ran for the catering tables.

He figured it out before she reached them and put on a burst of speed himself, knocking platters and trays aside as they both snatched up the ice troughs. They were half melted already, long sticks of ice floating in cold water. Cam spun around with hers, spraying salt water back at the group they'd escaped from, then bellowed, "*Margrit!*" at the top of her lungs.

Margrit's gaze snapped up. Cameron threw a stick of ice at her, water dripping as it flew through the air. Margrit caught it, bewildered, then yelped as its cold bit her hands. She licked one palm instinctively, trying to warm it, and her eyes widened before a grin split her face.

The djinn were already suffering the effects of the first splash, exacerbated as Cole flung water the same way Cam had. He threw a second ice stick toward Alban, who caught it with inhuman grace, then slammed it across the faces of the djinn trying to get past him. It streaked them with salt water, binding them to corporeal form, and Biali gave an ugly howl of pleasure as his next blows landed to great effect. Cole spilled more ice water onto the floor, sending ice sticks skidding toward the fight. Rebecca Knight, of all people, picked one up, though she didn't begin to fight with it. She used it defensively, though, moving elegantly and smoothly. Her surgeon husband was more efficiently brutal, clobbering the now-solid djinn with the skill of a man who knew where a body's most vulnerable areas were. Beyond them, in the wider ball room, selkies were starting to realize what Cameron and Cole were doing, and ran for the buffet tables too, arming themselves with the one weapon that could equalize the fight.

Maybe more than equalize it. The selkie were *strong*, not as strong as the stone-born gargoyles, but they had the physical strength of the seals that were their natural form, and that, translated into human bodies, was disproportionately powerful. The djinn, it seemed, lacked that strength: their power was in their ability to phase in and out of physicality, and with that talent neutralized they were suddenly as out-matched as the selkies had been minutes earlier. Cameron's stomach lurched again as the tide turned, the fight turning bloodier and messier by the moment. After a minute Cole caught her shoulders and turned her away, tucking them both beneath one of the catering tables, out of sight and out, she hoped, of harm's way.

Cameron was tall, strong, physically fit. Not ever the sort who seemed to need holding or taking care of, which was part of what Cole loved about her. She'd crawled out of a car wreck mess as a teenager—not literally, but physically and emotionally—and had become someone who helped others, not somebody who often needed help herself. But she curled tight in his arms as they hid beneath the table-cloths, her face buried in his shoulder and her breath coming short and hard against his chest. Cole knotted his hands against her spine and held on as tight as she did, trying to keep his own breathing steady, but they both flinched and gasped quietly into each other's bodies at the sounds and screams from beyond.

It wasn't heroic. It wasn't the stuff legendary men were made of. It wasn't even in any real way protecting his woman: they were both hiding, no bones about it. And given his hackle-rising reaction to the Old Races, Cole thought he should have a problem with that.

Turned out he didn't. There were more important things to worry about, when it came down to it. Surviving, for example. Making sure Cam survived. He'd thought that would mean needing to fight, needing to make himself visible among the Old Races, needing to prove his place. But putting himself out there in the middle of battle, having seen even just a minute or two of it, seemed stupid now. Kaimana had been right: there was no chance Cole could compete physically with the Old Races. He wasn't afraid of them anymore, but he no longer had any impulse to try himself against them or worrying about—in Cam's words—who was the alpha dog. He wanted to live and he wanted Cameron to live, that was all. It didn't feel cowardly, just smart.

It ended faster than he expected, but he stayed still, hanging onto Cam and waiting. The djinn could be so silent, slipping in and out of reality, that he didn't know how he *could* know that it was—

"It's safe to come out now. You may…wish to keep your eyes closed." It was Rebecca Knight who came for them in the end, her unfailing calm in some ways more unnerving than the sounds of battle had been. Cole glanced at Cam, then nodded when she did.

"Sounds like a good idea." His voice was hoarse. He swallowed, then caught Cam's arm as she started to climb out from behind the tablecloths. "Maybe you should use your cummerbund or bow tie for a blindfold. I...it's going to be hard not to look."

Cam shuddered and nodded again, unwrapping her cummerbund and offering Cole her bow tie. Neither of them tied them in place, just held them over their faces with one hand as they crawled out from beneath the tables. Rebecca took their free hands as they stood, murmured, "I'll move slowly," and led them through the nearly silent ballroom.

Cole couldn't resist one glimpse, and wished he'd been able to. The opulent Daisani ballroom was streaked and sprayed with red, bodies lying in unrecognizable lumps and pieces all around. The floor was pink with water-thinned blood, darkening where it still drained from the dead. The food he'd prepared was smeared in a macabre mess among the bodies, a few plates strangely still pristine and untouched, as if nothing untoward had happened. Cole's stomach roiled, bile rising behind his teeth, and he clapped the fabric over his face again.

It had been impossible to tell, at a glance, who lay among the bodies, whether more were selkie or djinn. Djinn, obviously, or he and Cam wouldn't be walking away with Rebecca Knight in the lead. But there had been so many of them coming for Kaimana that it seemed unlikely the selkie leader was alive. Without him, Cole wasn't sure the selkies could hold onto their newly-gained empire, and for the first time he actually cared. It wasn't so much that he wanted the selkies to hold it as he didn't want the djinn to, given the ruthlessness they'd shown again and again. The idea of their tribes with that much power and influence in the human world scared him, though when he got right down to it, anybody with that much power and influence was alarming. The djinn generally seemed actively malicious, though, whereas the selkies had seemed to just want to survive.

Right now, that was something Cole felt a lot of sympathy for. He stumbled as Rebecca led them up the first of the balcony stairs, then found his pacing and climbed steadily. Rebecca murmured, "It's safer to remove the blindfolds now," and Cole dropped his to see a few remaining smears of blood, but far less carnage than had lain below.

Margrit burst out of a hallway and flung herself at both of them, offering a hard hug Cole could feel her trembling through. "I'm sorry. I'm so sorry. I never imagined—"

"Of course you didn't." Cam's voice was shaky but a little teasing. "C'mon, Grit, in what universe would you deliberately ask Cole to cater a bloodbath? Is everybody—your mom's okay, but everybody—?"

"Dad took a couple of good hits, but he's okay. Alban and Grace are fine. I think Biali's still jumping on the pieces of people he ripped apart." Margrit smiled wanly, then drew herself up, pulling on a mantle that Cole recognized as much as he knew her lawyer body language and jargon: she was becoming The Negotiator, the human woman entrusted with the fates of the Old Races. "There are some people who would like to see you two, if you don't mind."

"Do we have a choice?"

Margrit, looking incredibly serious, met Cole's eyes and nodded an affirmative. "You do. You can walk away right now and they'll let you. But they would like to see you first, if you're willing."

"You're the one who's said nobody gets to walk away from the Old Races."

"You've earned an exception." Margrit moved her hand, though, gesturing them to the door she'd burst through, and Cole exchanged glances with Cam, who nodded and went so far as to tug his hand a little, ushering him toward the door. She was braver than he was, he thought, but right now his fear was pretty much wiped out, so he went with her.

The room beyond was a boardroom, oversized and lush: the party could have been held *there* without losing any of its ambiance. There were two men in it, two Old men, or however they named themselves when they met in human form. One was Kaimana Kaaiai, whose genial smile broadened as he saw the relief that swept Cole.

The other was, from his coloring and clothing,

a djinn. His hair had steel in it, grey slabs against black, and he wore a short gnarled beard, which the djinn Cole had seen previously did not. He exuded power the same way Eliseo Daisani had: naturally, charismatically, overwhelmingly. He rose when Cole and Cameron entered the room, and came forward to stop not more than an arm's length away. His eyes were such a pale brown as to seem gold, much lighter than the other djinn—or the selkies, for that matter—and long lashes shuttered those gold eyes as he bowed slightly in greeting. Cole, watching the djinn's lashes tangle together, wondered just *how* unwise it would be to describe them with the obvious word—feminine—aloud, and didn't risk finding out.

The djinn straightened, studying both Cam and Cole a moment before he spoke. "I wish to make apology to you, and to thank you for your quick thoughts this evening. I regret the deaths of so many of my own, but they were rebellious fools who very nearly succeeded in setting us on an unstoppable path of warfare and bloodshed. They would have succeeded, had it not been for you, and I am therefore in your debt."

Cole looked over his shoulder for Margrit, half expecting her to be holding a "PRANKED!" sign, but she shook her head very slightly: this was real, and the djinn was serious. Cameron, more gracious if no less surprised, squeaked, "You're welcome. Um, excuse me for being rude, but who are you?"

The djinn exhaled, not as if insulted but as if shedding a lifetime's worth of weariness before answering. "I am Amar Beqi Rusel di Hefze al-Kaleek, and I have argued with my people for a very long time that the way to go forward in this world is with the hand of humanity in our own. I would like to offer that hand to you now, in hopes that we may put this incident and all others like it in our past."

He did exactly as he said, offering both his hands to Cameron and Cole. Cam instantly moved to take it, then stopped the motion and looked at Cole, who twisted a faint smile at her. Even in the immediate aftermath of the fight below, even with all the unanswered questions, it was in her to assume the best of people and hope for a better future. He couldn't do that. He wasn't that good and he had too many questions, but there was something he could do, something that he hadn't had the option to do since the Old Races had first come into his life.

Cole said, "I love you," to Cameron, took a deep breath, nodded at Amar al-Kaleek, and finally, for the first time since Alban had revealed himself as a gargoyle, *chose.*

BETRAYALS

THE WOMAN DISTURBS HIM. There is nothing overtly *wrong* about her, not to human eyes. She has a gift for stillness; well, some people do. But he sees more, a stillness from within that is uncomfortable to him, because mortals do not hold that still. Not while they live, at least, and she is fully alive. But he knows the stillnesses of the Old Races, and the woman does not have that, either. Not exactly. Not entirely.

And then there is her hair. This is Japan: everyone has black hair, silky straight and smooth. Those who do not have altered it chemically, dyed it bright colors or forced waves and curls into it. Hers is black, but it has none of the undertone, none of the gloss that naturally black hair has. There are no hints of blue or red in it: it is flat, matte, dyed. Very few of even the elderly in Japan bother to dye their hair black again, as age is venerated, but this woman is also not old.

Nor is she Asian, of course, but that somehow seems unworthy of comment: her features, with a slight downturn to her eyes, a straight but not narrow nose, full lips and skin that would probably brown under sun it never seems to have encountered, *could* be Asian, if one didn't look a second time, or if one simply chose not to think about it. In many monocultures, not thinking about it is both easy and forgivable; that which appears to be approximately like the whole, is. He is not Asian, either, but his disguise runs deeper and is far more difficult to see through. More difficult to obtain and retain, too, for that matter, but that's unimportant.

She knows by now that he's watching her, and curiously, she is not distressed by it. Many women — many people — are; it is the hunter in him, ancient and more primal than humanity cares to remember. He is the thing they fled in their infancies, the thing they built fires in the night to ward away, the thing about which they still tell tales, all the while pretending not to believe. Most of them look away, move away, finally break and all but run, when he has been studying them as long as he has watched this woman. Even, perhaps especially, those who consider themselves strong, leaders, men of action and challenge, tend to find excuses to be elsewhere.

This is part of why he is so very good at dominating board rooms, and how he has rebuilt an empire taken from him by others of his…kind, though even in his thoughts he uses that word with caution. His own kind are buried beneath human holy places, and there they must remain. The others, the selkies and djinn, the dragons and gargoyles, they are of the Old Races and therefore *of his kind,* but they are no more vampires than this strange still girl who sits a dozen feet away, and does not flinch as he examines her.

What is equally extraordinary is that now that she knows he's there, she makes no move to encourage a meeting. Most people are not content to be studied without demanding some other kind of acknowledgment, but although she has glanced his way—her eyes are as dark a brown as he has ever seen—she returns to her reading without neither a come-hither smile, a cold shoulder or any sign of discomfort.

It is precisely because of intriguing behavior like this that he has gotten into trouble in the past. If he were Janx—but no, and it has been many years since he has allowed himself to think that way, which means he is more unsettled than the woman is. In the end, he rises from his own seat, a small dip in an otherwise unadorned concrete slab, and approaches the woman where she sits in an identical hollow.

She looks up, as expressionless as he has ever seen anyone. It is not curiosity on her well-formed features, nor is it displeasure. There is no fear, no distrust, no anticipation. She is only waiting, waiting to see what happens next.

Her utter neutrality causes him to make a choice. He says, "Eliseo. Eliseo Daisani," and with those words reclaims a name, a man, that he has chosen not to be for quite some time.

She is not surprised, although if she knows the name she should be: his face is not as it was when last he used it. So perhaps she does not know it, and assigns no importance to it. But no, that is almost certainly not true, not with what she says, not with the stunning simplicity of her response: "My name is Hajnal."

Memory hammered him, all the sides of a story gone untold. Four centuries past, in the year that London burned. More than the city had burned then. So too had need, desire, even love, all hot enough to leave marks that still ached hundreds of years later. Hajnal, whose family name was Obsidian, but who in the human fashion had taken her mate's last name, because the Germanic-sounding *Korund* raised fewer eyebrows than her own name. That, and it was only the most powerful of royal females at the time who might dominate their marriage with their own name instead of taking their husbands', but that was a detail of the future intruding on the past.

She had been small for a gargoyle, and dark: obsidian indeed. Small and dark had meant of a height with modern women, golden skin tones, and black hair, rather than six feet tall and alabaster and white in coloring, as most of her kind were. She had been particularly striking beside Alban, who was monstrously tall even by gargoyle standards, and whose paleness was emphasized by her color. And Alban had been —was still—romantic, where Hajnal had a pragmatic streak as wide as the Thames. She had chased Janx away when a human woman needed space to breathe, and Janx, who could not be cowed, had gone, though he'd been hissing and spitting fire by the time he returned to the estate he owned and Daisani had taken up uninvited residence at.

With *that* response, Daisani had been obliged to go and meet her, this Hajnal, this gargoyle who could order a dragon around without fear or consideration. And she had met him outside the small but stately church-like home she and Alban kept; had met him under the stars, as her kind were forever barred from daylight; had met him as though she expected him, and had said without introduction or remorse, "You're a fool. She's human and fragile, and you're going to destroy her."

"I do not even know of whom you speak." He met her eyes precisely: she was no taller than he, but neither was she smaller. Obsidian was glass: it would fracture easily, if hit at the right angle. But there was nothing of fragility in Hajnal Korund, not that night nor any other for long years, until bullets fired in the rain brought her down.

"You are a terrible liar," she said, and even today he was uncertain if she meant he lied badly, or if the lies he told were dreadful ones.

The latter, he thought, had always thought, if only because most of the Old Races lied well. "Do you pretend to tell me you haven't gone to glimpse the woman Janx is so taken with?"

A shudder ran down Eliseo's spine, rare emotional response. His voice thickened and his tongue swelled in his mouth: "She works in the slaughterfields. I went to look, aye, but it was unwise to stay."

"Then you may be a trifle wiser than your companion, but neither of you is wise. Do her a kindness, Eliseo Daisani. Stay away from her. Keep Janx away from her as well. We are not good for them, and you know it."

"They," Eliseo recalled saying, recalled saying it as clearly as if the words were only just now passing his lips, "they are not good for us, Hajnal Korund."

A crack in her facade: she glanced over her shoulder, as if expecting Alban to be there. The motion said everything it needed to about the sentimentality of the two gargoyles; about youthful Alban Korund and his much older mate, about how she recognized the truth in Daisani's words, and about how she would protect Alban, and indeed the humans he became enamored of, from the dangers they represented to one another. "What," he said, surprising himself, "if it proves that we are the fragile ones instead? Will you be as fiercely protective then?"

"Would you accept it?"

"Of course not."

Hajnal Korund's mouth twitched, as much humor as he was ever to see from her. Then she turned her hands up, a human gesture of helplessness that made him like her because it said she was lying, as badly as he had. She would protect him too, and Janx, if she could, because that was a gargoyle's nature. They would be lost without the gargoyles, all of them, because they and their steadfast ways were the bedrock of the fractured Old Races community. Daisani barked a soft *hah* on a breath, dismissing the pun as unworthy of explaining when Hajnal arched an eyebrow. "You and Alban must come to dinner soon, I think. There are not so many of us in London that a gathered few would garner attention."

"You may come here," Hajnal said, "you and the dragonlord both. But I will not come to you, not while Sarah Hopkins is your pet. She may need refuge, and I will not compromise Alban or myself as a source where she can find it."

That, then. that is the essence of *Hajnal* to him: uncompromising, wise, perhaps wry beneath the stern visage. But also *dead*, dead for well over a century, and this girl who lays claim to the name is Asiatic, pale, and most important, sitting beneath an afternoon sky. A cloudy one, to be sure, but it is fully daytime, and gargoyles cannot be abroad in day. The girl is *not* Hajnal's daughter, nor Alban's, and there is no comprehensible way she can carry the stillness of the Old Races within her and bear that name.

Eliseo Daisani, who has not been truly, fundamentally *surprised* in longer than he can remember, sits down heavily beside the girl who calls herself Hajnal, and eventually, as if a fool, says, "...who?"

"My father's name is Biali."

Inside a breath, the pieces fall into place. A jolt zings Eliseo's spine, making his posture more perfect than usual. "Isabel. The Mexican woman. Alban—Biali—"

As if he has spoken coherently, the woman—Hajnal, though he cannot yet think of her that way easily—nods. "Yes. I believe I owe my life to you, for saving my mother's. Thank you."

"Your mother." Eliseo remembers her, though he saw her only once, and nearly dead at that. She was small and dark like Hajnal. Darker than Hajnal, with African blood mixed with the Mexican Indian and European Spanish to make a singularly striking woman. That was whence this Hajnal's epicanthic folds came: not Asian stock, but American native. Biali had left his mark too, in the whiteness of her skin; Daisani could see it now, all the reports of her heritage written on her face. "Your mother gave you the sunlight."

"A gift beyond measure."

This girl has no evident humor in her: he has rarely seen such a solemn and unchanging face. But then, what little he knows of the gargoyle gestalt, of the vast overmind of memories that they share, it is possible that a half-blood chimera like Hajnal the younger dares not release her hold on sternness for fear of being overwhelmed by it. It is a mental discipline, navigating the gestalt, and there is a real possibility she has no idea what manner of thing it is that presses constantly at her mind. She speaks suddenly, a spark of hope breaking in the words: "You knew my father."

"I know him."

There: that change of tense is what she hoped for, and it changes the tension in her as well. Her shoulders become less like the stone that is part of her, and her jaw softens. Daisani, who is alive with curiosity, says, "You haven't met him, then. And your mother—"

"Dead."

Of course. He gave her a single sip of blood, a sip for health. For healing, to drive away the pain that had been visited on her, but it would have taken a second sip for Isabel to survive through as many years as have passed since that night. Twelve or thirteen decades now, and that is as long as any woman Eliseo has given the second sip to has lived. One is simply not enough. It takes two, to extend life. "But you know who I am," he says cautiously. "What we are. She told you that much before she died."

"No." Only with that word, to which his ear is attuned to hear as an English one, does Eliseo realize they are speaking Spanish and have been all along. Quietly, as to not be overheard, but the conversation is not taking place in Japanese, which in this city offers them a measure of privacy beyond their lowered voices. Hajnal—it is hard to think of her that way. He wishes he had a human name to assign her, even a surname so that he might differentiate between the woman he knew and the one sitting beside him now. But he did not know Isabel's last name, and is strangely reluctant to assign Biali's daughter her father's clan name. So it is Hajnal, and he will have to become accustomed to it.

Hajnal takes up the story after a moment to gather breath, perhaps to gather courage, though there is no uncertainty in her voice or eyes, which remain as stoic as any gargoyle might offer. "She knew my father had secrets, of course, but not their depth. Not until I was born at night, and became stone at dawn. Then she understood, at least, why he always left her before the sun rose. And you, of you she knew only the name, and the blood. You…are an easier guess than the stone. *Eres un vampiro, no?*"

Eres. The familiar verb, not *usted.* That is part of why he didn't notice the language they spoke: she has no qualms about using the personal and intimate terms, when most people default to formality when they speak to him. For a moment Eliseo Daisani wishes he had known Biali's lover Isabel better, because it appears she was not only formidable enough to draw a gargoyle's eye, but also to instill an unswerving sense of self-worth in her half-breed daughter. "*Si,*" he answers, "*soy vampiro. Eres una gargola.*"

"And the others? Because there are others," she says with certainty. "The way my father spoke of his people to my mother…there are others." This time it's a question, though the lift in the words is barely audible.

"Dragons. Djinn. Selkie. No others that I know have survived. You're well over a century old, but you've never met any of us before?"

"How would I know?"

Daisani's eyebrows draw down. "You knew me."

"No. You knew *me*. And I knew your name, when you said it. You began this dance, *Señor* Daisani. Why?"

He does not know the answer before he says it, and that is as rare as any of this, to a creature his age: "Because you're a thing that's not supposed to be."

And memory again, rushing through him more powerfully than the blood in his veins. This time, a girl whose mother's beauty only showed through in flashes. His stamp was stronger on her: the sallow tint to the skin, the black hair and the not-quite-handsome features tainted with rage. She had all but lost control of the gift—the other gift—that was a vampire's real power. It was true that no one saw a vampire's true face and survived to tell about it, but anyone looking on Ursula Hopkins might sense what they ought not see. It was the one thing vampires and djinn seemed to have in common: a form that was always human. But no; djinn turned to dust riding on the wind, and vampires turned to something nameless, vicious, always hungering and ready to feed. That other face stretched Ursula's in the moment she met her father; in the moment she met Eliseo Daisani, and learned what he had done to their people.

Betrayal was not an expression intended to be featured on the faces of vampires. *Expressions* were not intended to be featured there, no more than a snake or a preying mantis might have expressions. But there had been betrayal in Ursula's eyes, visible even through the fire and smoke filling the room. She had made one move toward him, toward his bleeding, dying body. Then she had stopped, fury greater than familial bonds or a child's curiosity about her parent.

And then she had been gone, gone as breathlessly fast as any vampire could move, and he had been left to die. No, never die, because vampires did not, but the recovery would have been unbearable, had it not been for the Negotiator. *There* was the source of all betrayal: a human woman, a lawyer, a player as fine as Eliseo had ever met, when nearly every player of note was of the Old Races. Margrit Knight had told him she would betray him, had betrayed him, and had then survived by offering her life for his.

It was not honor that had driven him to that final choice, the offering of the second sip, the blood of life. It was a hope of revenge. The dead could not be preyed upon, and he had made a promise, kneeling beside her in the gouting flames: if they crossed paths again, her life would be forfeit.

She may not have known it then, but he had: the world was too small for them not to meet again, and the Old Races far too few. She had changed everything for them, had made them reconsider their laws, sacrosanct from time immemorial. Only one had remained untouched, but it was the one he had cast off long ago: *do not kill one of our own.* He was the master of his kind, and would not be held to such demands, not when his people verged on destroying themselves through their lack of discipline. That was what Margrit Knight had seen, that Ursula Hopkins could not: that his choice had been the necessary one, and that, among other things, was why she had been granted the title *Negotiator.* In a lifetime of uncounted years, she was one of perhaps five humans to be granted a title by the Old Races, and the only one to have earned it so quickly. Weft and warp, tangle and trouble. In all those years, very few women had undone Janx and Daisani so thoroughly, so swiftly. Fewer still had lived to tell about it.

Do not tell humans of our existence. Do not breed with them. Those were the laws that had changed profoundly, and in changing them, the loss represented by Ursula's retreat was far greater than anything Margrit Knight might have anticipated. Bad enough, if inevitable, to have lost Sarah; to have lost Ursula's mother. Time would have taken her away regardless, even with the two sips of his blood in her veins. Perhaps Janx would have taken her before time did; Janx's fire was difficult to resist, even for Eliseo, who had spent millennia warming himself with it. Losing her to Janx would have been infuriating but acceptable, because in time he would have found a way to repay that particular gift.

But losing the daughter, the half-human child he never imagined to have: *that* was an offense beyond repair. *That* was a place inside him given over to outrage, a place so cold that he buried it as he had buried Eliseo Daisani, as a name, a thing, too fragile to consider resurrecting. His face, changed by the slipping, shifting skill of a master vampire, could never betray him, and so he could never permit himself to look at the wound, the insult, the damage hidden within, for fear it would betray what his face could not. For years already it had been tucked away, less fuel to his fire than the pursuit of money, which had always been his mortal persona. That, if he thought about it, was Janx's influence too, a dragon's treasure the only thing precious enough to garner a dragon's rivalry and friendship, and a dragon was the only friend a vampire might have. So the acquisition of treasure had become part of Eliseo's life as well, though what he regarded as worth coveting was never quite the same as what Janx desired.

Well, except for the women. So very often, the women. That, though, was not a matter of rivalry, or at least not most often. It was that a woman who could draw one of them was the sort who could draw any of them, and he and Janx were in perpetual orbit around one another, exposed to what the other discovered. Even Vanessa, who had never looked a second time at Janx, and in whom Janx had never been truly interested: even she, Janx would have stolen if he could, in the name of habitual competition.

It was not a comfortable thing, admitting to himself that he missed Janx's companionship. Less comfortable still was the fear that it had been lost forever; that he had gone too far in the capturing of his brethren. That Janx, for all his disdain of the ancient laws, might never admit to the wisdom of it, and hold Daisani in censure for all time.

Too much. Too much had been lost, and it stung, which it was not meant to do. He was too old, too cold, to care, and yet. And yet.

And yet there are things now in this world that were not meant to be, and he has all unintended sat down beside one of them, and that changes the game. Again, still, for always. She remains very still, absorbing the impact of his words against skin that might well be stone, and into that stillness he asks, because he has need of the knowledge: "What is your family name?"

"Jefferson."

For the third time in a matter of minutes, Eliseo Daisani is surprised, and this time he shows it with a blink. "Hajnal *Jefferson*?"

"Hajnal Maria Jefferson. My grandfather was a Buffalo soldier, and my mother never married. His is the name I was born with."

A gargoyle's forename and a black soldier's presidential surname. Daisani's mouth twitches as he murmurs, "A thing that should not exist, indeed. Hajnal." The name is easier to say, now that that he can hang its full, unexpected weight in his mind. "There are very few like you, Hajnal. Very few children of the Old Races and humans, and until a very little while ago, you would have been killed if you were discovered."

He is not entirely certain of that: *he* would not have killed her, because a curiosity is of more interest than a death. The selkies, who saved their race by breeding with mortals, certainly would not have killed her, nor would Janx or Alban, and Biali would certainly have made an exception for his daughter. It is possible, perhaps likely, that there are far more half-breeds than Eliseo is aware of, and suddenly, for the first time in years, he has purpose again.

Hajnal is neither afraid nor surprised at what he says, and for the space of a breath Eliseo wonders at that. Only the space of a breath: then it is obvious, that she has lived the entirety of her life aware that discovery would mean death. Humans are good at many things and excel at a few, among which *destroying that which is different* is chief. Hajnal, as if she was waiting for him to realize it, only speaks after he's come to the conclusion: "And now? What has changed now? Why would I not be killed?"

"Because our people have, as a whole, opted for survival instead of slow dignified death. Children like you are our hope."

"I am no longer a child."

She is, of course: anyone who says otherwise always is, though by human standards she has certainly long left childhood. From his perspective—but then, from his perspective, entire cultures and faiths are infantile, so perhaps his perspective hardly matters. So he nods, because there is no use in giving offense. Not when he wants something from the girl, even if it's something still forming in his mind. "Not by years or experience, no, but in the sense of inheritance and perpetuation. There are relatively few young among us—"

For the first time, real humor flashes across her face. It cracks the stone facade that is her father's legacy and brings her mother's beauty into play. She was disturbing, then intriguing; suddenly she is appealing as well, though the brilliant smile disappears as quickly as it came. It leaves her voice so solemn that it laughs, though, and the hidden laughter is as warm as Janx's fire. "Hence the name *Old Races?*"

The first and truest answer is, "No," though a moment's reflection begets a dry, "and yes," as well. "We call ourselves the Old Races because we came before humanity. Before this world had decided on its form, on the four limbs its creatures would have, before it had become what it is now. But also yes, now, and perhaps it has always been, that we are Old because we have so few young."

"How can we be older than the world?"

There is a response there, one that burns deeper in him than any he will ever voice. *The vampires say they are not from this world at all.* But that is not an answer he will give this girl or anyone else, and so he says something else, something that is perhaps equally true: "There is a serpent at the heart of the world, a thing of fire and power and fury, and it is mate to the earth itself. Perhaps the Old Races came from that mating in its earliest incarnation, before there was a dream of humanity."

Having smiled once, Hajnal is more willing to show expression. Her eyebrows furl, not even making a line between them. "Is that true?"

"It's certainly true that there's a serpent at the heart of the world," Daisani says almost blithely. "I've known at least two people who have met it."

She is suspicious, an emotion that sits well on her flawless features, but she is not willing to ask again, for fear she is being made a fool. A child indeed, even if her years are many.

"We need you," Daisani says to that fear, as much as anything else. "We need children of both worlds, Hajnal, and you...can walk in sunlight. Your father can't. You are proof that our children can be greater than the sum of their parts, and neither part is lacking."

"What do you need me *for?*"

"Revolution." The word escapes him before he's thought it through, which is as well, because the other answer is *revenge.* "Not war and blood, though that will come too. But to move forward, to become part of this world, to belong to it the way humanity does, there must be revolution. We must put ourselves forward quietly and boldly all at once, and our children are best suited to do that. There is a woman." Daisani sucks his teeth, then spits the words, giving credit where it is due: "A lawyer, in New York. The Negotiator. Margrit Knight. She has begun all this, began the changes that make children like you...permissible. She will lead this revolution, or her children will. I can teach you what it is to belong to the Old Races, Hajnal Jefferson. She can show you how to belong to the world."

A glimmer of hope unclenches from within Hajnal, and Eliseo recognizes what it is she desires. She's cautious, though, saying, "Why would you teach me what it is to belong? I'm nothing to you. Is my father your friend?"

"Your mother sipped from my veins, and blood is all. You are something to me for that alone: within you beats my own pulse. But it is also—" Daisani draws a sharp breath, allowing himself a revelation: "It is also that I have seen children who were raised apart from us, and they have their own rules, their own laws. That's their right, their prerogative. But I think it's a lonely way to live—" and he has hit on something there, something that runs as deep in the half-human gargoyle girl as it does in the full-blooded vampire, alone these several years, "—and within the Old Races you might at least be allowed to relax the human facade a while. It may be decades before you can do that among humans."

"Centuries," she says with a pragmatism he was trying to avoid for fear of driving her away. "But you've just said the Old Races have only just begun to acknowledge half-bloods. Would they really accept me?"

"Enough will. Biali will," he says gently, and in that moment she is his. This is what she wants: to belong, to have a father, to understand whence she comes. It is a very human need, but she has known nothing of the Old Races, and thus is vulnerable to a promise of them.

He knows the rituals of human affection, and slips his arm around her shoulders, drawing her close to kiss her hair. From here he can scent the dye in it, coloring it to the social normative of black. From here, too, he can feel the incremental relaxation of the stone that holds her, of the face she wears so mortals cannot hurt her.

They can hurt her, of course. They can hurt

her far more badly than they will ever hurt him, but that is what revolution does: demands pain. It demands sacrifices, it demands martyrs, and it demands blood before it begets change, and no one, not even the Negotiator, can manage a revolution without blood. So be it: Margrit Knight is not wrong. The Old Races must become part of the world or die, and Eliseo Daisani chooses not to die. More, he will do all he can to be certain of who *does* die in Margrit Knight's war, and of all those he intends to protect, the girl who ran from him in shocked betrayal is first among them.

Ursula Hopkins is her father's daughter: she is rash, easily angered, prone to acting without thinking. It is her nature to be on the front lines, her nature to put herself in danger without ever believing it will touch her. Daisani is much older than that, and knows better. Knows, too, that there is no easy way to dissuade an angry child; that it is easier to redirect one than change its mind. And so redirect he will: Biali's daughter is perhaps more temperate, but little is as unchangeable as a gargoyle determined to follow a certain path. He will get Hajnal Jefferson killed in the name of belonging, and is easy with that. For that cost, his own daughter might survive, and that is well worth the price.

"It will be all right," he murmurs, and knows he tells a lie.

AFTERMATH

I HAVE LIVED IN DESERTS all my life, never
entering the human world. I have watched as
it has encroached upon us: watched the yellow
dust kicked up by their vehicles racing across
sand, watched the engines of their jets draw
white lines across the hard blue desert sky. I
have been curious, even eager to explore their
world, but it is not the way of my people, and
particularly not the way of our females. I have
waited for this to change, and as I have waited,
some things *have* changed. Amar, the male I
refused to marry, has become a power in the
human world. Not a power for good, but one
who feeds and encourages mortal vices, hoping to help their seven billion souls destroy
themselves. Many of the djinn are sympathetic
to his cause, but I think him a fool. There are
too many of them, and there have always been
too few of us.

It was still to him that I went so that I could
for the first time leave the desert sands and
cross the ocean, there to meet the woman who
killed my brother.

#

Margrit ran during the day now, and the one-time cadence of *ir-ra-tion-al* that matched her feet pounding against the pavement had faded. She was faster than she'd been before Daisani's gift, her feet slapping quickly enough that the syllables would only blur into a word anyway, but mostly the interminable repetition had been born of the scoldings and lectures she'd received for the late-evening jogs. Those had stopped when she'd changed her schedule. That, and there was nothing to match the irrationality — or at least the impossibility — of what her life had become anyway, so the word had lost its power. A breeze pushed her along as she glanced skyward and smiled at the slowly-setting sun.

Her mother was pleased that Margrit had stopped working so many long hours, and rightfully attributed the change to Alban Korund's presence in Margrit's life. Furthermore, Rebecca Knight knew, at least on a surface level, that Alban was no more human than Eliseo Daisani or the djinn Tariq. Margrit had never, would never, understand the reserve in Rebecca which allowed her to *not ask*, to accept Daisani's impossible speed or Tariq's dissipation without needing to know how and what they were.

But that reserve was a gift, as well. Rebecca had not asked about Alban's unusual hours, had adapted without question to the occasional very late, post-sunset dinner in summer, and had made an effort to visit or invite Margrit and Alban to Queens for meals during winter's earlier nights.

That was a far cry from the mother who had argued with Margrit over dating a white boy, especially when Tony Pulcella had been considerably browner all around than Alban's alabaster skin tones and shining white hair. It made Margrit wonder what exactly had happened between Rebecca Knight and Eliseo Daisani some thirty years earlier, but it wasn't an inheritance of Rebecca's reserve that kept her from asking. It was common sense: her mother would talk about it if she wanted to, and so far hadn't wanted to. In the meantime, there was no point in rocking a surprisingly stable boat.

Curiosity was killing her, though. Margrit reached the end of her route, stopping to stretch against a park bench and smile again at the sky. She was still a good lawyer, still dedicated to Legal Aid, but even she had to admit her life was more balanced now. With Tony, they'd struggled to fit a relationship in between their careers; with Alban her work day began and ended on the sun's schedule, so the hours they had together were uncompromised. It had seemed impossible at first, but the gift of healing blood from Eliseo Daisani had decreased Margrit's need for sleep considerably. Another breeze wrapped around her, cooling sweat on her body enough that she shivered. Feeling chastised, she bounced on her toes, doubled over to grab them and grunted happily at the stretch in her hamstrings, then straightened again and left the park at speed, determined to make it home before the sun set.

The wind chased her, but that was only usual in New York's canyon streets.

She does not look like a killer.

I have known killers; the male who wished to marry me is one. His gaze is always calculating, though not always cold. Margrit Knight's gaze is forthright and discerning, but not edged. She seems to me a woman of resolution, difficult to turn aside once set on a path, and I wonder if that resolution is how my brother's life ended at her hands. It is not difficult to imagine the contempt he would have held her in: she is petite, curvaceous, and as dark-skinned as I, though her hair is dark brown and full of corkscrew curls to my straight black, and to my brother, all of those things would have spoken of weakness. But then, her very femaleness would have seemed weak to him, and he was never one to understand there are different strengths in different people.

I drift through street lamps, following her as she runs at a speed that seems to me to be one of those strengths. I had not thought humans to be so quick. But then, there is something of the Old Races about her, a lightness in her step and a grace in her movements that I would not have expected in a mortal. I wonder at that, because she is not, I am almost certain, the chimerical daughter of one Old Race parent and one human parent. We are too cautious about breeding outside the tribes, and the few laws all the surviving Old Races live by forbid it.

Or they did, before Margrit Knight challenged those laws on her own behalf and on the behalf of two women nearly as old as I: the daughters of Eliseo Daisani and Janx, called dragonlord. The truth is I owe Margrit Knight my very presence here: had she not put our world in such disarray, I, a female, would not have been permitted to leave the tribe, not even to confront my brother's murderer. Perhaps they could not have stopped me, if I had been determined to go; perhaps I could have traveled the long way around, chasing the wind across continents and small bodies of water until I reached my destination, but it was faster and easier, certainly, to take a sky-scarring jet over the ocean, and to drift from a private air field to the tall glass city that is New York. I would be overwhelmed if I allowed myself to be, but I cannot allow that, not if I am to see this thing through.

So I focus on Margrit, chasing her through the streets until she chooses a building and enters. There, she ignores the small rising box and takes the stairs instead. I slip through the door behind her, and am struck with the ease of infiltrating her home. Perhaps Amar was correct, once upon a time: perhaps, had we moved much earlier—thousands of years ago, long before my own birth, or even his—perhaps we might then have conquered the humans, who are so blind to our existence. They could not have stood against us, we who can move with the wind, but it is far too late now.

The home she has led me to is unremarkable: two rooms for sleeping, one for preparing meals with a small, busy room beside it that might be meant for eating those meals, but which cannot possibly be used as such, not with the papers and books piled all around it. The final room is for visiting, and in the corner of that room rests Alban Korund, the exiled gargoyle who has changed the Old Races and their destiny as much as his human lover has done. The sun has not quite set yet, and he is bound to stone as are all his kin, and I study him while the human makes use of the room they call *bath.* I can hear water running there, more water than we would dream of using in a day in the desert, but her wasteful ways are not, at the moment, my concern.

Korund is massive, but then, gargoyles are. Even the smallest of them have weight far beyond the largest of the djinn: we are air, and they, earth. He is also beautiful, more delicately formed than the finest sculpture: I can see blood vessels in the wings that fold over his shoulders. His face is noble, proud, solemn even in sleep, and white hair cascades over white shoulders, all but hiding the upswept tip of his ears.

Margrit Knight does not look like a killer; Alban Korund does not look like a changer of ways.

Sunset strikes unexpectedly: Korund changes without warning, an implosion of air that is familiar to all the Old Races. The transition is impossible to see, from one moment a monster to the next a man. Still massive, but less so than in his natural form, he would be unremarkable among humans were it not for his astonishing paleness. White hair surrounding a face not old enough for it; skin that has never known sunlight's touch. He is my opposite in size, in coloring, in strength, and it strikes me that he is as much Margrit Knight's opposite in these things as well.

Margrit, as if she knows the very moment of sunset in her bones, calls, "Alban, can you come here a moment?" over the sound of still-falling water.

His smile is swift and heartbreaking. The djinn are not given to admission of profound love, and to see its presence writ across his features, even so briefly, startles me. Then he passes through me as he goes to his lover, and I follow.

Margrit, to my astonishment, is in the meal-preparing room, not the bathroom. She is sitting on the small table at its far end, and holds a small, bright green object casually in one hand. Alban stands aside, blocking off city light from the door that leads to their tiny balcony.

They are both looking at me, which should

not be possible. I am as the wind, ephemeral, unseen: they *cannot* know I am here, not unless I take mortal form and show myself to them.

"Look down," says Margrit Knight, and I do.

I am standing—drifting—in a ring of blood. Revolted, I back up, only to bounce off a wall I cannot see. It stings, a dull burst of sensation that fades quickly, but I would not care to experience it again. My gaze, which she cannot possibly see, jerks to Margrit, who says, "Vampire blood" as if this conversation is nothing of note. As if speaking to the wind of creatures that barely exist is usual, and for her, I fear it is.

"Did you know," she says conversationally, "did you know that a vampire's blood can cage a djinn, just as salt water can render one physical? That's what's in the water gun, salt water, so you may as well show yourself before I have to soak you, because you're sure not going anywhere until I decide it's all right."

Flushing with fury, I solidify.

Margrit's breath left her in a rush, more relief in the sound than she wanted. Alban, echoing her thoughts, murmured, "Not Tariq after all," and Margrit nodded. The djinn was female, the first female she'd ever seen, and showed naked emotion on her face, which most of the djinn Margrit had met did not.

The ones who had, though, did tend toward rage, which this woman shared. Her eyes were startling, aquamarine in a dusky face, and her thick hair was drawn back in bands. Margrit had the impression it, too, would crackle with anger if loosened, and for the space of an instant felt sympathy for the woman. She'd be furious, too, if she'd been caught sneaking around after someone. Unfortunately, the thought made Margrit grin, and the woman dissipated again, whipping around the confines of the blood circle in a whirlwind temper. Margrit sat back, watching and wondering if the circle would hold. An actual vampire's blood circle certainly would, but Margrit had drawn the circle from her own blood, which was at best only tainted with a vampire's gift.

It held long enough, at least. The woman snapped into focus again, hands clenched at her sides. She wore loose pants, banded at the ankle and waist, though her midriff wasn't bared like a Disney princess's might be. Shifting silks followed her curves instead, shimmering like wind as she breathed. Margrit thought she was lovely, but most of the Old Races were, and the ones who weren't tended to make up for it in charisma. "How did you know?" the woman demanded. "How did you know I was here?"

Margrit cast a glance at Alban, then shrugged and looked back at her captive. "I should be asking the questions, you know. You're the one in the cage. But okay, I'll give you one for free. The lights kept flickering when the wind gusted. Djinn disrupt electricity, and I might be a little paranoid these days."

The woman sniffed. "As you should be if you've made an enemy of Tariq."

"Are you working for him?"

Surprise wiped the woman's fury away, answer enough. "Okay, who are you working for, then? Who *are* you?"

The woman spat, "My name is Tahira Firaz Galia al-Shareef di Nazmi al-Massri." Margrit's stomach twisted in horror before Tahira finished with, "Malik was my brother."

"I'm sorry." That was slightly better than *I didn't mean to*, which was equally true, but pathetic. Margrit set her water gun aside and lowered her head, aware she was hiding behind her hair and momentarily unashamed of it. Then she lifted her gaze again, meeting Tahira's squarely. "It was an accident, and I wish to hell it hadn't happened, but at the time it was him or—"

"All of us," Alban rumbled when Margrit broke off. "I am sorry for your loss, Tahira al-Massri, but Malik pitted himself against a gargoyle and a dragon—"

"And a resourceful human," Margrit said.

Alban nodded before finishing, "And that challenge cost him his life. If I understood, his intention had been to win back lost prestige, a place in his tribe. Perhaps a position of leadership within it. I have never known how he lost his standing. Perhaps he never spoke of it."

Tahira paled, but didn't strike at the blood circle again. Margrit's stomach twisted a second time, the impulse to free the djinn almost stronger than wisdom. "Why are you here, Tahira? If it's vengeance, you probably should have pulled my heart out in the park, or wherever it was you started following me. But you're not a murderer, are you," she said softly.

"Because I do not look like one?" Tahira asked bitterly.

"Because I'm still alive."

The djinn's mouth twisted as sharply as Margrit's stomach had done. "I thought, when I saw you, that you did not look like a killer."

"Nobody does or doesn't. Killing is something that happens in war or passion and occasionally in psychosis, and just about anybody can do it if they're pushed far enough."

"Were you pushed so very far?" Tahira's aqua eyes were dark with accusation and hope, as if an affirmative might give her succor or strength.

Margrit picked up her water gun again, slumping against the wall as she turned it around in her hands. "Maybe. He was coming to kill me. To kill Janx, if he could. To kill Alban. I had this with me because I knew salt water solidified your people. It was the only way they could hit him. The only way they had any chance of stopping him, though Alban could have turned to stone and waited him out. Malik wasn't very patient. But he — Alban — was trying to protect Malik from Janx."

"He was what?"

Margrit looked up from the gun, sympathetic once again to the djinn woman's predicament. "It got complicated for a few months there. Malik was in danger and Janx set Alban to protecting him. But then Malik betrayed Janx and came after him, and Alban tried to protect him from Janx's retaliation, and—oh, God, Tahira, it was a mess, and I'm so sorry. But Malik was coming after me, and I had the damned water gun and I soaked him with it, and Alban didn't know and jumped him, and —I'm sorry." She got up and sprayed the floor with water from the gun, erasing the blood circle in spite of Alban's choked objection. Tahira held very still within its remains, eyeing the water gun warily.

"I'd be dead already if she was going to kill me," Margrit said to Alban, "and I'm not going to start keeping prisoners now. I'm sorry," she said to Tahira yet again. "I was afraid you might be Tariq. I thought the plan might be to kill me here so it looked like Alban had done it and—" She waved a hand in frustration. "And start the whole mess up again. I have put far too much work into the Old Races to let you set everything on fire all over again. But if you're not here to kill me, why *are* you here?"

Tahira straightened her shoulders, making the most of her scant height. Margrit felt another flash of sympathy: she had done the same thing more times than she could count, though usually out of sight of others. She was a lawyer, and the body language of enlarging herself was too much of a tell. Others might see it as a weakness, and she couldn't afford that in the courtroom. Tahira probably had less cause to make those adjustments off-screen, and really, had Margrit just been freed from prison, she might well have done the same thing, telling or no. Already half-prepared to accept whatever Tahira said, what the djinn woman asked for still took her entirely off-guard:

"I am here to seek asylum with the Negotiator."

Margrit Knight, who is as dark as I am, almost certainly does not blush easily, but I have brought her to it with my request. I have taken her breath as well, and left an astonished brightness in her eyes. Her companion, the gargoyle, simply becomes still in the way of the Old Races, more still than any human could hope to achieve. I am still, too, unmoving within the broken circle of blood. Everything, *everything* hinges on Margrit's reply, and I am not certain she will grant me what I ask. I am, in truth, not certain that she can, and so the question is truly whether she will try.

What breath she had left finally leaves her in a rattling rush, a sound just shy of laughter. "Asylum. From *what?*"

"From the ways of my people. From the laws and traditions that forbid a female from leaving the tribes or from becoming more than ornaments on the arms of our males."

"God," Margrit says under her breath, "sometimes you Old Races are much more human than I want you to be."

I ignore her, and finish speaking my need: "Asylum, so I might help shape our future, and in time change the lay of power within the djinni tribes. My life has been dictated by males, Margrit Knight. A male I did not love, or even like, wanted me as his wife, and tortured my father to gain permission. Only Malik heeded my wishes, and fought Amar for my right to refuse. You did not kill my brother. I did, decades past, when his loss on my behalf cost him his place in the tribes."

Margrit and Alban exchange glances, a different sort of surprise on their faces now. She looks back at me with interest, and says, "We knew he'd challenged someone in the tribes, that he'd lost and had had to leave. We didn't know why. That's, um."

"Softer," Alban rumbles, and Margrit snorts an agreement. "Softer than we'd imagined from him," she concludes.

Despite the intensity of my need I smile, brief and rueful. "I was his single weakness, perhaps. His only softness. I think exile would have burned it out of him."

"Yeah," Margrit says after a moment. "He didn't like anyone, and I had the impression he especially didn't like me. But then, I didn't see him interacting with any other women, and

God knows I've met enough men who just don't see women as human." She pauses, exasperated. "You know what I mean."

My mouth quirks. "I do. And you are not unlike me, Margrit Knight. You may have reminded him of me, and that may have made things worse."

"I'm not that much like you, either," she says, though I can see in her eyes she recognizes the similarities of height and skin tone, even of bone structure. Enough similarities, at least, that Malik may have seen them too, and hated her all the more for reminding him of the sister and the home he lost. "Anyway," she says, then glances around the room with a frown. "Why are we still standing in the kitchen. Come on into the living room. I'll order some…" She squints at me. "I don't suppose you eat pizza."

Absurd excitement blooms in my chest. It is silly and I know it, but the thought of trying foreign foods, of tasting unknown dishes, delights me. "I have not, but I would like to."

Alban murmurs, "I will never understand how you keep your figure, eating the way you do," to Margrit as she takes the calling device—the phone, I know this word from what little I've studied of the human world—as she takes the phone from the floor, puts it back on the table she had been sitting on, and presses buttons on its surface. She smiles at Alban while she does so, saying, "You sound like Cole. I've told both of you a hundred times, I run ten or fifteen miles a day so I can eat whatever I want. Besides, my metabolism's been perfect since — yeah, hi, I need to place an order for delivery."

The tantalizing *since* lies where it is, untasted. Alban escorts me to the living room while Margrit speaks on the phone, and for a minute or two we sit across from one another, Old Race to Old Race, and have nothing at all to say.

I have met very few of the other races. The selkies, our old enemies, were thought lost to time, and the vampires, too, had disappeared. I met a dragon once when I was young, a vast white wyrm called Rumi, but he left the hot desert sands and never returned. I know gargoyles the best, for they come from time to time so the histories might be recorded and preserved in the memory kept safe by their stony forms. Even so, females are not expected to speak with them, and now, faced with one, I do not know what to say. Except, after long moments, "Will she grant me what I ask?"

Margrit herself answers, and there is no offense in Alban's face that she does so. "She is disinclined to send someone back to a situation they find untenable, but she doesn't know what kind of asylum you think she can provide."

She comes to sit, not beside Alban, but in the same lumpy green couch I have settled on. It is not uncomfortable to me, because I can become so light that my weight barely dents it, but it also does not appear to be uncomfortable to *her*, who is sucked down into its bumps and crevasses like a stone falling into water. "I've earned myself a place in your hierarchy, Tahira. A title, 'The Negotiator', and I know that's significant. So yes, maybe I can get you some kind of asylum. I'm certainly not sending you home if you don't want to go, but if the djinn come for you—and there's a lot of them in New York now, you know that, right? They've taken over Janx's empire and the selkie have taken over Daisani's. So if they come for you, I'm going to have to give them something else, not you, in lieu of you. And I don't know what that something else is."

A shiver races over my skin, insubstantial as I am. I have tried hard not to think about my burden, about the cloth-wrapped weight that lies inside the bag I carry. Amar, thank the sands, thought nothing of it, only assumed it was whatever niceties I might need in traveling across the world, but it is more dangerous and more precious than that. Or so I am told, at least: what I bear was given to me by my mother, from her mother before, all the way back to the edge of time when the desert was small and our people difficult to hide within it. I have never dared to look at it, much less dared to touch it, and it is with trepidation I remove it from the bag now and offer it, wrapped in silk, to Margrit Knight.

Her eyebrows quirk, curiosity barely contained. She glances at me, making sure of her permission, and when I nod she begins to unwrap the thing. Layer after layer, the soft cloth I have put around it only the newest after thousands of years. Its shape becomes clearer as older silk is unwound, and Margrit's eyebrows draw down in perplexity, then crinkle as she begins to imagine what she holds.

In less than a minute, a puddle of cloth lies between us on the aged green couch, and Margrit Knight holds in her hands an ancient earthen lamp.

"You...this..." The pounding strength of Margrit's heart weakened her voice. That, and a childish giddiness, because what she held in her hands was both obvious and impossible. "This is, um. I mean, it can't really be. It can't really be," she said again, looking at Tahira.

The djinn woman's sea-green eyes held no hint at all of humor. Fear, in fact, was her chief expression: the wariness of a cat afraid to get wet. Margrit wheezed laughter, took up a piece of the cloth she'd unwound, and made to brush some of the dirt from the lamp's round sides.

Alban's sudden throat-clearing stopped her. She startled, dropped the lamp into the pile of cloth, and sat on her hands to rein in the polishing impulse. "The genie in the lamp is *real?*"

"The lamp is real," Tahira whispered. "Or I believe it to be. It has come down through my mothers since before history began. We do not dare touch it, for fear it will pull us in."

"How is that even *possible?*" Margrit almost laughed at her own enthusiastic wonder. She had met members of all the surviving Old Races, and yet a fairy tale lamp dropped in her lap could still astound her. It looked roughly like the representations of Aladdin's lamp: a round body with an elongated snout and an uplifted handle opposite. Every lamp carried by Aladdin, though, had been brass, and this one was cruder than that, pottery instead of metalwork. *Earth,* Margrit thought: earth to hold the air in. "Who made it?"

"A witch."

Disbelief flashed through Margrit, then quenched itself as a sharp memory rose: Grace O'Malley, the street side vigilante whose assistance had helped Margrit to secure the future demanded by rival djinn and selkie tribes. Grace, who had the uncanny knack of being somewhere more quickly than she should be able to, and who could stand up to a dragonlord without fear. Margrit had brushed with death before she had seen Grace's secrets, and those were still not hers to tell. But Grace had laid the circumstances of her own creation at the feet of a witch, and had dared Margrit to disbelieve when she already trucked with Old Races. "Witches," she murmured instead of arguing. "What race are *they?*"

"Human," Tahira said as if it was obvious, and Alban nodded.

Margrit, still sitting on her hands, peered at

Alban. "You know about witches?"

"Very little. Only that they exist, that they command human magic, and that they are dangerous even to each other. What they can do, what they cannot do, I do not know. We… avoid them."

"You, gargoyles, or you, Old Races?" Margrit looked at the earthen lamp and answered her own question: "Old Races. Alban, I didn't even know humans *had* magic."

"You have legends of it," he said in mild surprise. "Why is it less likely that your legends of mortal magic are real than it is your legends of vampires or shapeshifters are real?"

"Up until about a year ago," Margrit said dourly, "I didn't think vampires were real either. All right, we'll table that for now. How does it work, Tahira? Does a witch have to force you into the lamp?"

The djinn shook her head. "Our legends believe it will capture us if we touch it at all. Please understand, Negotiator, that this lamp is as much a legend to us as it is to you. It is used to threaten children—and sometimes adults—into good behavior, but no one quite believes it exists. My grandmother's mothers back ten generations have passed it down from one to another, keeping it hidden always, and sharing its story with the eldest daughter alone. We believe it contains the whirlwind. That the first of our kind outraged a witch, and in exchange she captured him."

"How long ago was that?"

Tahira shrugged, a motion so soft it reminded Margrit of wind through leaves. "Too long for words. The oldest of my kind do not remember it happening."

"Uh-huh. And how did your family come by it?"

"The witch died, and my grandmother's mothers, who remembered the taking of the whirlwind, stole the lamp away."

"And didn't free the whirlwind?"

"We cannot. We cannot touch it."

"And everybody knows you free the genie by rubbing the lamp. If nobody ever released the captive djinn, where did *our* stories come from? How do we know there's a djinn in the lamp for Aladdin to find?"

"Perhaps there was another witch," Alban suggested. "They are known to hunt each other. Or perhaps more than one has been imprisoned over the years, and only the most recently or lately captured escapes."

Margrit sighed, scowling at the lamp. "It doesn't matter. I can't help thinking of the story about letting the djinn out of the lamp, you know what I mean?" Both Tahira and Alban shook their heads in the negative. "Ah. In this story, after the first thousand years he decides he'll grant three wishes to the person who let him out. After two thousand years he thinks he'll serve the person who lets him out for all time. After three thousand years…"

"He will make his savior king of all the

world?" Tahira guessed.

"No," Margrit said grimly. "After three thousand years, he decides he's going to spend the rest of eternity torturing the poor luckless bastard who lets him out."

They all fell silent, studying the lamp, until Margrit stood up in a burst of energy and paced the room. "If it's the lamp that captures djinn, it's a hell of a bargaining tool. We could either make a straight trade: Tariq gets the lamp for leaving Tahira alone—"

"Amar would want it," Tahira murmured, but Margrit waved it away.

"Internal politics are their problem. But I think it's just as valuable if we keep it. Maybe more valuable. Leave Tahira in peace and we won't use the lamp to protect her. Or us."

"Margrit," Alban said gently, "no one will believe you would use a device meant to jail someone, even to protect yourself."

"Of course I would." Margrit deflated, sitting in another chair with her hands over her face. "Just not for very long. And it would only be a credible threat if we're certain the lamp works, anyway."

Tahira stood. "You have a djinn upon whom to test it."

My heartbeat is so quick a hummingbird might have lighted in my chest. I was not afraid in coming to America, not like this: that was only the beginning, and this could easily be my end. There is no promise I will escape from the lamp, no guarantee that the Negotiator can free me. I do not wish to spend the rest of my days in a small black space, neither corporeal nor able to ride the wind.

But I do not believe Margrit Knight will leave me in the lamp if she has any choice in the matter, and so afraid or not, I am willing to try. After all, I ask a great deal of her in return. I know she is not in a position to offer asylum; perhaps no one is. But she will try, and so will I.

She finds her voice as I try to reassure myself: "That's a bad idea, Tahira—"

Beneath her objection, Alban Korund laughs. Margrit looks wry, her passion briefly annulled, and she explains, "Alban is always telling me my ideas are bad. A lot of people tell me that. They're usually right," she admits, "but the trouble is—"

"That there is rarely a better solution to be had?" I ask, and Margrit's shoulders slump in admission and defeat. I have won my opportunity to test the lamp as quickly and simply as that, and am not certain I am glad of it.

"I could just rub the lamp and see what comes out," Margrit offers, but if my idea is a bad one, we can all agree, unspoken, that hers is worse.

"Do not leave me long, Negotiator. My people are of the air and sun, and I do not like the thought of being kept in the dark." Before my courage can fail, before Margrit speaks again, I put one hand on the lamp's belly, and my body is torn apart.

Pain is not the right word. It is too shocking, too quick, to be *pain*. It is as if transforming to air has been enhanced, made faster and larger and more dangerous. My thoughts fly apart, words darting separately from one another until I am left clawing at them, trying to hold a sense of self together. *This is human magic,* I think, and that is the end of me. I am nothing, dissipated and incorporeal forever, my sense of self drifting apart, away, fading.

And then I come together again in the darkness.

Djinn didn't erupt the air when they melted into their insubstantial form. Selkies did a little, a slither and slip of air and space as mass changed from one shape to another; gargoyles did more substantially, a clap of air rushing in or out as they became distinctly larger or smaller. Dragons knocked Margrit off her feet when they shifted, the unleashing of mass so vast it created concussive force. But djinn, airborne and ethereal, did nothing but fade when they took to the air.

Tahira exploded.

Not bloodily, not messily, but her very self flew apart so visibly Margrit could see the colors of her clothes spray into the air. They expanded, spreading further, then whipped together in a fine thread and were sucked into the lamp with a violence that left it rocking. For an instant, Margrit and Alban were both still, shock holding them more strongly than alarm. Then Margrit swore and lurched forward, seizing the earthware lamp and scrubbing its belly furiously. Dirt and dust flaked off, leaving a streak of polished clay bright and clean amid the muck. Margrit whispered, "Come on, come on *come on*," then, in a fit of desperation-born absurdity, blurted, "I wish Tahira would come out of this lamp!"

The reverse explosion was as dramatic as Tahira's disappearance had been. Color rushed out, stretching as if to spatter the walls, then slammed together again, leaving Tahira staring blankly at a spot beyond any Margrit could see. She was pale, all the sun-browned color leeched from her skin, and her shocking green eyes were huge in a haunted face. Margrit seized her hands and hissed at their chill, then squeezed hard, trying to bring Tahira's distant focus back to her. "Tahira? Tahira, come on, wake up. You're out of there, you're safe now. Tahira?"

The djinn's gaze drifted to Margrit, and she came to life with a body-jarring twitch. Her color returned and her hands warmed in Margrit's grip. A blush mounted her cheeks, dusky skin flushed hot. "No. Oh no."

"What? What is it? What happened in there?"

"The whirlwind, Margrit Knight. Legend speaks the truth. The whirlwind is contained within the lamp."

Nervous excitement thudded in Margrit's chest. "The first of your kind? The first djinn is in there?"

"No. Oh no. And yes, perhaps, but no. The first of our *tribes*, that is what lies within. The whirlwind is not one djinn, Negotiator. It is thousands, and they are mad."

KISS OF ANGELS

Part I

THERE WERE A *LOT* OF DAUGHTERS, now. Six at least, assuming Margrit Knight hadn't already gone and gotten herself with child. There was the one, the stumpy gargoyle's daughter, that nobody was even supposed to know about, but then, Grace knew a lot of things she shouldn't. And the *other* gargoyle's daughter—but she was dead, which was just as well, because she'd been mad and dangerous both.

Bloody Janx and Daisani had four between them: the half-breed girls Kate and Ursula, who had at least gone away after their fathers wrecked a good chunk of Manhattan, and then *these* two. Jana, the first full-blood child born to the dragons in Grace's long life and more, yet barely a century out of the shell. She took everything seriously, an emerald-eyed child whose black hair held red highlights that reminded Grace of her father, and whose slight human form carried the weight of a dragon with it. Jana, and then her sister Emma, who was half a vampire and half a *witch*. *That* one flitted about, sweetly interested, hardly tethered to the world: even her hair floated, black strands idling along with her as if they been exploring and then drawn away before they were quite finished. Her guileless blue gaze made it easy to imagine she didn't realize when she poked her pretty nose where it didn't belong, but Grace didn't believe that for a minute. If they'd had the decency to go away like Kate and Ursula had, then Grace could have put them out of her mind and forgotten about them. Kept herself and her world beneath the city streets safe and quiet a while longer, no itch to search out the impossible or answer questions that had been left lying for centuries now. At least the *mother* had left, that cold-blooded Russian creature who was *all* a witch and had been Baba Yaga's daughter besides. She claimed she was no longer that at all, but neither did she take a name to define herself as anything else, and there had never been a witch's daughter whom Grace had known who didn't owe something to her mother.

"*Witches*," Grace spat aloud, if softly. At her side, the police detective cast her a questioning glance. Grace, casting a sidling glance back, thought if she were to be honest, it might not only be the damned witches who awakened the itch to answer unexamined questions. But then, *honest* wasn't a word Grace used to describe herself, and if history books did, she no longer knew if they might be liars.

The stolen light beneath the city did Tony Pulcella no favors. He was meant for sunshine, where his olive skin glowed and his brown eyes lit half to gold. He could have been cast from the opposite mold used for Grace herself; she was moonlight pale and had been long before she took to the tunnels beneath New York to live. But he came down into the tunnels to visit more often than Grace went above. She had her excuses; Grace always did. The runaways and street kids she helped shelter and keep warm needed her presence to maintain order, or a homework group needed a tutor, or there was trouble in the tunnels that only the likes of Grace O'Malley could chase off. Tony found the time to come to her, delaying going home from work, or coming in early to spend an hour or two beneath the streets. Some nights he went from his shift at the precinct to the tunnels and back again; she didn't remember, quite, when he'd begun leaving a clean suit in the cool brick-work chamber she called her own. It had been years—decades—since a man had tried so hard, for her.

It had been decades—centuries, even—since she'd allowed one to.

And that thought lay too close to the itch to answer impossible questions for Grace's comfort, so she leaned in to kiss the detective before remembering that the daughters were still there. She muttered, *"Witches,"* again, against his mouth this time, and less bitterly.

"What about us?" Emma's sweet voice drifted across the chamber: round concrete walls had bounced Grace's curse to her, though if the young witch heard the distaste in Grace's word, her tone said she'd taken no offense.

"Witches get Grace's back up," Grace replied. Emma chuckled, but a spark lit in Tony's gaze. She'd touched too hard on her own mysteries there, and though he was patient for someone who solved puzzles for a living, he wouldn't wait on it forever. That he already knew more than most made no never mind; a mystery wasn't solved unless all the pieces fell into place. And she had no fear that her secrets would drive him away: Tony Pulcella had been glad to learn of the Old Races' secret existence alongside his own world. Margrit Knight had underestimated him. Grace didn't want to do that her own self, but the habit of silence was hard to break.

But break it she must, and soon, or lose the man, and she'd lost enough loves in her long life already.

"Which witch was it that cursed you?" Emma asked, oblivious to—or, Grace thought with a sharp look at the ethereal girl, *privy* to—Grace's most secret thoughts. Emma looked up from her task—repairing jeans, a dull chore she appeared to enjoy—with such a gormless gaze that Grace snorted disbelief. A smile touched Emma's lips and she returned to her mending, but her attention, sharper now, remained on Grace.

"Fúamnach. Her name was Fúamnach, and she was said to be a daughter of the Tuatha."

"The people beneath the hills," Emma murmured to her mending. "Perhaps she was the only Tuathan to ever truly exist. You know how witches are made, after all."

Tony blurted, "I don't!" with the air of a man knowing he's overplayed his hand but desperate not to let the moment of revelation slip past. Jana, who, though in human form, was lazing beside a heating pipe that protruded from the wall, let go a laugh. "And of all of us, you should, as you're the only one who could."

"Detective Pulcella doesn't carry any secrets dark enough to bring a witch to life," Emma said in a pleasantly disagreeable tone. "Not even if it lay bursting from the earth, all but alive already."

"The very definition of a good man." Jana settled again, though she'd truly barely moved at all, as Grace watched Tony's expression twitch between pleased and chagrined.

"A man needn't have dark secrets to be a man, Tony. We don't all need to carry darkness inside us."

"I know, I know. It's the patriarchy, isn't it. Convincing us that men have to have dark sides to be really manly." A thread of rue wound its way through the detective's words, but Grace's smile grew.

"That it is. A witch is born from human secrets, mo chroí. Secrets whispered into the earth until they take on life of their own, for there's power in secrets. There's blood and hate and anger and lust in secrets, and there's love and laughter and joy. More hate, though, or at least that's what births most witches."

Tony shot Emma a startled look. The girl laughed aloud. "Not I. I was born the usual way, as was my mother, who was the daughter of a man *her* mother later ate. But my grand-mother." Emma nodded. "*She* was born of the earth, and secrets, and no living mortal will ever slay her."

"Baba Yaga," Jana said from where she lounged. "Mother says she has grimoires full of secrets about the Old Races, but she won't let me fly to Russia to steal them."

Grace saw it, the protest that flew to Tony's lips and went no farther: *Baba Yaga?* that protest said. *The Russian fairy tale? The witch from folk-lore?* She saw, too, what he thought then: that he had—albeit unknowing—tracked a drag-onlord's criminal activities for years, that his ex-girlfriend was in love with a gargoyle, that he sat amongst fairy tale creatures even now, and that he had known, accepted, that Grace herself had long since been cursed by a witch. She saw all of that in his indrawn breath and the silence he kept with it. His next breath, though, he spoke with, and said, "I guess if there are witches it's not surprising we know the names of one or two. But I didn't know the one you said," he said to Grace. "Fooam... nack?"

"Fúamnach." Grace emphasized the *noch* at the end and Tony repeated it under his breath. "The Tuatha dé Danann were the fairy folk of Ireland, long ago. Human-sized, not the twee things like Tinkerbell. They were said to live beneath the hills —"

" —and witches are born from the earth," Tony finished, almost triumphant. "*Was* she the only one?"

Grace shrugged one shoulder. "The Tuatha were before even my time, love. Ask Daisani, or Janx."

Tony, dryly, said, "I'd rather not," and laughter rippled around the chamber.

Then it was Emma, the witch's daughter — of course — who asked the question no one, not Tony, not the massive gargoyle Alban Korund, not even endlessly curious Margrit Knight, had been bold enough to ask: "What happened?"

A smile pulled at the corner of Grace's mouth. "I got involved with a girl."

She wasn't meant to be at sea at all. Had never been meant to be: the price of being a girl, even if she was the only child of the O'Malley and his wife. She remembered still the day she had asked her father if she might go to Spain with him. Remembered his booming laugh and his mocking answer that she could not, because her long red hair would be caught in the ship's ropes.

Remembered, too, his face as she had drawn her belt knife and sawed her braid off as she stood there in front of him, and how the plaits sprang free into rivulets like blood upon the earth when she threw the severed hair at his feet.

They called her *mhaol* after that, cropped-hair or baldie, but the O'Malley let her sail with him to Spain, and she returned to Ireland's western shores with a good command of Latin, and the skill to write it. She was nine then, and the next seven years she spent at her father's side, learning the art of leadership and the skills to sail a ship. She was years married and the mother of three when her father died, and not a soul, not even her father's son by another woman, disputed her claim to being the O'Malley, head of her clan. Nor did anyone dare decry the O'Malley when she took to the seas to protect their westward-facing lands, as every O'Malley had done before her.

And neither, more was the pity, did anyone dissuade her of the taking of a bad wager: that she herself alone could navigate a small little currach from miles beyond Clew Bay back to the safety of shore on a morning when a red sun rose warning of storms.

It had seemed a fine idea at the time. Saint Brendan had done it, after all. Had taken himself and nine monks all the bloody way to the Americas, if legend could be trusted. In the small hours of a morning, having taken deeply of the drink, Grace, trusting both legend and her own navigational skills, had been fool enough to let someone drop her off in the hide-hulled boat in the middle of the ocean. The night had been clear, though, with no hint of the upcoming storm. Now, at dawn and still half-stupid with drink, Grace scowled at the scarlet sky as if the weight of her impotent gaze might cow it into fair blue. The sky cared not at all, and the storm would care even less when it drowned her. Grace swore, once at those who had laid the bet, and thrice at herself for taking it.

The currach was a wee little thing hardly long enough to lie down in, with no mast and a single bloody oar. A child could paddle it around the bay for a week without tiring, but the bay would bring a child back to shore with its tides. The ocean would offer Grace no such help, and besides that, if she didn't come to a casual docking at her own castle on Clare Island she would be laughed out of being the O'Malley; making landfall in north Mayo, or down the country at Galway, would nearly be worse than never making landfall again at all. She took the oar in her hands, feeling it settle familiarly against old callouses, and set off with one eye on the sky and the other on the horizon, where a shadow marked Ireland's placement in the cold northerly sea.

A pleasant ache settled into her shoulders and arms as she worked her way east, and the thought struck her that, so long as she beat the storm getting home, rowing across the ocean wasn't a bad way to spend a morning. There were no children wanting attention and no men seeking advice, no ships to collect taxes on and no squabbles with the other clan lords to tend to. Just herself and her sweat and the cool sea air, with the sound of gulls complaining and water slapping the boat to keep her company.

That and the wind coming up. More than was safe: enough that she was only holding her own against the sea rather than being driven back to the west, and then in a little time, she was no longer managing even that. Waves swelled, tossing the currach as they wished; it became Grace's duty to lash the oar down, that she might not lose it, and do what she could to keep the boat from filling as rainwater pissed down from the sky. Her fingers went numb with the cold, and in due time, so did her mind. *Dry* was a thing of the past, a distant memory not to be dreamed of in the moment; indeed, drawing another breath above the water was all that *could* be dreamed of, in the moment.

She was too wet and too cold and too tired to even realized it when the currach capsized.

A Serpent slept beneath the ocean's surface. Far beneath: it wound around the ocean floor, squeezing and flexing, stretching and sighing. Earthquakes rumbled when it did, and mountains rose, or great belches of gas erupted in bubbles that reached the sky. A bubble had caught her, and drifted downward again, as if her weight was enough to anchor it but too little to send her falling through its curve into the cold water beyond. It sank until it bounced against the bottom, and with each bounce, brought her closer to the serpent.

It was the devil himself, she decided: if there'd been a serpent in the garden, it had to be this one, large enough to end the world. Though it didn't look interested in ending the world, or anything else. It might even have been said to save her. "Sure and of course it did," Grace said beneath her breath. "I'm the O'Malley, after all," and laughed at her own audacity.

The Serpent opened its eye at the sound of her laughter, an eye three times her height and full of its own glittering light. There shouldn't be any light this deep at all: she shouldn't have been able to see the Serpent, or anything else. But then if she was applying good sense, she ought to have drowned an hour or more ago.

Maybe she had.

The thought made her shudder from her bones out. She was cold, as the dead were meant to be, but so was the fathomless water, so that was no signifier. She breathed still, but perhaps the dead breathed, on the other side of the night. "What do you want of me?"

An answer came, but not in words. Hardly even in images: it was as though the *sense* of what the mighty beast wanted overwhelmed her, took her thoughts and mind and self away to be replaced by a knowledge as endless as the sea. Mortals skimmed the surface of the sea, fighting battles with each other and the weather, all almost too small to notice. All just large enough, together, to sometimes disturb the Serpent's sleep. To make it *aware*, as a creature so vast could hardly be, of the lesser beings in the world it encircled. Very few other living things came to its notice: sea serpents, perhaps, for they dove so deep as to find the Serpent himself, and brought with them whispers of the world above. Perhaps it was those smaller serpents who had made him aware of humans at all. Other sea monsters, squids and great whales, brushed by him from time to time, carrying stories of the small things that hunted on the surface. And sometimes a ship sent its crew into the deep as well, but very few, very few indeed, of those drowned sailors brought with them enough of a spark to draw the Serpent's attention. More of those luckless seafarers were taken by the siryns, whose songs had once soothed the Serpent's slumber, but who never swam into the deeps where he coiled around the heart of the world. For all that they lived in the ocean, they were closer to belonging to the other, his counterpart, the green thing that grew through all the land and nurtured the life that had crawled from his domain into hers. The serpents were his, and perhaps even their winged brethren who flew the skies above, but the dragons never came into the sea, and the Serpent was —

"Lonely," Grace breathed, "and curious, I'd say. What has that to do with me?"

The world as she knew it, blue and green and grey, came to life as if the Serpent woke every memory she had at once. The sun raced through the sky and hid behind clouds, a thousand days of living, of dying, of birthing and fighting. Clear moments she remembered without prompting: her red braid bleeding on the ground, her childrens' first squalls. Moments she had forgotten and many of them better left so: unwarranted cruelty and unbearable shame awakened to haunt her, for she wouldn't easily forget them again. Moments that lay in between, forgotten in the daily business of life but recalled with a certain scent or taste. Memory even seemed to cast forward, as if the Serpent couldn't quite understand imagination or anticipation, and saw a dream of what might be as something no less real than the recollections of what had been. The one constant was Grace herself, a fixed and always-changing point, weighted, going forward, with a sense of observation: the Serpent, seeing her world through her eyes.

"Hah! And what do I get out of this?"

Water pressed in, sudden and cold and unforgiving. Salt filled Grace's lungs, and a sensation of fish nibbling at her fingers, at her flesh, at her very bones, gave a seafarer's answer to the question. She flung her hands up as if she could protect herself from the surging ocean and found no water clawing at her face, but still felt the weight of it in her chest and throat. As quickly as it had come, it vanished, leaving her coughing and doubled as she gasped for air. Wiping her eyes, she wheezed, "You'll throw me back to land, then, like a fish too small to keep? It's a devil's bargain, beastie, but it's better than drowning. I'll take it, and sing a song for my supper, too."

The Serpent's eye glittered again and its whole head settled a little, like a cat expecting a bit of meat thrown to it if it lay quietly enough. Grace ran her hand over her eyes again and frowned at its glimmering gaze. "You wouldn't really want me to sing, beastie. My brother Donal has the voice for it, but mine is only passing fair." The Serpent waited, and she sighed. "Though who else would sing for you here in the depths, I suppose. Those mermaids you put me in mind of haven't sung in a long time, have they? All right, but the decision is yours to regret." Her voice, she knew, wasn't as bad as all *that*, but even when they were no taller than her knee, her children went to their father or uncle for lullabies when they could. Grace found one of those tunes and brought it to life for the Serpent, and then another, for she knew the words and melodies as well as anyone might, even if her song wasn't as sweet as another's might be. And then for the sake of singing, she sang a third, making bold enough to sit by the Serpent's jaw and close her eyes while she drew jigs and poems and laments from memory, until her voice was gone. She had been hours under the sea, she thought, though the cold no longer seemed to touch her. It was magic at work, and she who had never done more than blow a kiss to the fairy forts to help pass safely by, was content with that: superstition could be winked at, but magic could not be denied. She stood, not surprised to find her muscles stiff, and looked up at the Serpent again. Its eye was lidded, barely a glimmer of light curving at the bottom, but something shone at the inner corner. Grace reached for it, then snorted at herself: the beast's *eye* was thrice her height; she could hardly hope to reach the distance up *to* its eye without climbing its face. Bold she might be, but not *that* bold.

As if it heard her, the Serpent opened its eye again. Grace swore she saw amusement flicker in its depths, before the monster shook its enormous head once and sent her bouncing across the sea floor and up into the waves.

She awakened on a beach, drenched to the bone and cold as a dead man's knuckles. She'd made a pillow of her hands and a stone while she slept, if sleep it could be called, and sat up rubbing at a sore spot where the stone had

poked against her cheek. Even under the dull
light of a dreary day—rain drizzled down and
the sky was so uniformly grey Grace couldn't
tell where the sun sat in the sky—even in that
light, the stone she'd used as a pillow shone a
deep grey opalescence, so liquid in appearance
she prodded it to make certain it wasn't a puddle. It wasn't; the ache in her cheek told her
that, but she prodded it anyway, then lifted it in
her hands. It filled her two palms, its gently
rounded bottom fitting against them nicely. The
whole of it was roughly oval, but swollen to a
nub at the top, like a tear frozen just before it
finished settling from its fall. It hadn't the
weight of a stone, either, any more than it had
the look of the rocks on the rest of the beach: if
she looked away from it, she could imagine she
held nothing in her hands at all. Grace stood,
the stone in one hand, and looked out to the
water as if she might see a serpent's coil break
the surface and sink again. There was nothing
there but the choppy white of small breaking
waves, and the arguments of gulls as they dove
at the water. At least the storm was over, and if
she hadn't come home direct to Clew Bay, then
she had still survived, which was more than
might be expected, even of the O'Malley.

She wrapped the stone in the extra fabric of
her shirt—its saffron yellow was dulled by sea-
water now, and would need to be re-dyed—
tied a knot to keep it from falling out, then
struck out for higher land and a sense of where

she might be. Far enough away from home that Croagh Padraig, the holy mountain, couldn't be seen once she'd found a hilltop to look from, but then, with the high fog, even the hilltop she stood on was shrouded. The wind, if it blew like it had done through all the summer, would be from the north, but Grace hated to set out only to learn she'd been going the wrong way once the skies cleared. By all rights the sea should at least be to the west, but she'd spent a night nestled with a serpent at the heart of the world, and she didn't like to chance it that all was as it might usually have been.

A cairn stood on a hilltop not so far away, and near the cairn, smoke from a fire made a line against the fog, before mist made the smoke its own. Grace, cursing the shoes she'd lost in the sea, made her way down the hill and through forest to the cairn-hill, where the smoke came from not near, but within, the cairn itself. She stopped short and cast another glance toward the sea, half-suspicious of mockery now. It was one thing to be faced with the Serpent of Eden itself, and another altogether to then march up a hill to a grave with living beings within. "I am the O'Malley," she shouted at the cairn. "If this is earth of the Tuatha dé Danann I mean you no harm and will leave you in peace!"

Silence met her cry: silence, and then the soft scramble of shifting earth before a child's face emerged from the cairn. A filthy child's face, with hair so matted and dirty it had no color of its own, and as human a child's face as ever there was. "My mother is Fúamnach of the Tuath Dé."

Grace crouched, her breath leaving her in a laugh. "And your father?"

The child shrugged. "A man."

"And yourself?"

"My mother's daughter, but nothing more. I have no old magics or godhead. I have run away," the girl declared. "I will not be of use to her in the only way the untalented daughter of a god might be."

"And what way is that?"

"She sups on my flesh and drinks of my blood to bring the power she wasted in making me back into herself." The child extended a hand to show Grace that three fingers were missing, and the dirty scars that said she had not been born without.

"Mother of God." Grim with curiosity, Grace added, "Why not eat you all at once?"

The child's gaze was flat. "Had I been born a son she would have, but a daughter has *some* power of her own, and not even a witch dares eat it all at once, for fear of losing herself to the rising magic. I cannot *work* magic, but neither can she eat me all at once."

"Mother of God," Grace said again. "How do I stop her from eating you?"

"Why would you do that?"

Grace's eyebrows rose. "We don't often eat

children, where I come from. Much as we might sometimes like to."

The girl's expression became so suspicious that Grace laughed. "Children try the soul, girl, but we don't eat them. If you've run away I suppose you won't be calling your mother here, so tell me how to find her." She glanced toward the sea, hardly visible now beyond the hills, and muttered, "And tell me if the sea still lies to the west. I don't know this land at all, and I would have said I knew Connacht like the back of my hand."

"Some witches live in houses that walk the earth, that they may not be easily found. Others cast a glamor on the hills they call their own, that the mind slips and cannot see clearly when it encounters the witch's home. My mother lives in Mabh's tomb, but you'll never find her by climbing the hill and calling her name. You must enter my barrow, and go always to your left, even when the path leads only to the right. When you've gone thrice sinister a circle, you will find her by her fire, gnawing on my bones."

Grace glanced at her own fingers, the ones the child was missing. "They're thin bones there. Surely she's eaten them all by now."

The girl, filthy as she was, managed an even filthier look, and dragged both herself and a stick from the cairn. With the stick's help, she stood, letting Grace look her fill at a leg half missing. "She ought to have taken both my legs at the start," the girl snarled, "so I couldn't run away."

Sickness rose in Grace's gullet, though she didn't look away. "How do I kill a witch?"

"With the secret that birthed her," the child said, and to Grace's drawn-down eyebrows, bitterly, said, "You don't. You might bargain with her, but no human has much a witch desires."

"All I have with me is my own life, and that, I already owe to my people and my children. How can I help you?" Wind crawled up Grace's nape, ruffling short hair and lifting bumps on her arms. She would have said that witches and magic were not for the likes of her to truck with, but fate meant to say differently.

"You might steal me away," the child said hopelessly. "I might travel safely over the water, or not, but even if I should die on the salty sea I would die my own creature, and not my mother's meal."

"Now that I can do," Grace said with a smile. "Why would you die on the sea, when you sail with the O'Malley?"

"Because a witch can't cross running water wider than her stride," the girl said in a withering tone, "and I am a witch's daughter."

Grace gently set her teeth together, thinking of her own daughter Margaret, who was thirteen years of age and obnoxious, and did not slap the tone out of the witch's daughter's mouth. "A daughter with no witchery of your own save the life in your veins, so perhaps not a witch yourself. Have you *tried* to cross water, child, or have you stayed on your hilltop here, like your mother Fúamnach before you?"

A look of guilt and shame skittered across the girl's face before she wiped it into defiance. Grace held up a hand, silencing the excuses that were no doubt about to come, then stood with a sigh. "Down the hill with me, lass, and we'll find a stream to see if you can cross it. At the worst I'll bring you home and wash you, and I'll find the filí to see what tales of witch's secrets he knows. And if I cannot squirrel you away, and I cannot defeat her, then thrice widdershins a circle I'll go and bargain with her, for there must be something a mortal lord can offer a witch."

The girl, leaning on her stick, swayed. "Why?"

Grace sighed again. "Because we don't eat children, girl, and *this* O'Malley, at least, knows what it is to defy fate and write it the way you wish."

The girl could cross a stream, though she stood a long time on the far bank after Grace waded through, staring at the water as if it might leap from its bed and drown her on its own. Grace waited, if not patiently, until the girl lurched forward awkwardly, with the air of one going to her own death. Her foot, then her stick, plunged into the water, and nothing more happened: no shrieking, no wailing, no melting, no—Grace didn't know, truth be told, what might happen to a witch trying to cross running water. Whatever worst it might be, though, it didn't come to pass, and the girl, astonished, came to stand at Grace's side on the near bank.

"There," Grace said. "We've learned a thing about you. What's your name, child?"

"I have none. A witch doesn't name her daughters, for a thing with a name is a thing defined by something other than its mother."

Grace muttered something not even she could understand, then said, "What name would you choose?"

The girl slid a glance laced with uncertain hope at her. "O'Malley?"

A bark of laughter broke from Grace's throat. "Well, you'll not be *the* O'Malley; that title is taken. All right, then. Máire," she decided, because to give a witch's daughter the Virgin's name seemed like the best way to draw her away from the witch. "Máire O'Malley. You're my clan now, girl, and no one will eat any more of you so long as I live."

They went south together, for Máire knew the way even when Grace didn't recognize the land. In only a little time the witch's glamour faded and Grace knew the way home. The serpent had thrown her far to the north, though: it was two days' walk before they came to the beaches that Grace called her own, and had the moon not broken through to shine half as bright as day, it might have been another morning before they found Grace's people.

It was testament to them, and to Grace's repu-
tation, that no one had yet begun funeral prepa-
rations, or to call her oldest son the O'Malley.
Grace kept the tale of the serpent to herself, and
claimed that Máire, an orphan, had found her
washed up on shore, and offered help. The clan
embraced the girl for that, and laughed good-
naturedly at her discomfort. Well, a mother who
ate her bit by bit wasn't one to show much affection, Grace supposed. Máire would get used to it
—or not—and soon enough she'd be judged on
her own merits, instead of simply being wel-
comed as the girl who helped the O'Malley. A
fire was built of driftwood, then built higher still,
to celebrate the O'Malley's return, and the night
ran long with joy. Grace went among those at
the beach, reassuring them that it was her own
self home safe again, and sent word to her castle
on the island that she was returned. The lads in
the boat warned her—as if she needed warning
—that her children would insist on fighting the
out-going tide, and come to shore to meet their
mother. In the warning was a question they
didn't quite dare ask aloud: why the O'Malley
meant to remain on the shore, rather than going
to her keep to see the children immediately. But
they didn't ask, and she didn't answer, and they
did as they were bid, bringing word to her family in their castle.

Her reason for staying a while longer stood
on the shore of Clew Bay looking toward Clare
Island with something like true fear writ on

her dirty features, though. "Crossing a stream is one thing," Máire whispered when Grace came to stand at her side. "A bay of sea water is another."

"What happens, when a witch tries to cross water?" Grace kept her voice low, though with a bonfire going and fish roasting over it, not many were nearby to listen to the O'Malley and her new ward. "Does it drag her down and drown her?"

"Maybe, if she can get onto it in the first place. I saw my mother try, from time to time. It was as if she walked into a wall. At the edge of the water, she could simply go no farther."

"And yet she tried."

"There's never been a witch yet who didn't try to take more than was hers to have." Máire wet her lips, watching the changing tide. "I stood at the stream so long for fear of feeling that wall, if I stepped forward."

"Do you feel it now?"

"No, but…" Máire gestured to the sea, inching backward from where they stood. Even the tide mark lay a few steps ahead of her: she hadn't nerved herself up to the test yet. If it were her own child, Grace would seize the girl and drag her bodily into the water, laughing while she screamed and played at getting away. But her own children had no fear of the sea, nor of their mother's intentions, and so Grace put out a hand, not making quite so bold as to take Máire's without the girl's consent.

Máire looked at Grace's outstretched fingers as though she'd never imagined holding someone else's hand, then carefully fit her palm against Grace's. Grace gave an encouraging nod and took a single step forward, waiting to see what Máire would do. She hesitated, then hitched forward, then again, hobbling through sand and stone toward the water's edge.

Grace stopped there, half a step before the retreating waves could reach their toes. "Feel anything, lass?"

"The sand is cold and wet between my toes," Máire said, revulsed and fascinated all at once.

"Well, aye," Grace said, amused. "But anything else? A wall?"

"No, but...." Máire shrugged. Grace clucked her forward like she might a horse, and together they stepped into the fading edge of surf. Máire yelped at the cold, but neither bounced backward as if she'd encountered a wall, nor fell foaming into the water as if determined it should drown her. A few more steps had them knee-deep, as deep as they could go without soaking their clothes. Máire stopped there, her breast heaving like a horse who'd run a race. "I feel its pull."

"Acht," Grace replied softly, "so have all of us, child. It's what draws us to the sea again and again, even when the storms take our lovers and our fathers and our brothers."

"That isn't—" Máire stopped, seeing that Grace knew that wasn't what she meant, and letting Grace see that surge by surge, Máire began to understand, too, what Grace had meant. "Will it take my foot out from under me?"

"If it can. Make no mistake, Máire O'Malley. The sea will drown you if it can, as sure as if you *were* a witch, but I think, my girl, that it won't do it *because* you're a witch. Now, will we go back to shore or wade in until we're wet through and through? There are blessings in the sea, a chuisle mo chroí, as sure as there are deaths."

"'Cushla machree'?"

"It means my pulse, or my heart."

"My mother had no such fond names for me."

"Your mother," Grace said pleasantly, "was an auld bitch, so to hell with her and her ways."

Máire O'Malley laughed for the first time then, and went into the sea to come away a witch's daughter no more.

Nothing, Grace knew, was ever that simple, and yet she was surprised when the witch came for her daughter.

She came at night, in the dark of the moon, two full weeks after Máire crossed to the island for the first time. She came to the edge of the bay and stood wreathed by flame that seemed to have no smoke, and there lifted her voice so loudly that she could be heard across the water, all the way on the island, where Grace O'Malley stood listening and watching from the height of her tower castle. Curses spilled from the witch's lips, but Máire, at Grace's side, listened and shook her head. "She's only raging. There's no power in her words. Even if there was, the water would stop it."

"I may be born and bred to the sea, but even I can't stay on the ocean forever," Grace said wryly. "What happens if I go to parlay?"

"She'll kill you."

Grace's eyebrows rose. "She can try."

"She is Fúamnach, witch of the west, daughter of the barrows, and she will kill you. Perhaps not all at once, but your death will be hers and every day you keep from dying will fill her coffers with a little more of the power of the O'Malley. Do not treat with her, or the price paid may echo down the centuries."

"So I must not go, I cannot stay, and I will not give you back to her. Where does that leave me, Máire O'Malley, once a witch's daughter?"

"It leaves you a fool for helping me," Máire said quietly, and slunk away with her head bowed in guilty relief. Grace watched her go, then stood, listening a while longer to the witch on shore roaring threats and anger across miles of shifting water. Below, keeping watch on the island shore, her own men shifted uncomfortably, clumping together in ways they usually would not. Some tested the wind, as if it blew ill, and others hunkered down with a scowl so deep it changed the set of their shoulders: they liked the witch not at all, even knowing nothing of who or what she was.

Well, they must be shown that the O'Malley was not afraid, whatever else might come of it. Grace went below to put on her finest léine, thigh length in saffron, with snug sleeves that stopped at the elbow, so the great loose cuffs could fall free. Over this went her coat, short and snug heavy wool dyed deep green, with the seam unfastened from the elbow down so the léine's cuffs could fall free, and the sleeves wrought with leather knotwork patterns that told of her own exploits—for while she might do the witch an honor of wearing her best, even a witch ought to remember who the O'Malley was, and what it meant to bear that title. She wore trousers beneath the léine to ward off the wind, and boots, but her head she left bare, to remind all who saw her that she was Gráinne Mhaol, the O'Malley, who wore her fiery hair cropped short that it would never tangle in the ropes aboard her ship.

Those who saw her stride out from the castle took heart: she saw it in the corners of her eyes, how they straightened and pulled their shoulders back, lifting their chins and finding defiance to replace fear. She went alone despite that, in a currach with a sail to go with its oars. The wind was with her, so she made a fine sight, leaving the island behind, and the truth was that curiosity, more than terror, writhed in her gut. She had never met a witch, and only believed in magic because she had sung to the Serpent at the heart of the sea.

She expected Fúamnach to stand twenty feet tall, so easily had she been seen from the water, but the closer Grace got, the more ordinary in size the witch became, until Grace leapt from boat to shore and found she stood taller than the daughter of the barrows, and had bathed more recently besides. Not even the wreath of flame could burn away the witch's scent, if flame it was at all: Grace felt no heat from it, and smoke still did not rise. Despite the stink, though, Fúamnach was not as Grace imagined, ancient and wizened and grey. She had the lines of beauty in her face, and her carriage was strong and certain. Máire, once clean and combed and dressed in more than rags, favored her, a thought the girl would hardly appreciate. Fúamnach herself wore — not rags, but a gown that should have long since tattered to thread. It was too aged or too dirty to be named any particular color, but its cut was exceptionally fine, and the fabric beneath the grease had once been expensive. Gossamer and gold, Grace thought, such as the fair folk were said to wear.

The witch spat the same words she had been speaking all along, in a language so old Grace was hardly certain it was Irish at all. As she touched the shore, the force of the phrases hit her, nearly knocked her back into the currach. She staggered with them, feeling the weight of Fúamnach's hatred, then gathered herself and stepped forward. Something flick-ered in the witch's eyes: fear, or surprise, or perhaps simply more anger, but it gave Grace a branch to hang on, and so a smile pulled at the corner of her lips. "I am the O'Malley. You have something to say to me?"

"You have stolen my child. Give her back to me." This time the witch spoke an Irish Grace could understand, though that was no surprise: Máire knew the modern tongue too.

"I can't give back what I haven't taken. Máire came with me of her own free will, as God intended she should be able to."

"She is *mine*."

"She belongs to her own self and no one else," Grace murmured. "What will it take to drive you from my shores? Our oldest filid have reached back to the stories of their fathers and their fathers before them, and the secret that made you is not among the stories that they know, so your death is not a thing I can command." The witch's eyes flickered again and Grace hid a smile: she ought not know of how witches were born, and it discomfited Fúamnach that she did. Pressing the advantage, Grace repeated, "What will it take to send you away?"

Fúamnach's lip curled, showing a bit of fine white tooth. She sniffed the air, though how she could smell anything besides herself, Grace didn't know. Still, sniff she did, then said, "You've the scent of magic about you."

"I am trucking with witches," Grace replied dryly.

The witch hissed like a cat, showing a whole mouthful of good teeth. Perhaps it was magic that kept them strong, for surely the witch was as old as the hills, and ought to be toothless. "*Other* magic," she snapped. "Deep magic. I will have that, and leave you."

Grace waggled a finger. "I might trade it, for Máire's freedom and your departure. But how do I know you'll keep your word?"

"Witches don't lie."

"I doubt that."

Fúamnach hissed again. "The Tuatha cannot lie."

"But there's never been a faerie born who couldn't twist the truth. I want a blood oath on it, that Máire is free and you'll haunt Connacht no more."

Rage glittered in the witch's eyes, but she drew a knife from beneath her gown and lifted her hands, shaking her sleeves back to expose her wrist. Grace stepped forward and caught the knife hand, staying the blow. "Blood spilled on the earth will do me no good if you break your word and return. I'll fetch a cup, and the deep magic besides. Wait on me, Fúamnach, daughter of the barrows, and cry your terrible cries no more. My men need sleep, and I have no patience with theatrics."

She took a perverse pleasure in Fúamnach's impotent fury, but then, since the day she threw her hair at her father's feet she had always enjoyed thwarting those who thought themselves more powerful than she. She wouldn't have grown up into the O'Malley, otherwise; for a woman to lead the clan she had to be more than anyone expected. And she was, it seemed, more than Fúamnach of the barrows expected, for the power in the witch's arm relaxed, and she strained no more against Grace's hold. Grace nodded once and released her, then returned to the currach and cursed her way back across the water to the island, in part because the wind was against her and more because if a witch was interested in the serpent's gift, there was more to the thing than a bit of shining rock. Though Grace, being no witch herself, could hardly imagine what good it would do her, so the bargain seemed sound enough.

She took herself into the castle whistling, and back out again as cheerfully, with a bag with her treasures at her hip. Dawn colored the sky gold and rose as Grace returned to shore and presented Fúamnach with a bowl of lacquered oak to bleed in. The witch glowered but cut her arm, dripping blood into the bowl as she snarled, "On my blood I will not return to Connacht so long as the O'Malley holds Umhaill," a vow that Grace considered, smiled at, and agreed to.

Fúamnach's eyes glowed with greed as Grace took the stone from the bag at her hip. It felt cool in her palms despite having been near her body's warmth, and its shimmer reflected her face back at herself as she offered it to the witch.

Fúamnach cradled it close, stroking the glimmering surface, then lifted her gaze to meet
Grace's with a furious smile twisting her lips.
"Hear this, Gráinne Ní Mháille, called Gráinne
Mhaol and Granuaile, called Grace, called the
O'Malley. You have taken three things from me:
my daughter, my blood, and Connacht, where I
have long since dwelled, and you have only
given me one in return. I take two more in
exchange, to make our bitter bargain equal. I
take your land for my child's life, and your death
for my blood. I am banished from Connacht; so
be it. Let all of Ireland be a stranger to you before
you die, for your life will be long and your death
longer yet. I curse you to walk this earth, Ó
Máille, until you taste the kiss of angels, for that
is the price of treating with a witch."

A silence filled the chamber as Grace finished her story, the sort of silence that didn't
know if it should applaud or gasp or question.
Jana was unlikely to break it, as she appeared
mostly asleep, but Emma's eyes were enormous
with interest. Tony finally spoke. "Did you all
really talk that formally all the time?"

Exasperation blew out of Grace in a raspberry. "Jesus, man, have you no respect for the
telling of a tale? There are *forms*, Tony, you
don't just—" She saw him laughing at her, and
subsided into mutters.

"I have a thousand questions," Emma whispered. "How could you have given up the Ser-

pent's Tear, even for someone's life? Don't you know what it can do? Did you lose the Ireland you knew? Did Fúamnach ever get to return to Connacht? Don't you know a witch couldn't harm you, not if you had a tear from the Serpent itself? What song did you sin—"

"Stop!" Grace held up both hands. "You'd ask all thousand if I let you. Yes," she said more softly. "I lost Ireland to the English long before my own death fighting the bastards. And Fúamnach regained Connacht even before that, for England made a county of Mayo, and all our kingdoms were subsumed. I lost it all, little girl, all for the price of a child. She died. My foster-daughter, Máire O'Malley, drowned on the sea not a year later. But she died free of Fúamnach, and perhaps I would have lived to see Ireland fall regardless of the old bitch's curse."

"You would have," Emma said. "You did. She didn't curse you. She couldn't."

"And yet here I live and breathe before you." Grace shrugged, throwing away the accuracy of the details.

Irritation crossed Emma's face. "You're not hearing me. How did you die?"

"In battle." Beside her, Tony made a surprised sound. Grace shrugged at him, too, as if to ask what it was he'd expected. He muttered, "I don't know," not loudly enough to interrupt Emma, who demanded, "And what happened then?"

Grace sighed. "I rose up a wraith, a ghost, young again in incorporeal body, but old of mind. I've walked the line between life and death ever since."

Emma, the witch's daughter, rose and came to stand in front of Grace. Behind her, still lazing near the heating pipe, Jana lifted her head as if making sure her sister required no support. For once, though, Emma's hazy gaze was focused, even intense. "Tell me what a ghost is. What it can do."

"You're mad. A ghost is a spirit of the dead. They walk through walls and—" Grace flung her hands wide, exasperated again. "They speak with the other side. They haunt people. They're ghosts!"

"They're usually tied to a place," Tony said. "A house or their place of death or even a person. They're often murder victims, or have some unresolved business to deal with before they can move on. Some of them have the ability to interact with the world, usually violently. Those ones are poltergeists. Ghosts are usually able to fly, or at least levitate. They're depicted as wearing sheets, which is probably meant to represent burial shrou—*what*?" he asked of Grace's half-accusing, entirely astonished look.

"When did you get to be such an expert on ghosts?"

"When I started dating one!"

A smile crooked the corner of Grace's mouth. "That's the nicest thing anybody's said to Grace in a long time."

"Well, what else was I supposed to do? A lot of my job is trying to understand things, and you're a hell of a mystery."

Grace tilted over to kiss him, then curled her fingers in his hair and drew the kiss out, long enough that Emma made an impatient noise to break them up. "Are you tied to a place, Grace? Were you murdered? Are you unnecessarily violent? Can you fly? Do you haunt anyone? Do you know *any* other ghosts?"

Grace sat back from Tony with a sigh. "In all my born days and all my long nights I've never met another ghost, no. Get to the point, witch's daughter."

"I've gotten to it twice already! A witch can't hurt you, Grace. She couldn't curse you. She *couldn't.* Not if you held the Serpent's Tear."

"I'd given it to her already, girl."

"Daagh!" Emma stamped her feet in frustration, an action swifter and more mercurial than any mere human could manage. Jana, lazily, came to her feet and crossed the room to put an arm around her sister's waist. "You're not hearing Emma, Grace, or you don't know enough about what you did. You spoke with the Serpent at the heart of the world, and he gave you a *gift.*"

"I know more of the Serpent now than I did before Margrit's stunt with the gargoyle council," Grace allowed. "What's that to do with the price of tea?"

"He is the *Serpent,*" Emma said, speaking

with urgent precision, like she was trying to impart something to a particularly obstinate child. "He's half the core of this world, Grace. He's half of what all magic is made of. And he *liked* you. Fúamnach didn't curse you to a half life. The Serpent gave you a tear, and with it granted you immortality."

Little enough in the world could render Grace speechless, but she sat wordless under the weight of Emma's declaration for nearly ever, turning it this way and that to see if sense could be made of it. It couldn't: she said, "I died," flatly.

"And you rose up young again. Reset to when the Serpent had known you." Emma sounded unflappably certain of herself.

"I walk through walls and turn iron to mist."

"Because you believe yourself to be a ghost." Emma's voice softened suddenly. "The Serpent's Tear, Grace—I've read about them in Mother's grimoires. There have only ever been a handful of them, and they imbue their owner with power. Not mortal magic, either, not even such as ours, but a whisper of the Serpent's power. You can do—" She caught her breath. "You can do anything, with a Tear."

"I gave the—*Tear*, if that's what you say it is, to Fúamnach centuries ago. Whatever power it might have is surely hers to command."

"You traded it." Emma sank down into a bundle, her knees drawn up and her arms wrapped around them. Jana went with her as naturally as if they were twins, though they shared not a drop of common blood. "A trade and a gift are two very different things. Had you *given* it to her, its power would be lost to you, but it was one thing offered for another. In all of these centuries, the Tear will have strengthened Fúamnach's magic, just as the heat from the pipes warms Jana, but she can't command its magic herself. The most she can do is siphon some of it, and it may be that your ghosting is from that little drain of power over all these years."

Grace closed her eyes, blocking out both Emma's earnest young face and the portents of what she said. She was cold, but she had *been* cold for centuries: ghosts were. Her heart, which had never stopped beating in all her living—or unliving—days, felt thick and slow and heavy in her chest, and knocked an ache into her lungs with each dull thump it made. That ache was almost a physical thing, which she needed: without it she thought sickness might rise and overwhelm her; the beads of sweat on her lip and hairline said it was all too possible.

Tony Pulcella's warm arm went around her waist. He pulled her closer to him, silent as she turned her face against his shoulder and breathed, long shaking breaths that did little to quell the roiling of her stomach. He rarely used cologne, for which she was grateful: even the scent of his soap and skin was nearly too much for her. A tremor started somewhere in her gut and rattled out, and came again in waves. Tony's warmth was suddenly welcome. "Tell me," Grace finally said in a harsh tone. "Tell me from the start, so that I understand."

Jana, into Emma's hair, said, "Mother would be better at this," and Emma murmured, "But Mother isn't here," before raising her voice and speaking to Grace. "A Serpent's Tear confers immortality to the one it is freely given to. In exchange, the Serpent…"

"Watches," Grace said hoarsely. "I remember *that* part of the bargain well enough."

"Watches," Emma agreed. "Barely, though. We're too small for him to really understand. But he watches, and sometimes bits of his knowledge slip through."

"Grace knows more than she should," Grace whispered, and from the corner of her eye saw Emma nod. "And?"

"The Tear—" Emma sighed. "Its ultimate power is to grant a wish, Grace. But if a wish isn't made by the one to whom it was gifted, then it…empowers her. The Serpent is…vast. What it understands…you died. You lived again. To you, that's a ghost. And so the Serpent's power…helped you become a ghost. You walk through walls. You turn iron to mist."

"*That*," Tony breathed against Grace's shoulder, "is a story I want to hear someday."

"Ask Stoneheart," Grace replied, while Emma went on, "Fúamnach knew what the Tear was. She knew what it would do to you, and I think she saw you *didn't* know. The curse was a trick, Grace. I'm sorry. She set you looking for the kiss of angels, knowing you'd never find it."

Grace finally lifted her head. "Why not?"

The child of a witch and a vampire, sister to a dragon, stared incredulously at the ghost. "There's no such thing as angels!"

A weak laugh broke the cold weight in Grace's chest. "Sure and there's not. Of course there isn't. What madness would that be? Angels and devils and gods, oh my. Hah!" A shiver brought some of the cold back, but she straightened out of Tony's arms. He let her go, but a part of her thought there would be a reckoning for that, soon enough. Not for pulling away, but for the thing in her that made her determined to stand on her own. The thing that had made her the O'Malley, and had set her fighting a losing battle against the encroaching English, hundreds of years ago. The thing that kept her under the streets, in fact, trying to save runaways like Máire, to make up for having not quite saved the girl *enough*, in Ireland so many years past. All this time she had told herself it was being a ghost that kept her apart, but the truth of that was coming undone, and aye, there was a reckoning to come. "So I'm a ghost by my own design, tricked by a witch to wander the earth a lonely soul, and now you tell me that there's a *wish* to be made, witch's daughter? I could have my mortality back, if I made the Tear mine again?"

"You could have whatever your heart desired," Emma said.

Grace, without meaning to, cast a glance at Tony. His slow smile warmed her as much as his arms had, and she told herself that a ghost couldn't blush, never mind that it seemed she wasn't a ghost at all. Centuries of believing it had to count for something. She did return the smile, as soft and slow, for she might as well be hanged for a sheep as a lamb, before saying to Emma, "How do I undo a trade with a witch?"

Jana, the dragon's daughter, whose hoard was her own sister and mother, shrugged. "Offer her something she wants more, or kill her."

Tony barked laughter. "I thought witches couldn't be killed. What's she going to want more than a wish-granting rock?"

Emma fixed him with a thoughtful look. "Perhaps a handsome young man to make another daughter with."

"She could find that herself," Grace said sourly, but laughed at the grimace that pulled Tony's face. "Don't worry, love. Grace won't trade you for a bit of shiny stone. You say the Tear is mine anyway," she added, to Emma. "Can't I just take it back?"

"It would work if you did," Emma agreed. "Whether you'd—" She stopped abruptly, and Grace smiled.

"Whether I'd survive it? I would, though, wouldn't I? Because I'm the Serpent's chosen." She pulled a face and got up to stretch, shaking leather-clad limbs and rubbing the numbness of sitting on concrete out of her bum. All three of the others watched, the girls idly and Tony with an appreciative tilt of his head. "She'll still be in Ireland," she said, mostly to herself, then frowned at Tony. "Fuck. It takes a passport to travel overseas these days, doesn't it?"

"I know a dragon who might bring you," Jana drawled. "For a price."

"When was the last time you left America?" Tony asked.

Grace shrugged at him and gave Jana a hard look all at the same time. "Grace has been here a long time, love. There was nothing for me in Ireland. I might have stayed and fought on against the English, but where? The clan had watched me die, so I'd have had to gone somewhere else, become someone new. I'd be no longer the O'Malley, and have to watch every day as the Ireland I'd known was eaten away by conquerors. I might have," she said, voice dropping low and seething. "Had I known I couldn't die? Oh, I might have fought on, and perhaps I'd have made a difference. But I had already been Grace O'Malley, whom the English called the pirate queen, and even as a queen I couldn't hold Umhaill, or treat with bloody Bess, or keep my country mine. And we fickle humans, we only love legends when they're safely dead and gone: had I stayed, immortal, among them, I'd have lost them sooner than later, and broken my heart all the more when I left." She fell silent, breathing through her teeth, then snarled, "Though it would have been worth it to walk unkillable through Cromwell's camp at Drogheda and rip the bastard's throat out with my hands. Damn!"

She spun away from the listening trio and slapped a palm against the wall, angry enough —but not fool enough—to hit it harder. She heard Tony's indrawn breath, an answering murmur from one of the girls, and knew that her lust for revenge over injustices three centuries and more in the past bordered on incomprehensible. Not one of them had even a third her years, much less the sudden, bitter insight that she might have done more, then, than she had known.

Tony, though, rose and came to her side. Folded his arms and leaned his shoulder on the wall she'd hit, his head lowered but his gaze cast upward, so he watched her through his eyelashes. In a woman—in another man, even—she might have called the gaze coquettish, but she had led men for too long to think Tony had come to flirt her into calmer waters. His was the look of a man ready to do as his officer required, but it was love, not mere loyalty, that drove the look in his eyes. Despite herself, Grace chuckled, and the hint of a smile played at the detective's mouth. "You all right?"

"No. Yes." Grace gave a loose-shouldered shrug. "I don't like finding out I've been a prisoner of my own mind for nearly half a millennia, but there's no taking it back, not any more than I could go back and tear Cromwell's throat from his miserable body. And if the witch holds no power over me..." She sighed. "Well, that's a better thing than learning my every breath is at her whim."

"Would you really want to give it up? Your immortality?"

Grace shook her head. "Ten minutes ago Grace didn't know she had a choice, love. Now? I don't know. But I'm none too keen on Fúamnach draining power that should be mine, either. And yet the bargain was made." She looked past Tony's shoulder, finding a middle distance in the chamber.

"Máire died young, though."

"I traded the Tear for the girl, not for her long life. How do I come calling four hundred years later, to say the deal's done and the stone is my own to take?"

"You were tricked when you made the deal to begin with."

"That's nothing to do with the price of tea." Grace sighed, bringing her focus back to Tony. "I suppose I ought to get that lawyer involved."

Tony laughed. "Margrit? Well, she'll give you her two cents on the moral and righteous thing to do, whether it's the legally acceptable one or not."

A smile pulled at the corner of Grace's mouth. "Will you never forgive her, then?"

"Aaaah..." Tony waved a hand. "We could

never really forgive each other for what we were. It's most of why we didn't work out. Even before all of this came along." He waved again, but this time encompassed the sisters, whose heads were ducked together as they murmured to one another. "So, sure, I forgive her. But that doesn't stop her from being sanctimonious." He paused, then, with a pull of his face, admitted, "Or me, either."

"And there, now, mo chroí, that's why I'm so fond of you. You admit the truth about yourself to yourself, which is rare enough. Take it from a woman who's been lying to herself for centuries."

"You didn't know you were." Tony stepped into Grace's space, sliding his hands around her waist and tugging her against him. "'My pulse', huh?"

"Did you not know what it meant?" Grace smiled against *his* pulse, pressing her lips against his throat.

"We call each other 'rigatoni' as an endearment in my family, not 'my heart'." Tony tipped his head back, sighing as she kissed his throat again, then chuckled, a tingling vibration against her lips. "This isn't talking to Margrit."

"Fúamnach has waited four hundred years," Grace murmured. "She can wait another night."

A moment later, Emma said, "Ew," with perfunctory sincerity, dragged Jana to her feet, and left the O'Malley and her lover to their business.

Part II

MARGRIT KNIGHT STOOD FIVE FOOT THREE in her bare feet on a good day, and made it a habit to never be caught flat-footed if she could avoid it. Grace O'Malley, though, excelled at catching people off-guard, and grinned lazily down at the petite lawyer, who sighed and left her apartment door open, invitation to come in. "Normal people don't show up at three in the morning without warning, Grace."

"And when was the last time you were normal people?" Grace slunk in after Margrit, bumping the door closed behind her. The apartment wasn't much different from when she'd visited last: two bedrooms down the hall to the right, a bathroom nearly across the hall from the front door, a kitchen to the left, and a dining room, then a living room, wrapping around behind it. A fridge twice Margrit's age still dominated the kitchen, but the dining room table was no longer impossibly laden with papers, and the living room had a new couch. New cushions and strong springs were necessary, Grace guessed, when one member of the household weighed in at several hundred pounds in his natural form. "Was it after you met Stoneheart, or before? I'd think that would have been the end of *normal people,* never mind supping of a vampire's blood."

Margrit gave her a scathing look that said she preferred not to be reminded of that incident. More fool she, Grace thought, when it was the two sips of blood that reduced her need for sleep and allowed her to live the double life she'd chosen with her gargoyle partner. Rather than address it, though, Margrit said, "You should talk," without particular heat. "I can still count the years since 'normal' on two hands. You, though…what do you want, Grace? You don't usually come knocking."

"I *never* come knocking, lassie."

"A point which I forbore to make, so thank you for making it for me." Margrit climbed onto a counter with the ease of a child and opened a cupboard, reaching for a bottle of whiskey that she withdrew half an inch before glancing at Grace for confirmation.

"Far be it from me to refuse a dram," Grace drawled.

Margrit rolled her eyes. "You do want something, if you're laying on the Irish." She still got the whiskey down, hopping off the counter as easily as she'd climbed up, and pulling out a couple of crystal tumblers from another cupboard. "On the rocks or straight?"

"Straight. Most people would have a step-ladder, love."

"Probably." Margrit poured the whiskey, handed one to Grace, and collected the bottle as she gestured toward the living room. "Come on and lay it on me. Last time you showed up here in the middle of the night it was to be dramatic and ghostly at me, so I'm braced for more of the same."

"You're not wrong to be." Grace followed her into the living room and took the opposite corner of the couch to where Margrit sat. The whiskey bottle went on the coffee table, in easy reach. "Where's Stoneheart?"

"Lurking over Janx's old territory. I've told him dozens of times that there won't be any trouble with the djinn and selkies, but he watches anyway." Margrit smiled into her whiskey, murmuring, "It's what he does."

"And you," Grace said, "give advice."

Margrit's eyebrows rose. "*You* need advice?"

"I've a quandary."

"This should be good." Margrit nursed her drink while Grace sketched the details of the deal she'd made with the witch, then she sat back, considering Grace's story. "So you're asking me if you have a legal standing to take the Tear back?"

Grace drained her own whiskey, which she'd left untouched. "I am."

"I'd say no. You both got what you wanted out of the trade, and like you said, it's not her fault that Máire died. At least, I assume it isn't, and it's centuries too late to tell. Now." Margrit lifted a finger along-side the tumbler, light bouncing off the gold liquid within and brightening the underside of her hand. "That's my legal interpretation of the matter, but legal code doesn't take serpents at the heart of the world into account. Have you asked him?"

Grace, dryly, said, "I don't have his cell phone number."

Margrit laughed. "I forgot to get it myself. But he's down there. There must be some way to commune with him, without…"

"Drowning? I wouldn't count on it, love. And what would I ask him, whether trading away his Tear was legally binding? I don't think the question would mean much to him."

"Didn't you say he watches through you, though? Which means you have a connection to him." Margrit moved her hand a little, pushing the question aside. "I don't know what you'd ask him. Whether he could recall the Tear, maybe. Or whether he knows—Foo-am-noch," she said carefully, then, with more confidence, "Fúamnach's secret. Something that would give you leverage over her."

"You're a bit of a conniving bitch, aren't you, Margrit Knight?"

"Says you," Margrit said in a half-offended tone, and then, with a twist of her mouth, "Bitches get shit done. You need leverage, Grace. Otherwise you're at a stalemate. Not that I'm condoning murder, but even if I was, neither of you can strike the other down, so you're going to have to find another way. Find something else she wants, or find her secret. Witches," she said under her breath. "Why do the Old Races seem easier to deal with than witches?"

"Because witches are human magic." Grace sat back, stretching her legs expansively.

Margrit leaned over to the coffee table, got the bottle, and poured more whiskey for both of them. "Humans aren't supposed to *have* magic."

"Most of you—us—don't. There are dream-walkers and a couple others, but magic is a thing they *do*, not a thing they *are*. The gargoyles and all, the whole lot of them, they can look human on the outside but once you know the truth, you know they've never been and never will be like us. And that makes it all right, in its way. They *are* magic. Sometimes we have it, but it's a thing inside us, not who and what we are in our bones. That's why witches feel wrong. They're human-born but made of magic, and that's not how human-born things are meant to be."

Margrit looked askance at her. "And how do you know all that?"

Grace pulled a face. "Grace knows lots of things she shouldn't."

"The Serpent's Wisdom." Margrit lifted her glass in a salute.

"So it seems." Grace returned the toast and drank the second glass in as swift a swallow as the first. Margrit, watching, said, "Do you not get drunk?"

Grace arched an eyebrow at the drink Margrit sipped. "Don't tell me you do. Not with all that vampire blood swirling in your veins."

"You know, I haven't tried? Maybe you and I should go on a bender. Drink all the boys under the table. Win a few bets."

"Before I find a way to end this curse."

"Except it's not a curse," Margrit said. "It's a gift. Do you really want to give up immortality?"

"Tony asked that too. Ask me again your own self when you've lived four hundred years."

Margrit smiled. "Implying that you'll be here in four hundred years for me to ask."

"Don't lawyer your way around this one," Grace said severely, and Margrit laughed. "Let's say I get the Tear back. What do I do with a wish, Margrit Knight?"

Margrit sighed, taking a larger swallow of her drink. "I don't know. I've never been able to decide if I should go big or go home, with a wish. There's all the legalese, you know?"

"Only a lawyer thinks wishes have legalese."

"You're wrong, though. There's literalism in wishes. Look at Midas, wishing everything he touched would turn to gold. That's obviously a terrible wish, because he didn't mean *everything*. He meant he wanted to be able to turn specific items into gold, not that his dinner and his daughter should be included. So when you have three wishes, is the first one 'I wish these would be taken in the spirit they're meant instead of the literal words I say'? Or do you just try to limit the wishes in a smart way? 'I wish, with no changes in my health or circumstances, that I would be the most miserable person in the world?' What are the effects of wishing for something abstract, like happiness? God forbid you should wish for no more conflict. That could kill everybody on the planet. Wishes have consequences. Even 'I wish I wasn't immortal anymore…'. Think about that, Grace. You could die on the spot. So you have to be careful with wishes."

Grace leaned forward and poured herself another drink. "I'd think wishes came along every day, the way you've thought out how they ought to be used. Anybody ever tell you that you think too much?"

"Many people, often." Margrit swirled her whiskey. "If they really came along every day maybe I wouldn't have thought so much about it. They're abstract, this way. And maybe a real wish *does* respond to intent instead of literalism. That would be…" She smiled. "Well, that would be more wish-like. That would be how magic is supposed to work. Like a dream. Like a wish. You know what I mean."

"I do." A key turned in the front door and Grace's head came up like a startled cat's, wary of what lay beyond.

"It's only Alban," Margrit said, amused. "He lives here too, you know."

"I know a gargoyle in a high-rise apartment seems wrong," Grace muttered, but stayed put as the big gargoyle came around the kitchen corner and paused, surprised, to see her.

"Grace."

"Stoneheart."

"'High-rise' makes it sound fancier than it is." Margrit rose to give the gargoyle—not that he looked the part right now, being in human form —a kiss. "Grace came by for some legal advice. Have you ever heard of a Serpent's Tear?"

Alban's eyes, yellowish even as a human, darkened in thought. "There are whispers about them in the memories. Why?"

"I had one," Grace said succinctly, "and I lost it. Traded it," she amended, because the detail mattered. "I'm wondering if I can get it back."

"Ask Janx. He's as close as anyone is to the Serpent." Alban retreated to the kitchen to get his own crystal tumbler, and even poured himself whiskey when he returned to the living room to sit, but didn't drink any of it. Grace watched the chair he took sink under his weight, but didn't offer to trade places with him. Margrit got her own glass and perched on the wide arm of his chair, bird-like in comparison to his bulk. They looked well together, though, as if they'd been designed to be aesthetically pleasing: Margrit, small and brown-skinned with a wealth of loose curls highlighted with gold that brushed the collar of a comfortable, bright shirt. Alban was over a foot taller and nearly that much broader than she, hewn of straight lines and pale shades beside her, alabaster skin and white-blonde hair falling down his spine in a simple ponytail incongruous with the grey suit he wore. Grace smiled, and Margrit lifted an eyebrow. "What?"

"You two should have a portrait done. A painting, not a photograph. Janx left the city months ago." She muttered, "Besides, Grace tastes good with ketchup," to herself, and though Alban looked baffled, Margrit laughed aloud.

"Do not meddle in the affairs of dragons. I don't think you've got much choice, though, Grace. Not if you want the Tear back. You need some kind of advantage. She traded it to a witch," Margrit said to Alban. A remarkable —for a gargoyle—expression of *you're fucked* crossed the big man's face.

To her own surprise, Grace laughed. "Stone-heart thinks I haven't a chance of recovering it."

Margrit twisted to look at Alban, eyebrows lifted in curious amusement. "Doesn't she?"

"Witches don't easily give up what they've taken."

"But the gargoyle memories might know something about Fúamnach. As much as any-one else might. Could you look?"

Alban lowered his gaze to the drink he hadn't sipped from, then lifted it again to meet Grace's eyes. "Is it a sign of friendship that you just ask me, or a sign you think I'm easily taken advantage of? You wouldn't ask Janx so directly. You'd sidle around, looking for a way to make him offer, or for it to seem like an advantage to him, and Daisani—"

"Daisani I wouldn't ask at all," Grace said with a shudder. "I'll wheedle and deal if you want me to, Stoneheart. You do owe me one, and I'll call that favor in if I must."

Interest glittered in Margrit's eyes, though she left the question unspoken. Alban, though, cast an edged smile at his drink. "If I were a wiser man I'd insist on it."

"But you're not a man at all." Grace flung herself back in the sofa, arms spread wide. "So you'll do it."

"I already have." Alban shook his big head once. "There are whispers, here and there. Memories of a memory. Not about Fúamnach, but about the birthing of witches. It may be that contained somewhere in the stone we have all their secrets, but despite our best efforts—despite our vaunted beliefs—even the gestalt has suffered. We're so few now that we remember less than we should."

"Some good you are," Grace said without heat, then, more slowly, "I suppose it's Janx, then."

"You could find out what Fúamnach wants now," Margrit said from contemplation of her glass. Grace frowned and the lawyer lifted her gaze. "Everybody wants something. Find out what Fúamnach wants *now*. Get it. Trade for it. The Tear for her newest desire."

"What could a witch want more than a wish-granting rock?"

"She can't *use* the Tear. Not for more than siphoning power, anyway. Which is good, as far as it goes, but she'll never be able to wish on it. Maybe there's something she wants more."

"Dragon's blood," Grace muttered. "A virgin's tears."

"Eye of newt," Margrit agreed. "There's a lot out there Grace can find, that someone else couldn't."

Grace drew her face long, giving Margrit a severe look that made her laugh. "I'm sorry. Are you the only one allowed to talk about yourself in the third person?"

"Grace is the only one who spent fifty years as the O'Malley. Try half a century of a title like that and then four hundred years of a half-life and see if you don't get a little strange with how you refer to yourself."

"Negotiator," Alban rumbled so quietly it was almost inaudible, but Margrit's spine straightened and she cast him a look that held an opinion or two about the use of that name. She didn't say anything else, though, and Grace rose.

"You've given me a path or two to follow, at least. I thank you for that. Alban, I'll call our debt even, for your efforts."

"That's generous," Alban said in a tone that suggested he expected loopholes. Grace didn't disabuse him of the notion, and let herself out through the front door like a normal person might, though the idea of wafting through a wall and giving Margrit Knight the willies stayed with and amused her as she returned home.

Tony woke up when she came home, instantly more coherent than he ought to be in the small hours of the morning. "It's hanging around with you inhuman creatures," he said when Grace commented. "I think it's rubbing off."

"I think you need more sleep, love." Grace dropped a kiss on him as she drifted through the chamber, looking for things that weren't there. She'd owned and lost, or rid herself of, a lot in her life: not much was left now. Not much to show she'd lived four centuries, but that was the idea. It was hard enough to gain teenage trust; carrying around loot a hundred years out of date only made her seem stranger than she was, and she had plenty of that going on already. So, although she still had the now-pitted blade she had carried as the O'Malley, it lay tucked in a teak chest at the foot of her bed, as did everything else from her youth. The concrete and brick room beneath the city streets reflected someone who lived sparsely: a bed, candles for light, a scattering of books. She'd seen Alban's lair before it was raided, and her own life didn't look so different, save she walked the world day and night alike, and the gargoyle was bound to night. She rarely felt the lack of *things*, but tonight, with dawn breaking above the city and only artificial light here to mark the difference between night and day, her world felt empty.

But that was the shock of revelations talking, for all that she didn't show much of it on the outside. A clan leader had to keep her own counsel, and a ghost even more so. Only she wasn't a ghost at all, but a creature half-damned by good intentions. Someone else might have wept and wailed and rent her breast; Grace O'Malley was made of sterner stuff. Or at least more inured to the improbable than most, by dint of having lived through more of it, if nothing else. Still, beneath the surface lay a whirlpool that could draw her down if she let it: not even centuries of existence made it easy to reconcile the idea that she'd been misled about the circumstances of that life for most *of* that life.

A rueful smile pulled at her mouth and she turned to look at the detective sitting on her bed. His black hair was tousled and the sheets were rumpled around his waist, his arms looped around his knees. She ought to be telling *him* all of this, not keeping it tamped down inside. Easier thought than done, though, for when she opened her mouth to speak again, what she said was, "Your lawyer had a lot of ideas," rather than offer any hint of her turmoil.

"Were any of them good?" Tony asked dryly. "She has a lot of bad ideas."

"She has a lot of *dangerous* ideas," Grace disagreed. "Most of them turn out well enough in the end. All of these were dangerous," she added after a moment's thought. "Would you take Janx or Daisani, if you had to choose?"

"Janx," Tony said without missing a beat. He scooted to the side of the bed and swung his legs over, reaching for his slacks. "I know he's a dragon, but I spent years on a task force try-ing to bring the man down. I understand some of how he works. Daisani…" He shook his head and stood, buttoning his slacks. "The high finance world is a whole different kind of evil, never mind the vampire part of it." He reached for his shirt and Grace, amused, said, "Do you have to get dressed?"

He lifted his eyebrows. "You didn't come to bed when you came home, which means you're not going to, not before I have to get to work. So I'm up and I'm listening. Are we going after Janx?"

Grace stopped the *we?* that tried to cross her lips, grateful and bemused by the offer all at once. "I've a witch to find, first, and a bargain to undo."

"Can you even do that? Blood oaths, and everything?"

Grace chuckled and knelt in front of the chest that lay at the foot of her bed. Tony tried not to watch too avidly as she opened it; she'd never done that before in his presence, and trusted he respected her enough to not have gone digging around in it himself. She took out a small, soft bundle of cloth, unwrapped a vial of ancient glass from within its folds, and shook the rusty dust inside the glass. "I can return her blood, if that's what she wants."

Fascinated horror paled Tony's face. "That's — that's — is that four-hundred-year-old *witch's* blood?"

"It is so."

Tony dropped to his knees beside her, an awful, wonderful grin twisting his mouth. "I bet you could sell that for a fortune on the internet."

Grace laughed. "How would I prove what it was? And if I did, how would I return it to the old bitch to gain her favor?"

"I don't know, but it just seems—" Tony reached for the vial, stopped himself, and crushed his hand between his thigh and calf to keep himself from doing it again. "It seems like you should hold on to some of it. Just in case."

"Magic isn't done with eye of newt and toe of frog, love."

Tony's eyebrows shot up. "Are you *sure* about that?"

"Sure enough." Grace dropped the cloth back into the trunk, closed it, and rose, eyes sparkling, with the vial still in hand. "Maybe we'll save a wee bit of it for ourselves. Just in case."

Sheer youthful delight brightened Tony's features. "Awesome. How did you even keep it this long? Shouldn't it have disintegrated?"

"I scraped it still wet from the bowl, stoppered it, and never opened it again." Grace gave the vial another little shake. "And perhaps there's a bit of magic in it, too. I don't know, love. I've never tried keeping anyone else's blood for nigh unto half a millennia."

"That…is just as well." Tony made a face as Grace tucked the vial away again for safe-keeping, this time in a bag that would do for traveling.

"It is. And if you're up for it, I thought on our way to Ireland we might pay a visit to the Serpent."

"*We?*" An incredulous note broke in the small word, more, even, than Grace would have put in it herself, had she said it.

"Unless you're not up for it, Detective."

"No, I just—*can* I? You're—" Tony made a swift gesture that encompassed Grace and, it seemed, the whole of her world. "You're magic, Grace. I'm just…me."

"I don't know," Grace admitted. "But I'd like you with me as far as you can go. If you're willing."

A smile lit Tony's brown eyes. "I wouldn't miss it for the world. How do we call on a mythical monster at the heart of the sea?"

Grace shrugged. "The only way I know is to drown."

"And you said *Margrit's* plans were danger-ous." Tony Pulcella stood on the stern of a ship, bundled in a winter jacket and still cross-ing his arms over his chest like he could con-tain another degree or two of warmth by doing so. Grace, beside him in her black leathers, didn't feel the cold, but then, she hadn't for centuries. She didn't even wear a hat, her blonde hair glowing in the autumnal sea sunlight, and Tony glowered at her like it might warm him up.

"We talked about this," Grace said with more patience than she felt.

Tony sighed explosively. "Talking about it is different than standing here watching you get ready to dive off the back end of a cargo ship, Grace."

"You took a month off work so we could do it. What did you think Grace would do, lose heart?"

A chuckle broke through Tony's scowl, obviously despite his best efforts. "I don't think that's even in your vocabulary." He leaned on the railing, cheeks scoured ruddy by the wind, and rubbed his hands together. "I still don't really…understand…."

"I told you." Grace's voice gentled. "I'm hard to see, Tony. Unless I want to be seen, I'm…"

"A ghost." Tony looked over his shoulder, not at Grace, but toward the bulk of the ship, where, somewhere, a small crew kept the behemoth running. He *had* taken a month off work, a vacation long enough to require real finagling to achieve, and he had bought only a single ticket for the cargo ship's handful of private berths. *His* passport had been updated and stamped on the way out of the harbor, but Grace herself had simply slipped aboard, unnoticed, while Tony dealt with the formalities. She had waited for him in his berth to let him know she was there, but the call of the sea was stronger than she'd imagined, and on the giant ship she couldn't feel the waves moving her at all. Once Tony was marginally settled, she'd abandoned him for the upper decks, barely willing to return to the berth at night: at night, she could see the stars unimpeded, as she hadn't in centuries, not in New York.

The truth was she could have stowed away even as a wholly ordinary, living human being, and she didn't see how the crew could have found her. Not as long as she brought food of some kind, at least. The ship was preposterously enormous, like a city block set on the sea. Shipping containers of all hues were stacked high, their size dwarfed by the ship, and the comparative handful of crew unimaginably small in the midst of it all. It had taken fifty men to sail one of her galleons; this ship, vastly larger, was staffed by barely half that. They were specks, and as a normal stowaway she would only have been one more, crawling over the ship's surface.

As she was, though, she was less than that, even. Grace O'Malley had become a street legend for a reason: always slipping in and out of places she shouldn't be, never caught by cops even when they swore half a second before they'd been staring right at her. They were right, too, but that was the ghost in her, able to fade away in a moment. Save that it wasn't ghostliness at all, but Fúamnach's draw on the Tear, stealing precious bits of tangibility from Grace, half a world away. "It hardly matters," she said aloud, and Tony looked surprised.

"That you're a ghost? If it really doesn't matter, why are we doing this?"

"Whether I'm a ghost or just a human stretched thin. Sorry, it was my own thoughts I was following, and not what you're after saying. We're *doing* it because Grace doesn't like to be tricked. Because I've been ill-used, and I won't have that if I can stop it. And because perhaps —" Grace caught her breath and let it out again. "Because perhaps a half life isn't enough, if there's more to be had."

Tony pushed off the rail and turned to lean on it the other way, his butt against the metal, as he put a hand out toward Grace. She took it and stepped into his embrace, smiling as she nestled against his chest. "The cold might not bother me, but the warmth is nice."

"What would the crew see, if they noticed me right now? A lunatic cuddling the air, or a woman in black who didn't belong on the ship?"

"The woman, and then I'd disappear, and in time they'd be telling tales of ghosts. If sailors are as superstitious a lot as they were when I sailed, they might put you overboard for consorting with me. I hate the size of this ship," she said, suddenly fierce and surprised at her own honesty. "There's no sense of the sea with it. It's only a floating fortress, beaten by the winds."

"Someday," Tony said against her short hair, "you'll have to take me sailing on a real ship. One with sails, I mean. One *you* can sail."

She smiled up at him, lips against his jaw. "Will you be my crew, Tony Pulcella?"

"For as long as you'll have me." Tony fell silent a moment. "Grace, before you do this, before you go into the sea…"

"Don't be giving declarations of undying love," Grace said, somewhere between serious and amused. "I can't take the melodrama."

"You bleach your hair almost white and wear black leather so you're a ghostly floating head while you skulk around the city streets," Tony said dourly. "Don't pretend you don't love melodrama. But, listen, I want to say this. I hoped it would be me."

Grace leaned back enough to see him more clearly, her eyebrows furled. His gaze was serious in the grey afternoon light, though his windswept hair did some damage to the noble intensity of it all. More matinee star than untouchable hero. "Hoped what would be you, mo cuishle?"

"The kiss—your kiss—the—Jesus, it sounds stupid, trying to say it aloud. The kiss of angels. I hoped it would be…a fairy tale. True love's kiss. It sounds worse the more I talk." Tony didn't blush easily with his olive color-ing, but he tried, neck stiff as he turned his face from Grace's gaze. "Talking about true love to a five hundred year old woman who's been married twice—"

"Thrice," Grace said softly, "though once only in my heart. That was all another lifetime, Tony. Another lifetime, a dozen lifetimes ago. Do you really think I'd be diving into the sea today, if it wasn't an angel's kiss I feel when your lips meet mine?"

His eyes came back to hers and Grace brushed her fingers over his mouth. "I'm bad enough at showing it, much less saying it, love. Grace learned to play it close to her chest long ago. But I was content, for all those long years. It's only since you that this half life hasn't been enough. Before that wretched witch's daughter opened her mouth, there wasn't much point in saying so, because what could I do? And even if she *had* opened her mouth, but I hadn't known you? Ah, Grace might have wanted the Tear back to settle a score. But immortality, love. You know how the song goes."

Tony said, "Grace," his voice suddenly thick, and she pressed her fingertip across his lips, silencing him.

"Not today, and not tomorrow. I've a Serpent to see and a witch to destroy, but when it's all over, love. When it's all over, then we'll find the words to say."

He closed his eyes, then nodded reluctantly. His voice was still rough as he opened his eyes to say, "You're a difficult woman, Grace," and Grace's answering smile was blinding.

"Acht, you think I'm difficult now, wait until I've supped with the Serpent again."

Before he could object—before *she* could think
—Grace spun away from him, ran, and dove
over the side of the ship in one long smooth
motion.

It had been decades—centuries, even—since
she'd swum in salt water. The memory of it
hadn't left her, though: the taste, the buoyancy,
the relentless cold, and the endless swell of
waves. Of course, had she been less a ghost and
more a mortal, the dive might have done her real
harm, a thought she didn't consider until she
broke the water forty feet or more beneath the
ship's deck. Nor had she needed to take into
account massive propellers driving the huge
ship forward, the last time she'd taken a dive
from a stern. The momentum of her dive had
taken her a fair distance away from those huge
props, though, and while she felt their pull as
they churned the water, it wasn't quite irre-
sistible. She kicked down-ward, swimming
deep, while the water filtered through her, not
quite able to seize hold and chill her into immo-
bility. As the water turned black, she stopped
kicking, waiting to see if she would drift upward
again. No: but then, she hadn't expected to.
Breathing was for the mortal, and she had long
since known she didn't strictly need to, though
she usually did, out of habit. But without real
breath in her lungs, there was little to buoy her
upward, and the water's pressure was more than
enough to keep her submerged.

Swimming all the way to the bottom of the ocean in hopes she'd find the Serpent in the dark had never been the plan, though. Once in his element, all she could really do was — *Grace is here,* she thought, and tried to make it an open, expansive thought, tinged with amusement. *The O'Malley seeks audience with the Serpent.*

The Serpent seemed to share nothing of her humor. Grace tried again, wondering how — if — it would recognize her at all. *Your watcher,* she said silently to the ocean. *The one who knows more than she should, through you. I've come back to you, Serpent. I've a question for you.*

It had a whole world to encircle, she told herself; a whole ocean to listen to. She should be in no hurry to have her call answered, though *that* was a thought that should have struck her earlier, before Tony had spent weeks arranging his month-long holiday, and before he'd gotten on a huge fecking ship to deliver her to the middle of the ocean. She could have done all of this by herself, including waiting for however long it took for a bit of flotsam in the sea to gain the Serpent's attention. Tony would have worried, to be sure, but he could have worried safely from land, and not wasted his holidays on a slow boat to Europe. It was sheer arrogance to imagine the Serpent would come when she called.

But then again, Grace had never lacked for arrogance. *On a grand scale, a day or a month or a year here won't matter, not to me,* she told the ocean, *but there's a man up there of whom I'm passing fond, and his days are only mortal in number. You know how fleeting humans are; it's part of why you chose me, so that you might have some sense of our brief lives, through one who was close to them. So I need to speak with you sooner rather than later, beastie, else all the sweetness you long to taste will be dead and gone before I return home.*

The water ought to have surged: it ought to have knocked her around with the Serpent's arrival, but there was no such thing. Its enormous eye simply opened in front of her, shedding light, without a drop of water disturbed by its sudden presence. Grace stood tall in the water, aware she was no more than half the size of one of its teeth, and one of the smaller ones at that. "I've some questions for you," she said again, then laughed suddenly, a sound that carried no distance in the heavy water but which bounced off the Serpent's scaly hide regardless. "That conniving old woman Chelsea told Margrit no one had ever spoken with you since the dawn of time. I fancy Chelsea thinks she knows quite a lot, and it was all I could do to keep from laughing at her theatrics. She claims it's you and the Green Mother who hold this world together, and both of you too remote to be known. But perhaps all we have to do is die, to meet you. There's a whole world of theology that might say so."

Water rushed around her as the Serpent blew through slitted nostrils as long as Grace stood tall. "No theological debates, then? All right. Is the witch's daughter right, Serpent?

Am I not cursed at all, but gifted with immortality since the first day we met? Was that stone I woke up with a wish in a bottle? And do you know Fúamnach's secret, so I might take it back from her?"

It—he, it, whatever it was—hadn't spoken to her before; why she expected answers now was beyond her, and yet seemed worth asking. The Serpent stared at her, sharing nothing save for his own size and presence, as if challenging her to doubt what it had granted her. Nor could she: looking into its massive eye she thought she was a fool for even daring to call on it, much less demand answers from it. With a sigh, Grace put her hand out like she might have for a dog or cat, and to her surprise the Serpent moved its huge head beneath her palm. Part of a scale on its head, at least; she reckoned its jaws could hold a blue whale or two whole, and the length of its head went beyond her ability to easily measure. But it put its head beneath her hand regardless, and once more the water didn't stir with its movement. "All right, then," Grace said quietly. "I've learned a tune or two since we last spoke, so I'll sing for my supper and then away with me, great beastie, with no more answers than I had before."

To Grace's relief, she was deposited back on the cargo ship, and not thrown all the way back to America, or even farther yet, to the shores of Ireland. The Serpent had known, she supposed, where she'd come from, perhaps because humans didn't belong in the middle of the ocean and the passing ships were the only way she might have reached him. She'd been much closer to land, the last time she'd encountered him, and overall she was grateful for the care it showed in depositing her where she'd come from.

That she returned two days after she'd left was only a problem in that Tony had worried himself pale in her absence, in a way the men serving the O'Malley hadn't, centuries earlier. But none of them had been her lover, either, nor as protective as the police detective tended to be. Margrit Knight—who had ended up with a gargoyle, hah!—had chafed under that protective streak, but Grace found it charming, perhaps because she hadn't met a man in four hundred years who could best her in combat, even if she *didn't* ghost on him.

A twinge made itself known along her jaw, and she rubbed it, chagrined at the memory it brought. It was true she hadn't met a *man* in four centuries who could defeat her, but Margrit had handed Grace her ass not all that long ago. Not that there was any shame in losing to a woman jacked up on vampire blood, but still, the loss stung a little.

"You're brooding," Tony said sleepily, at her side. His color was better now that she'd been back a few days, and he'd regained the weight he'd lost worrying about her. Grace dropped a kiss on his temple and nestled back down in the mechanical-quiet of their little room. Her sailing ships had been quieter, for all that the wind snapped the sails and shouts of sailors threaded the days and nights alike. They'd been natural sounds, not like the grinding engines and roaring propellers, or groaning steel and hard boots against metal floors. "Are you sure he didn't say anything useful?"

More awake, the detective wouldn't have asked that again; Grace had already snapped at him about it more than once. But in the dimness of night all she said was, "I'm sure, mo chroí."

"Then we'll figure it out in Ireland. We'll find an answer." He was quiet a moment, his breathing drowned out by the ship's sounds. "I thought I might see it. The Serpent. I stayed up on the deck, looking."

"For two days?" Grace pulled back a little, as though she could see him better that way, in the dim light. "No wonder you looked like death warmed over, love. Why would you do that?" A dry note came into her voice, half teasing and more serious than she wanted. "Don't you trust Grace?"

His eyebrows furrowed, though his eyes stayed closed, and he moved closer, putting his lips against her skin. "Of course I do. I knew you'd come back if you could. Didn't stop me from worrying. But I wanted to see it, if I could. I don't…think you realize how extraordinary you are. Any of you. Not even Margrit, anymore. But

I still see all of you through human eyes. I'm as close as any mortal is going to get, but I'm still on the outside looking in. I've never—" Grace, her own eyes closed now, felt the quirk of his smile against her shoulder. "—I've never danced with the devil in the pale moonlight. Which is all right. I've seen what it's done to Margrit. But I can't help wanting to be more a part of it. So I looked for the Serpent."

"Did you hope it would grant you a Tear, too?" Grace murmured.

Tony rose up on an elbow, surprise visible on his face when she opened her eyes. "No. I didn't even think of that. I just wanted to see it. The ouroboros. The Serpent. It's at the heart of so many myths, and it's real. I wanted to see that."

She traced a finger over his jaw, stubbly with a day's growth of beard. "Perhaps that's what Grace will wish for, then. That the good detective might see the Serpent."

He closed his hand over hers. "Don't you dare. What a waste."

"Then what should I wish for, Detective?" Grace turned her back to him, drawing his arm over herself to nestle in his warmth. Easier to whisper of wishes and dreams when there weren't brown eyes gazing on her, weighing her words and her thoughts.

"I don't know, Grace. You don't have to rush it. The Tear has sat around unused for centuries. Another year—or seventy—isn't going to hurt you any." Tony kissed her shoulder.

"True enough," she said, but kept the rest of it, that seventy years would be far too late for *him*, within. "What would *you* wish for?"

"I don't know. World peace. An end to hunger. To see the earth from space. That one's selfish, though."

"If the Serpent grants a Tear to a single person, it might be said it's expected to be used selfishly, love. It's not a magic lamp, there for anyone to find through luck alone."

Tony chuckled. "A lucky find means you have to make unselfish wishes?"

"It's a gift from the world if you find a magic lamp," Grace said. "You'd best offer the world something in exchange."

"Is that general Irish philosophy or a Grace O'Malley special?"

"No idea, love. It's a long time since I've been home."

It had been long indeed, and though she felt a fool saying it, the words left her lips anyway: "It's changed."

Of course it had changed; she had known Cork passing well, but it had been sacked and burned and sacked again, all the way up into the twentieth century. If anything was left that she knew, it was buried beneath the roads and sidewalks that had been plastered over the myriad islands that had once held the city between the streams of the River Lee. She knew it wouldn't be the same, of course: she'd seen maps and drawings from before photography, and thousands of pictures since. She *knew* what it looked like now, but knowing and walking down a broad lamp-lit street that had been river in her day were not the same.

Worse was Clew Bay, which she'd once known like the back of her hand, and which now looked wrong in a hundred ways. The shoreline had shifted until she, who could have walked it blindfolded in a storm, would no longer trust herself to do so. What had been a track was now a road: the road they drove in on, with Tony swearing every time a car passed him on the right. Grace, who walked everywhere anyway, was more bothered by the different beach and the modern scents carried on the wind.

Perhaps it would have been better if she could have come by water, but no: by water, the first thing to break her heart would have been her keep, her castle on Clare Island, which had been home to no one and nothing for centuries now. "My children still live here," she said abruptly, to the water.

Tony, unburdened by troublesome memory but astute enough to leave Grace to hers, turned from a dozen yards down the beach to stare at her in astonishment. "What?"

"Descendants," Grace corrected herself, still gazing at the water. It, at least, hadn't changed: it rolled slate grey under an equally dark sky, until the distant horizon made them one with each other. "They're Browns now, but I've granddaughters still alive. Four hundred years and the blood of the O'Malley still lives on."

"You should meet them!"

"No." Grace smiled briefly. "I wouldn't know them to see them, and it might be worse if I did. What if I saw my own children in their faces? And they may not be properly *here* at all, not anymore. The house—it was never mine; there was a fort there, in my time—left the family a little while ago." She fell silent, jaw clenching before she spoke again. "I thought she'd had me by the gut when I left here after the Nine Years' War, but the witch's curse gives no quarter. The O'Malley blood may survive, but there's nothing left of Umaill at all anymore. No house, no lands, no name. Only my own self alone."

"Immortality." Tony's voice was pained.

Grace offered a thin smile. "It's not what we dream it to be, is it? It sounds a grand adventure, and it is. But that adventure comes at a price. A tragedy in unending acts."

"So you don't want to go out to the island." Now Tony sounded wry.

Grace laughed, her humor turning. "No, but you do. You want to see where I once lived."

"I want to see where you ruled."

A rush of fondness washed through Grace. She prowled to the detective, curling herself around him and smiling. "You know just what to say to warm my old, cold heart, a chuisle. It's not what it was."

"But it was yours. What is left, it's still part

of who you were. And who knows?" Tony smiled. "Maybe when Fúamnach is dealt with, Umaill will be restored."

"Will I come back and declare myself the O'Malley again?" Grace asked with a smile of her own. "Throw down the gauntlet at the British crown and demand Ireland be free and whole once more? The people rallied to my name for forty years after I died. Will they come fight for me again? Once they've finished putting me through a battery of mental tests and locking me away for my own safety? No, I don't think so. We'll sort the witch and go back to New York, Tony. My life hasn't been in Ireland for a long, long time."

"If this was a decent fairy tale, that's exactly what would happen."

Grace shook her head, still smiling. "There are no fairies, love. Not even Fúamnach herself is of the fair folk, but only the daughter of the barrows, as any witch might be. You'll need to walk in another world, if it's sidhe and druids you want to see."

Tony, grinning now, said, "You've gotten more Irish in the half day we've been here. All right, O'Malley. How do we find us a witch?"

"You're the detective," Grace said with a sniff. "Detect." As Tony pulled a face, she looked back toward the island she'd once called home, indistinct in the afternoon gloom. "I know she's *not* there, and perhaps we've only half an island to search, as the canal has intersected this country for two hundred years. She may be caught on one side or the other."

"Does a canal count as running water?" Tony wondered.

Grace elbowed him. "I'd hope so, save I've no way to know which half of the island she might be caught on, which leaves us the whole of it to search anyway. I ought to have left you in America, love. I'll be half a lifetime searching every inch of this place, and you've only a month's holiday."

"I've already used up half a lifetime," Tony said. "I can't waste the rest of it waiting for you to come back with a Serpent's Tear. We're going to have to do better than that."

Grace muttered, "You're only thirty-two," but spread her hands in invitation. Tony muttered, "Arguing over semantics is a lawyer trick," back, and more clearly, said, "Can you find your way back to the hill you met Máire on? If Fúamnach can be summoned, that would be a good place to do it from."

"I'm not half sure it was in this world at all," Grace replied, but nodded anyway. "I'd know it well enough. North of here, two days' walk."

Faint alarm splashed across the detective's face. Grace snorted. "No, I'll not be making you walk it, you great lump. I'll make you hike up a mountain, though, to be sure. Get in the car, Tony. It's only an hour or two up the road."

#

She stomped, she swore, she shouted; she even cut open a vein and dripped blood on the earth, bellowing for Fúamnach to answer her call. She called her by Máire's name, and by the names of the Tuatha de Danaan who were said to be Fúamnach's parents, and after a while Tony sat down to watch instead of keeping an eagle eye out over low hills slowly disappearing into rising fog. "Are you sure you've got the right place?"

"As sure as I can be after four and a half centuries," Grace snapped. "I should have done this on the shores of Clew Bay. She would have expected me there, at least."

"You banished her from the bay."

"Only for so long as I lived."

"You haven't died yet."

Grace shut her teeth on the rising objection, scowling down at the seated detective. After a moment, her ire fleeing, she said, "I did, though, you know. I was after dying at Rockford, for all that I live now. Had I lived my years as the unaging O'Malley, my own people would have turned against me as a witch."

Amusement creased Tony's brown eyes. "'After dying.' I don't even know what that means, you increasingly Irish weirdo."

"It means the thing's done and over with," Grace replied irritably. "You're lucky I speak your bloody, colonizing language at all. I didn't, when I died."

Tony's eyebrows rose. "Didn't you? I thought you talked with Queen Elizabeth."

"In Latin." Grace turned away from the detective, frowning at the foggy hills, though the frown faded. "It was like this, the day I met Máire. Foggier yet, even, but it had that other-worldly feeling."

"What was she like?" Tony fumbled audibly. "Elizabeth, I mean, not Máire."

"A conniver and a bitch with fetid breath. But she held the room." Grace's voice softened. "By God, she held the room. It wasn't that orange hair, either, or the jewels or the paint she hid her age beneath. It was the woman herself, all power and unafraid to use it. She was only three years my junior, and in another world we might have been friends. What a world that might have been, with a free Ireland at Bess's side, rather than beneath her heel. There," she said even more softly. "There, do you see it, mo chroí? The path in the fog?"

Tony rose. "No." But he took Grace's hand, and let her lead him down the hills. "What do you see?"

"A shining path. Light in the fog." It glowed ahead of them, twisting across the land, but the closer they came to it, the more quickly it faded. "Ask me something else."

"What was it like to be a pirate?"

The question came so quickly that Grace laughed. "Been sitting on that one a while, have you, love? I wouldn't have called myself a pirate, though I'll take any title that names me a queen. It's true we took tithe and taxes from any ship in our waters, and true again that the English, feeling those waters should be theirs, hated me the fiercest for it. But they were my lands and my waters, and I protected them as any leader might. It was brilliant," she added with a sudden grin. "Dangerous, cold, wet, often hungry, but brilliant. It's a path through the past," she said, confident now as the fog trail brightened. "Linking who I am now to who I was then. To the O'Malley Fúamnach knew and treated with. Ask your questions, love. I'm never more likely to answer them than now."

"Did you really have a baby on a ship and fight off marauders the next day?"

Grace laughed again. "You've done your reading on Grace, haven't you, love? I did. Wee Tibbot, and I held him in my arm as I came swinging down from the mast to fall upon the thieves, a knife in my teeth, as neat and far more dangerous than any film star you ever did see. And in betwixt that husband and the first, I found a lover in the sea, who stirred me more than any other man for four hundred years. But he was slain and I married again less from fondness than for a need for an army that I might take my revenge on the bastards who took him from me. But you won't want to hear about that; men get jealous too easily."

"I'm secure enough to not get jealous over somebody who's been dead since long before my country was a country," Tony said dryly. "Would you do anything differently?"

"Knowing then what I do now? I might not give up that Tear." They stepped across hills grown small in the fog, and rivers only the width of a trickle, as if they wore seven-league boots while walking the shining path. Grace watched carefully, knowing Tony trusted her to lead him through. "But for Ireland? I don't know. I tried to ally with the Spaniards to crush Bess and keep Ireland free, but the storm took their armada and left me with nothing to show for my troubles. I might use the knowledge of that to send their ships another way, but even then it might have been too late. Áth Cliath belonged to the English already and had long since."

"Áth Cliath?"

Grace glanced toward Tony, then returned her attention to the glimmer through the fog. "Dublin. No, to keep Ireland free of English hands I'd need not only what I know today, but to cast myself back in time a full thousand years from now, not the mere five hundred I've got to my name." She fell silent a moment, urging them forward over land that shifted with every step, then added, "I might act to preserve much of what was lost. Histories. The language. Write them down and hide it away." A thin smile pulled her lips. "Ask Janx to hoard it, to keep it safe for my eventual retrieval, perhaps, in exchange for some future favor. And for my own satisfaction I might see Cromwell dead before he came to power, but to change it all? I'm not sure one person could do that, love. Not even Grace O'Malley. Ah!" She stopped as the path ended in water, Tony catching himself from a stumble at her side.

A river lazed by them, eddies on the grey surface twirling and promising that greater speed ran in its depths. Every swirl caught a bit of fog and whipped it away, until a stretch of water reflected blue from the clearing sky. An island no wider than Grace stood tall emerged, and beyond it the fog remained dense and cool, unaffected by the brightening day.

"Where are we?"

"You can see this?" Grace chuckled at herself. "We've come to the River Shannon, love, a hundred miles or more from where we started."

Tony turned sharply, as if he could follow their path with his gaze. "We've only been walking a few minutes."

"Sure and you can't expect witches to follow the laws of physics, now, can you? But we've not reached the end of the path yet, love. It doesn't end until there." Grace nodded at the streak of blue water leading to the island.

"Gosh, and I forgot my boat. It's a six foot island with two trees on it, Grace. Nobody's out there. Even if there was, it wouldn't be a witch. How could she get out there?"

"Now there's a fine question." Grace prodded the water with a leather-booted toe. It gave and chilled and, when she pulled her foot back, dripped like any other river water would. "The water's real enough. Do you swim, love?"

"Not in rivers!"

"Then perhaps you'd best stay on shore, and be a beacon to guide me home." Grace unlaced her boots and pulled them off to set aside while Tony looked at her with a mix of horror and dismay. "I've come this far. You wouldn't have me go back now, would you?"

"No, but—" He gestured at the river, as if it said everything he needed to.

"It's hard to drown a dead woman, Tony, and I swim well besides."

"You didn't take your boots off to go swim with the Serpent."

"I trusted him to cast me back out. I wouldn't trust a witch as far as I could throw her." Grace stripped her coat and leather pants off too, leaving her in a pale pink t-shirt that fell past her hips, wrinkled at the bottom from where it had been tucked into her pants. She slid her bra off, too, discarding it through a sleeve. "It isn't the leather. It's the metal in the steel toes and zippers and even underwires. Magic is neutralized with iron, so they help anchor me."

Tony cocked his head, a question in the stance, and Grace brushed her fingers over his cheek. *Through*, really: the touch didn't land, though it raised goosebumps on his skin. He lifted his hand to close it over hers, and she barely felt the pressure. From his expression, it was clear he didn't feel much of anything, either. "I forget," he said after a moment, his voice low.

"I prefer that you do. I work at staying *here* for you, love. I walk and I climb and I lift, because it's what mortals do. But it *is* work, for solidity hasn't been my natural state for four hundred years and more. So I can take myself to that island without ever getting wet, and if there's nothing there, then Grace will be back again safe and sound in a heartbeat."

"And if there *is* something there?"

Grace smiled and kissed Tony, a whisper of air against his lips. "Then we bargain."

Resistance met her at the island's edge, a warning of danger. It would sink, it would shake loose and float downstream, it would catch an unwary traveler by the ankles and drag them down. It wasn't enough to make her panic, nothing so strong that it would awaken greater curiosity in an explorer, but touching the little hump of earth in the river's heart made Grace ill at ease. Had she been only mortal, she would have heeded that twinge of discomfort, perhaps without even knowing it, and pushed away to find some other shore. Instead she drifted downward and stuck her toes into the mucky earth, grounding herself.

There wasn't a thing to be seen save the two trees, both tall and slim and, to Grace's mind, with an air of pride at having claimed this spot of isolated land as their own. Grace chuckled and put her hand on one of them, digging her toes into the dirt more deeply. "Well done," she said to it. "But you're not what called me here, are you. You're no more my destination than the bottom of the sea was, the day the Serpent gave me that Tear."

Fury given physical form exploded around her, the earth torn up and a whirlwind of rage smashing into the unseen walls that barricaded the little island. It spun and whirled and slammed itself around, disturbing Grace not at all: she let it breeze through her, no more impacted by it than she might be by a summer breeze. Finally it slowed, as if spent, or disgusted with her lack of response.

"Is it yourself, then, witch? I might have thought you a djinn, with all that storming, save a djinn is stopped by salt water, not a running river. Come, Fúamnach." Grace's voice softened without gentling. "Show yourself."

Fúamnach did not, as Grace half expected, coalesce as a djinn might, but instead expended a final wave of rage and burst from the earth, filthy but familiar. Her nails had grown too long, and her hair was matted and dank, but the beauty that had once been hers still lived on, with large eyes and a jaw that would please even a queen. Her hands curled in on themselves, nails bending every which way, and she stood hunched, like an animal ready to lunge. Only the knowledge burning in her eyes prevented her from bothering: she knew already she couldn't harm Grace, and hated the knowing.

"What happened?" Oh, there were better places to start, bargains to be made, but simple curiosity got to Grace, because Tony was right. The middle of a river wasn't a place to find a witch, and yet here a witch resided.

"Trickery," Fúamnach spat. "Wretched, miserable trickery, and you its mother."

Surprise lifted Grace's eyebrows. "Me? I swear to you, daughter of the barrows, I had nothing to do with this. How long?"

"Five thousand moons."

"Five thou—" Grace did the sums in her head swiftly, and her eyebrows rose farther. "That's most of the time I've been as I am. What *happened*, Fúamnach?"

"What should the O'Malley care, and why should I answer her questions?"

"Ah, now. The one doesn't matter, and the other...I might strike you a bargain, witch."

Fúamnach's lip curled. "You have nothing I want."

Grace smiled. "I can get you off this island."

Sudden feral interest lit the witch's face. She crept closer, still hunched, her hands clawed against her chest now. "How?"

"I've done less likely things. But surely you know what I want in return, Fúamnach."

Rage flickered in Fúamnach's eyes again, contorting her mouth. "The Tear."

"You're a wise one, you are. It's not yours to begin with, is it. You've never made a wish, for I'd guess you'd be well away from this island if you could have. So I might take it, for all that it was squarely traded between us, but then, the girl died, and the bargain was broken. But I'll bargain again: your freedom for the Tear."

Fúamnach's shoulders rose, neck disappearing until she had a turtle's guise, angry eyes gazing out from shadows. "Its power…"

"Does you no good, trapped here. You've siphoned off it for four centuries. Surely that will leave you something to gnaw on, as you once chewed your daughter's bones. And *I* will have my body back again." Grace thrust her hand out, passing through the witch's chin until she found her hidden throat, then lent herself enough solidity to squeeze. Fúamnach squealed like a pig and scuttled backward as a lash of pain made Grace release her grip. "Don't imagine I can't take more than that," Grace whispered. "Knowing the secret might be all that can kill a witch, but then again, who knows? How many people have gotten close enough to try a knife across the jugular? You knew," she said more forcefully. "You knew what the Tear was, and let me bargain without understanding what it was I bargained with."

"Your ignorance was no concern of mine. Besides." Fúamnach's eyes narrowed and a nasty smile pulled her lips. "You'd have made the bargain anyway, for the life of the child."

"I'd have bargained," Grace agreed, shrugging one shoulder. "Perhaps I wouldn't have bargained *that*. Do we have a deal, witch, or do I leave you to rot in the current of the River Shannon?"

Hatred spasmed across the witch's face again. "We have a deal."

Grace smiled and turned her palm downward, miming slicing it open. "Your blood on it, witch."

"You have my blood already. Burn it, and the binding's made." Madness crept into Fúamnach's gaze again. "Or have you lost it, Gráinne Ní Mháille, as you have lost your land and your people and your very name?"

"I have it still," Grace replied. "Not with me."

"Neither is the Tear with me. Burn the blood and the Tear will return to you, our bargain sealed. But take me from this island, first, or I cannot call the Tear back again."

"You wouldn't be lying to Grace now, would you?"

A snarl creased the witch's mouth. "I told you once the Tuatha cannot lie."

"And I told you the fair folk were well known for twisting words, even if I'm fool enough to believe you're of their ilk. But lie to me, witch, and I'll bring you back to this island the same way I'll free you from it, and you'll rest here forevermore."

"Nothing," Fúamnach snarled, "is forever."

"Close enough." Grace stepped forward, nostrils pinching at the witch's scent: astringent and sour, not rotted but not healthy, either. "Close your eyes, Fúamnach, and hold tight. This will not be pleasant."

The witch eyed her warily. "Are you sure of yourself, that you can do this?"

"Sure enough, at least, and if I'm wrong you're no worse off than you were before, save that I'll know you don't have the Tear and can't stop me from liberating it on my own." A surge of cheer ran through Grace at Fúamnach's filthy look, and she beckoned the witch closer again. "Come on, then. Hold on, and close your eyes."

In four hundred years and some change, she had only rarely extended her intangibility onto another. More often she spent her hours concentrating on being solid, so the kids she helped and the adults she interacted with weren't spooked away by a woman who flickered and faded like a ghost. The last—and hardest—time she'd put herself to such a task was to free a gargoyle from his iron chains. That had *burned*: the pain had stayed with her for days, settling in the creases of hands that shone with heat scars. It had left a chill in her chest, too, one that hadn't been driven away until she grew close to Tony Pulcella, as if only ordinary human warmth could heal the trauma of trucking, uninvited, with the Old Races.

Carrying Fúamnach, Grace thought, was not quite as bad as that had been.

It wasn't *good*: the witch writhed and screamed like an angry cat, though Grace didn't think she meant to. Every scream seemed torn from Fúamnach's throat, pain resonating from the sound, and every twitch felt dragged, protesting, from the witch's bones. And that was with Grace drifting as high as she could: down was easier. She could step from the top of New York's tallest buildings and sail unconcerned to the ground below, but floating upward required more effort. She'd long since learned a superhero's jump to start, driving herself farther into the air—much farther—than any mortal could achieve, but even that only took her a few stories up. In New York she could bounce from building to building, using fire escapes or window ledges to gain height, but there were no such edifices to be used along the shore of the River Shannon. She could only leap as high as magic and insubstantial muscle combined would let her, and Fúamnach was fortunate that once aloft, Grace didn't sink down again until she wanted to. She could float along at any given height, guided more by will than wind, but not often at any great speed, either. She could—she did, at times—wink from place to place, skipping the intervening distances, but that took its own kind of toll, rendering her ghostly for longer periods after she'd done it.

Halfway across the river, a screeching witch in her arms, she wished she could do that wink with a passenger, but a single attempt sent bone-shattering shudders through *her*, and dropped them a dozen feet closer to the water's rushing surface. Fúamnach's shrieks intensified, each one deeper and more dreadful than the one before. Grace whispered a curse under her breath, and when they came staggering to the river's far shore, dropped to her knees and let the witch go in a rustling thump. Fúamnach clawed her fingers into the earth, breaking her nails as she pulled herself away from the river's edge, then lay gasping on the greenery. Grace's shudders stopped, but Fúamnach's continued, wracking her body while Tony stood above them both making helpless gestures with his hands. Grace waved him off, croaking, "I'll be fine," as she pulled her clothes on.

He crouched by her. "You don't sound fine."

"Mortal creatures aren't meant to be dragged through the..." Grace had no word for it, the insubstantial place she lingered. It wasn't the same space djinn moved through when they became incorporeal, for she'd ghosted a time or two when they were nearby, just to see if she could see or sense their presence. She couldn't, nor they hers. "And a witch is born of humanity, no matter how long her years might be or how hard her death is to achieve."

"Are all witches women?"

Grace, dressed now, sat on her butt to put her boots on. "All the ones I've met have been, and all their children, too."

"Mothers are what matter." Fúamnach spoke, her voice rawer than Grace's. "Any man could be a father, but a mother is always known. Mothers and daughters: therein lies the power. The sons...*pfaugh!*" She spat, then hauled herself to sitting, which seemed as far as she could go.

"And *phaugh* on some of the daughters as well," Grace murmured, but Fúamnach's hate-filled glare silenced her.

"On all of them, and on more than you think. Where is my blood?"

"Where is my Tear?" Grace rose, dusting dirt off her pants.

Fúamnach's lips curled, revealing snarling teeth. "I cannot call for it without my blood. Five thousand moons in running water, Ní Mháille. No witch can work magic after such torment. Not without all she has lost to breath and bone returned to her."

"You're screwed, then," Tony said thoughtfully. "Máire was your blood too, wasn't she?"

Loathing filled Fúamnach's gaze. "*That* faithless creature is long since a creature of her own. The blood spent there is no longer mine to call on. But the blood I swore an oath with..." She turned her eyes back to Grace and lifted a hand, fingers scrabbling greedily at the air.

Grace sighed and lifted her chin at Tony. "Go on, then."

"Are you sure?"

"As sure as I can be."

Tony shifted his shoulders as if to say *it's your funeral,* and dipped a hand into his coat pocket to withdraw a stoppered vial with rusty flakes dusting its sides. Fúamnach squealed with greed, reaching for it, but Tony folded the vial in his hand, stepping back and looking to Grace. She nodded and he repeated the shrug, then took a lighter from the opposite pocket and opened the vial to flick the flame inside it. The ancient blood vaporized. Fúamnach shuddered and moaned, a disturbing sound of ecstasy, and though the tiny bit of blood could hardly be enough to revitalize her, color returned to her cheeks. She threw her head back, power coursing through her almost visibly, as if she had been a dry riverbed now flushed with water. Rags and grime fell away and her hair came clean. The earth itself clothed her, greenery and soil becoming a gown. Within a heartbeat she had taken on the guise of a queen, if a queen was one with the very world around her.

Tony exhaled, sharp and surprised, and Grace, who remembered Fúamnach's beauty from centuries past, barely stopped herself from doing the same. She took a breath to ask *why*, though: Fúamnach's beauty had been incidental, on the shores of Clew Bay; now she clearly reveled in it, eager to share it with the world. But before the question left Grace's lips, she thought she had an answer: left powerless and isolated on an island, she, too, would reach for the best of herself in the first moments of freedom.

Then Fúamnach took a sauntering step or two toward Tony, a smile curling her mouth, and Grace nearly laughed at her own naïveté. She nearly stepped forward herself, about to block Fúamnach's approach, but held herself still at the last moment, waiting and watching. The witch moved into Tony's space, placing her fingertips against his chest. Tony, looking bemused, wrapped his hand around hers and moved her hand away before letting her go. "Friend of mine reminded me a while back not to go around touching people without their permission. You should probably learn that lesson, ma'am."

Fúamnach shot Grace a look as if she couldn't believe she'd properly understood the word *ma'am*. Grace burst out laughing and spoke in the Irish she'd used, without realizing it until now, on the island. "You heard him right, love. You can take it to mean you're too old for him." She laughed again as Fúamnach snatched her hand back from Tony and spun haughtily, dismissing him as unworthy. Tony, eyebrows arched and a quizzical smile playing at his mouth, glanced at Grace, who said, "You got your point across," in English. His smile turned to a grin, and Grace laughed aloud a third time before challenging Fúamnach with her gaze. "The Tear, Fúamnach."

A cunning look narrowed Fúamnach's eyes. "I've given it to safekeeping in another's hands. From me you have it freely, but from him…"

"I will kill you, witch. I will bind you with

iron and stake you with wood, drown you in water and bury you in the earth itself." The words rose up from within Grace as if she spoke with someone else's knowledge, and she thought: *thank you,* to the Serpent at the heart of the sea.

Fúamnach laughed, sharp and shrill. "There's a recipe for capture indeed, but not for the likes of me."

"Are you sure?" Grace spat. "Has anyone tried it? I will put you back on that island, witch, and leave you to rot.

"You ought to have left well enough alone to begin with," snarled another voice, and Máire, once of the Clan O'Malley, rose up from the river a witch.

Part III

THERE COULD BE NO DOUBT she was a witch: the power poured off her just as the river water did, sluicing and cascading like a thing with a will and a mind of its own. She carried a staff wrought of reeds in her crippled hand, and the river itself shaped a limb for the leg Fúamnach had so long ago supped on as her own. She stepped free of the river's current, fury contorting features grown more mature and experienced since Grace had last seen them, but whatever words she might have said were lost beneath Grace's astonished protest. "You *drowned*!"

If Máire had an ounce of gentleness in her, it was nowhere to be seen: the look she bestowed on Grace was as scathing, as loathing, as the one she had for the mother of her body. "I did."

"I *searched* for you." The strength left Grace's voice as swiftly as it had come, ancient distress rising in her breast. "I went into the waters myself, swam as deep as I could, as far as I could. You *drowned*, Máire. You were lost to me. How—?"

"I thought witches couldn't cross water," Tony said in a quieter, but equally mystified voice. "How can you be *in* it?"

Máire's blazing anger snapped between the two of them. "The answer's one and the same. Know you how a witch's daughter comes to be free of her mother, mortal?"

Though the title—or insult—could be aimed at no one else, Tony glanced between Grace and Fúamnach before answering. "She was trying to eat you to get her magic back, so...by dying?"

"Not just dying." Fúamnach stood in a hunch, her hands clawed against her chest and fury raging in the stance. "Had she been struck with a knife, her magic would have fled back to me and made me whole again. But the filthy salty *sea* took her, and in so doing, broke the bond that held her to me."

"But a witch can't survive the open water," Grace said, bewildered. "It's what kept you from her to begin with."

"A witch cannot," Máire snarled. "But a witch's daughter might, especially when that daughter is the foster child of one beloved to the Serpent."

"*Beloved*?" Grace's voice cracked with disbelieving laughter. "I'd never say so, but if it's the thread that draws you back to life, I'll take it, child of my heart."

"How dare you make such a claim, when you yourself freed the one who tormented me?"

"I didn't bloody know you were alive, did I!

What *happened*, Máire, how —?"

"The storm snatched me, as it will. My mother's ancient enemy, the sea, confining her to the green isle. I thought as the waters closed over my head that at least she would never have me now, that a death by drowning was better than living to be eaten some day when my foster mother was no more and could no longer protect me. So I let the water take me, waiting for it to drown me, and instead I felt more alive than I had ever been. It was as though the very blood left my body and took the salt sea in instead, freeing the last bonds that tied me to the daughter of the barrows. And once emptied of what she had been, I filled again with magic, a witch in my own regard. But even that wouldn't have been enough to save me, had the Serpent not lifted me from the drifting currents and cast me on land once again."

"Why didn't you come to me?" Grace whispered. "It would have gladdened my heart to see you again, and you must know I would have believed your tale."

"You would have, and perhaps the clan would have too. And then where would I have been, or you? No one would welcome a witch save perhaps yourself, and if you did, you would lose the clan."

"I lost it anyway. I lost it all, just as the witch of the west cursed me to."

Fúamnach spat a sound of pleasure. Grace

caught her arm, a threat in the gesture. "I can bring you back to that island, witch." Her gaze snapped to Máire. "You put her there?"

"It took *so long*." Máire sounded like the child she'd been centuries ago, something akin to a whine in the agreement. "I had to coax the waters away and leave the island dry, and bait it with a thing she wanted more than life itself."

"The Tear?" Tony sounded uncertain.

Máire spat as well. "*Me.* Me my own self, seeming weak as a kitten and dripping with power that she might have for herself, if only she could eat me up. I lured her, and when she finally came—"

"She left me there," Fúamnach snarled. "The river rose and she fled across it, laughing on the shore as my power died. And there I've lain ever since, dying without death, weak and waiting for the day of my release."

Anger crackled in the air, power coalescing around both witches; Máire's had a heavy feeling to it, like the weight of water, and Fúamnach's felt dark, as if it came up from the earth itself. Tony touched Grace's elbow, his voice low. "Maybe we should get out of here before they throw down."

"Not without the Tear, love." Grace stepped between the witches, hairs standing on her arms as their power washed over her. "I'm sorry to have disturbed your revenge, Máire. Had I known..." She shrugged. "But I didn't, and then again, if I had, perhaps I'd have chosen this path anyway. I need the Tear back, Máire."

"And why is that? Have you a use for it?"

"Not as such, but I know now what it does. And it's having it in *her* power that keeps me a ghost." Grace reached for Máire's reed staff, slipping her fingers through it rather than grasping it. For a heartbeat, Máire was the girl Grace remembered, pale with uncertainty that bordered on fear. Then the memory was gone, replaced by the older, wiser mask. She favored her long-dead father, perhaps; the lines of her face weren't Fúamnach's fine-boned beauty, but something rawer and more wild. Her hair was still loose and brown, waving like ripples on the water, and her pale gaze remained forthright. The magic in her lent her presence, but even without it, she seemed a woman to be reckoned with.

For once in her long life, Grace had no particular urge to face that reckoning, and yet it stood before her, expecting action. "I'm only half in this world, love. I want to be all in, or —"

Behind her, Tony caught his breath, and the words she might have spoken went unsaid. They weren't true anyway; she wanted to be all in, not all gone, and if in the end her choice came down to her half-life or a quick death, she would hold on to ghostliness for as long as she could. "Do you know where the Tear is?"

"She gave it to a dragon to keep, but the dragons have all been sleeping a hundred years and more."

Grace threw her head back and groaned. Tony said, "Not *all* of them," and stepped forward to face Máire. "It has to have been an Irish dragon, right? Because she wouldn't be able to draw on the Tear's power if it was across the water—"

"She's been in the midst of running water all these years," Grace said, "Would that not have broken her connection to the Tear, if it could be broken? And yet I'm a ghost."

"Any other item and it might have," Máire conceded grudgingly. "But the Tear is of the Serpent himself, and water is his element."

"Will you do nothing but talk?" Fúamnach demanded. "I have five thousand moons of torment to settle upon—"

A tremendous fist of water rose from the river and seized the older witch, dragged her screaming to the island, and dropped her there as Grace and Tony startled, having all but forgotten Fúamnach's presence at all. Máire spat after her blood mother, whose rage rose and echoed against the water, impotent as her magic. Grace gazed out at her, then turned a shrug on Tony. "I suppose I didn't say she'd be *kept* on dry land."

"You've a lot to answer for yet," Máire said darkly. "Freeing Fúamnach—"

"Broken record," Tony said. Máire stared at him and he shrugged. "We can go around on this forever, but it's a broken record. Grace took Fúamnach off the island, found out—sort of—where the Tear is, and you put her back. It's over. Let's get the Tear. Did she give it to an Irish dragon or not?"

Máire, sullenly, said, "There are no serpents in Ireland," and Grace laughed aloud.

"Surely even good Saint Patrick couldn't have driven a dragon away, daughter. But if not an Irish dragon, then who? In four hundred years I've met two, and only know of one other who still walks the waking world."

"He was a great red *péist* who came at Fúamnach's call, though he was no more bound by her spell than one might bind the storm. Curiosity drove him, and he carried the Tear away in a great and terrible paw, promising to keep it safe."

Grace exchanged a glance with Tony, who shook his head. "Can't be. Can it?"

"I know two red dragons, love, and only one of them was alive centuries ago. But he fled New York after the fire."

"What, don't you have his cell phone number?" Tony asked, ruefully exasperated.

Grace sighed. "No. But Margrit does."

"I'll call he—" Tony broke off, patting his pockets. "Or I *would* call her if the *phone* wasn't in the *car, a hundred miles away!*"

"That," Máire said, "I can help you with, for a price."

The waterways of Ireland took them back to the car more quickly than even Grace had imagined, though the journey wasn't a direct one, and there were stretches that even a witch had to traverse on foot. Grace herself might not have needed to, but ghosting a man and a witch both together seemed likely to wear her out, especially after the struggle with Fúamnach at the river. Still, they were no more than half a day going, and while Tony hiked the last piece of road to get the car and the phone, Grace sat at a stream's edge with Máire at her side, watching ripples in the water. "So you had magic in you after all. Has it treated you well?"

"It gave me vengeance." Away from the witch Fúamnach, Máire's anger had fled, and she threw pebbles into the stream like any child might. "I haven't asked much more of it. I've never known what to ask. A life of my own, away from my mother, was more than I dreamed possible, and you granted me that before the magic found me. You shouldn't have traded the Tear, though. I wasn't worth that."

"But you were." Grace smiled. "Perhaps if I'd had something else that appealed, or if I'd known the worth of the Tear, I might have tried another bargain, but in the end I would have made the trade. It's only a rock, Máire. A magic rock, to be sure, but still, only a rock, and you're a human being."

"Am I?"

"A person, at least," Grace amended. "No rock is worth more than someone's life."

Máire cast her an amused look. "I expected

you to protest my humanity."

"Grace knows a lot of people who aren't human, these days," she said dryly. "I'm finding it doesn't matter so much. You're my daughter still. That's what I care about."

"Me and that man," Máire said, teasing.

Grace glanced toward where Tony had gone, and nodded. "I'd not have started down this path at all without him. I'd still think myself a cursed ghost, not gifted with a shaky grasp of immortality. It's not using the Tear that's important. It's having it back and not fighting to keep myself attached to this world. What do *you* want, Máire? What's your price, for taking us halfway across the island?"

"I want to go with you." Máire lifted her chin, gazing at an unseeable horizon. "I've never left Ireland, and it's time I did. Fúamnach is imprisoned and will stay that way or won't, but I've had enough of being her jailer. I've seen all there is to see here, and watched it change through the centuries. It's no more the land of my childhood than it is of yours, and I might be best off breaking all ties with it."

Grace breathed a laugh. "I think you'll find that's impossible, my sweet. Even now, coming back after so long, with it so changed…it sings to me. It says it's my land, where I come from and perhaps where I'll someday rest. But most ties," she agreed with a nod. "Most ties are long since gone, and it would do you no harm to see more of the world. Why did you never go, if the water couldn't stop you?"

"I've made my own prison, I suppose. I would never have believed I could break free of Fúamnach, even when I tried as a child. It was a token protest, one I knew would end in being eaten all up, whether I willed it or not. And then, free from her, I tied myself to the O'Malleys, and when they were gone, to Ireland, for I had nothing else that I knew. But seeing you again gives me strength. I didn't know," she added more quietly. "I didn't know you still lived, after your death. I might have come to find you, if I had."

"I'd certainly have come to find you, if I'd known you lived past *your* death." Grace shook her head. "What a strange world we live in, Máire. Is it still Máire, or did you take a name of your own?"

"Máire O'Malley is the only name I ever wanted."

Grace put her arm around the witch's shoulder and drew her close to place a smiling kiss in her hair. "Then come with me to—"

"Indonesia!" Tony drove down the hill, leaning out the car door and waving his cell phone at the women. "Janx is in freakin' *Indonesia*. Grit says we don't need a visa, we can just get on the plane and g—dammit, neither of you have passports!" He stopped the car and got out, running his hand through his hair until short black curls stood up. "The modern world is not equipped for magic, dammit!"

"More like magic isn't equipped for the modern world. Get yourself a ticket, love. Surely a witch and a ghost can slip onto a plane unnoticed, and travel in peace, if not comfort."

Tony pointed the phone at Grace. "I don't know if that's cool or deeply concerning. What if you were terrorists?"

Grace looked at Máire. "Are you a terrorist?"

The witch girl's expression went shifty, then sweetly innocent. "Not for decades, that anyone might prove. You?"

"Never once. A pirate and a soldier, but never a terrorist. At least not by my own definition."

Tony put his face in his hands and walked away to the sound of the womens' laughter.

They joined Tony again outside of the airport, Máire with her hair damp from traveling through fog and Grace stepping free of the shadows with her usual nonchalance. Tony's eyes were bright with anticipation. "I've never been farther than Italy, before. The air smells different here."

"Does it smell like dragon?" Máire muttered. "Indonesia's got a population of two hundred million or more. How are we to find a dragon's hoard in all of that? Or is Jakarta his hoard?"

"We've got an inside man," Tony told her. "I just hope she doesn't show up for a few days. I want to see the city."

"Hate to disappoint, but there's our girl." Grace nodded toward a redhead pulling up in a little snub-nosed green car. "We'll go sight-seeing once we've got the Tear, love."

"You say that like we're not going to be stealing it from a dragon and running for our lives. Kate!" Tony raised his voice and waved to the woman driving. She waved back, gesturing them over, and Tony muttered, "I thought Irish cars were small. Will we all *fit* in this?" as they went.

"It's not that Irish cars are small, it's that American ones are stupidly huge. And yeah, I've got really good hearing. And a better sense of smell. And neither of them are half as good as my sister's." The redhead reached back to unlock a door and eyed her passengers. "Kate Hopkins," she said to Máire. "You should probably sit in back. You're the smallest. Grace and Tony can wrestle it out for shotgun."

"Máire O'Malley."

"Really." Kate nodded at Grace, who got in back with Máire. "Any relation?"

"In a manner of speaking."

"Your sister's not here, is she?" Tony asked as he climbed in the passenger seat. "No offense, but your father's bad enough."

Kate slid a glance at Grace in the mirror. "How should I take that?"

"As a statement from a man sensibly wary of dragons."

"And even more so of vampires," Tony said.

"Dragons," Máire half-asked, and Kate transferred the glance to her.

"Didn't they tell you? My father is the dragon you're looking for. I wouldn't have come, if Margrit hadn't called asking me to. What is it exactly that you want from him?"

"A stone," Grace said. "It was mine, and I lent it to a witch, who gave it into his safekeeping when you and I were young. I'm coming to reclaim it."

Kate chuckled. "Good luck with that. What are you bringing him in return?"

"A wish," Grace murmured, and looked out the window as Kate drove them north and east through towns that hardly stopped from one to the next. Deep green mountains rose up to the south, and eventually to the north as well, until they reached a shoreline built up in one stretch and forested up to the water in the next.

Kate got out of the car in a rangy movement, not as graceful as her father, but not as ponderous as he could be, either, and stretched like she was twenty-two, not just past her third and a half century. "Anybody bring a snack? We're here until nightfall, anyway."

"Why's that?"

"Because you can get to his island two ways: by boat or by wing, and if you take a boat he'll come out and eat you."

"I bet I can get there another way," Grace said in tandem with Máire. They laughed, looking at one another, and even Kate smiled.

"You probably could, and he might not even eat you. But if you want something from him you probably shouldn't sneak up on him."

"Is it sneaking if he knows we're coming? Margrit rang ahead."

"I'm pretty sure any time you visit a dragon's hoard you're sneaking, whether you're actually sneaking or not."

"'I smell you, I hear your breath, I feel your air,'" Tony said.

Kate pointed an approving finger at him. "Just like that. Sometimes I wonder if Tolkien knew my father, or if he just got lucky."

"Can a witch fly on dragon-back?" Máire wondered, soft and hopeful as a child. She stood on the shore already, a new staff of braided kelp in hand; Grace had no idea what stiffened it, other than the young witch's will.

"Kate's half-sister bears *her* sister the witch on her back all the time, and their mother, who was Baba Yaga's daughter, besides. They've traveled the whole world that way. The mother says the power of the Old Races betwixt herself and the sea disrupts the magic that holds a witch to a bit of land."

"Now *that*," Máire said sharply, "is a prize worth knowing."

"Keep it to yourself, then, girl," Grace said in a mother's tone, and all three of them younger than she looked at each other and laughed. Grace tried to find a scolding face, and found a laugh of her own instead. "All right, then. Will you be flying us, Kate, or will it be Janx himself?"

A strange look came over Kate's face. "I think the last person Janx flew on his back was my mother."

"And how long ago was that?" Máire wondered, but Grace lifted her hand to silence Kate, who arched an eyebrow while Máire turned a filthy gaze on Grace.

"Witches trade in secrets, love. Watch what you say."

"Do you not trust me, Mother O'Malley?"

"I do," Grace said, honestly, "but I don't trust witches. It puts me in a bind."

"Unpack that later," Tony suggested. "The sun is setting. Or do we have to wait until the dark of night to fly out?" All three of the women looked at him and he rolled his eyes. "Okay, okay, the *middle* of the night. Margrit was right. Hanging out with you people makes ordinary humans use melodramatic language."

"'You people,'" Kate said, amused, and Tony pointed a not-particularly-threatening finger at her.

"Don't you start."

Kate laughed and looked up the beach. "Sunset is as fine a time as any, but midnight makes it harder to get caught on satellite imagery."

"Are you big enough?" Grace asked, curious.

Kate gave a liquid shrug. "Not yet, not until I get bigger or they get better, which happens faster than I grow. Better to be in the habit of safety. Unless the witch can call up a fog to hide us?"

A genuine smile split Máire's face. "So I can, and no satellite will think anything of a girl standing on the beach as fog rolls in." She spoke in Irish then, her voice cajoling and sweet, and though Grace heard and understood the words, they slipped away from her memory like cotton candy melting in water. There was a cadence to them, almost a song, but the tune faded as fast as the words, all of it the sounds of magic.

No natural fog came up the way Máire's did: it gathered around her ankle, twining like a cat as it inspected the kelp staff and the one-legged woman leaning on it. Then, as if satisfied, it billowed like a spinning skirt, whirling around her waist and growing fuller with each turn. Máire's song went on, lifting from the mist that swallowed her up. Tendrils of fog brushed Grace's face, startling her with their warmth. She took Tony's hand so she wouldn't lose him. He chuckled, dropping his voice in the way people often did in the fog. "You could just drift away on it, couldn't you?"

"I could, but that would be a cold and lonely fate." Grace tipped her face up, searching for the leading edge of the fog. "How deep does it run, Máire?"

"Not deep enough for a dragon." Máire's voice came dreamily, still half a song. "Another few minutes."

"This dragon can change as slow as the fog." Kate came through the mist like a wraith, wings already tearing away from her spine. A ripple ran through her, distorting her ribs, expanding them; the next breath she took disturbed the fog, drawing it into her, and in the next her arms were forearms, burnished red and clawed with gold.

"*Jesus.*" Tony's hand went cold in Grace's, and even she fought the impulse to step backward. Kate's form flowed again, lengthening, wings enlarging, and again, until there was nothing human left in her at all, only a dragon whose size spiraled away into the fog. Whiskers danced around her face, and she dropped her jaw in a laugh that vibrated Grace's bones. Her wings flickered and she dropped to the lowest crouch she could, four tremendous feet digging into the sand and her belly rubbing against it. Her tail lashed in the distance, disturbing the fog, and Tony's voice cracked: "That's a *baby*?"

Kate jaw dropped farther, a hiss erupting from her throat. Tony put his hands up and did back away, voice cracking again. "Sorry. A, uh, an adolescent? You're just so fucking *big.*"

Kate's offense softened and she spread her wings farther, invitation to…*board,* Grace supposed. "She's only a quarter the size of her father," she murmured as planted her hands on Kate's spine and vaulted up. "Perhaps not even that."

"I know, but she's still huge!" Tony, still gaping, took Grace's offered hand and let her haul him up. Kate shifted beneath them, settling and shaking until she decided she, if not they, were comfortable, then turned to Máire, who still stood at the water's edge.

The young witch offered the flat of her hand to the dragon. Kate dropped her muzzle, one nostril large enough to cover the girl's hand, and huffed like an enormous horse. Máire, smiling foolishly, brushed her hand back over Kate's snout, rubbing vigorously between the dragon's eyes. "I never dreamed of seeing such a thing."

"You won't again," Grace said. "No pureblood dragon can shift so slowly. The chimeric children of the Old Races are wonders unto themselves. Now, come aboard before she takes you in her claws and flies you like a child with an airplane."

Both Máire and Kate turned speculative looks on Grace, who felt the warmth of Tony's snorted breath against her shoulder. "I'd say don't give them ideas, but it's obviously too late. Come on." He sounded five years old. "I've always wanted to fly on a dragon."

Máire came around, trailing her fingers against Kate's shoulder until she reached the dragon's spine. Water whirled upward, lifting her onto Kate's back, and no sooner had she settled than Kate sprang upward, a shockingly smooth and soft departure. Tony shrieked with joy, making Grace and Máire both laugh. Even

Kate rumbled with laughter, a deep tremble through her long bones.

The fog came with them, swift and graceful as the dragon herself, but thinning below them so the moon ghosted along over the water, a brilliant crescent that reflected in scattered pieces across the quiet ocean. Tears pulled from Grace's eyes and her teeth went cold from smiling into the wind. Tony shouted something about mosquitoes and she laughed again, then twisted on the dragon's back to kiss him fiercely. He smiled, startled, and Grace turned back again, overwhelmed with emotion. She had lived too long on the edges, her half life souring her connection with the world. It was easy to be cynical, when nothing could touch her unless she wanted it to, and easy to protect herself by wanting nothing to. The street kids she helped kept her from drifting away entirely, but she knew now that she kept even them at an arm's length, as afraid of feeling the glory of their highs as the sorrow of their losses.

Kate roared, a sound that rolled on and on over the ocean. Grace thought there might be words in it, perhaps a warning to Janx that another dragon approached his territory, but then the young dragon dove toward the water, skimming so closely to its surface that her wingtips cut into it and sent sprays into the air. Moonlight caught them and made rainbows, faint and flawless. Máire spread her hands and the spray hung in the air, traveling with them, racing along at eye-watering speed until they flew in the midst of a passage of silver fog and rainbows. Grace wiped her eyes with the back of her hand, then pressed her palm against Kate's back, unsure if a leviathan would even feel such a small touch, but unable to express her thanks in any other way.

The dragon roared again, sounding pleased, and Máire, pointing ahead, cried, "Look!"

Beyond Kate, at the leading edge of the fog and rainbows, dolphins leapt from the water, not silver and grey, but teased into a hundred colors by the reflected light. They arched and dove, innumerable creatures moving in tandem and in waves, so that there were always some above and always some below the surface, where they raced so close to the surface they broke the streaks of moonlight into thousands of bright curves. Kate, so much larger and faster than they, overtook them in a few wingbeats, and only when one leapt beside them did Grace realize what Máire had seen at once. Tony whispered, "Oh my God," into Grace's shoulder, and Grace, speechless, curved a hand back to find his.

Siryns, not dolphins, sped through the water below and beside Kate. Easily twice the size of a human, they took their color not from stolen moonlight but from their own rich palette, deep oceanic blues and astonishing oranges, bright yellows and vivid greens, all the shades of a coral reef painted on swift bodies that held a place somewhere between man and oceanic mammal. Their hair was as brilliant as their skin tones, streaming down their spines to make a play at being dorsal fins; they dove with their hands folded in front of them, making a dolphin's nose at a glimpse, but clearly *other* at a second glance.

Kate tipped to the side, dipping a wingtip in the water and spinning on it. Laughter burbled up from below as siryns whipped after her, creating a whirlpool with Kate's wingtip at the center. Máire cried out, hands extended and trembling, and there was a plea in her voice, a hope that ran as deep as the ocean. She sang again, bringing a wall of water to life beyond the siryns' wheel: a wall that widened as she sang, thickening until it could carry a siryn in it comfortably. One, and then another and another, of the siryns leapt from their whirlpool to Máire's wall, and Kate slowed in her headlong rush until her wings barely beat enough to keep them aloft as they glided, escorted by a host of merfolk once thought lost.

Grace bellowed, "*How*—?" to Kate, though a dragon's throat was never made for mortal words, and it was one of the siryns who emerged from the waves to answer.

"Blood calls to blood, ancient one. The beast who bears you saved us, and so when she called, we came. It is our honor."

"It is *mine*," Grace whispered through a throat gone tight. "Grace bears a message for you, lady siryn, from the Serpent at the heart of the sea. He misses you, and all of his kind who once peopled the oceans."

The siryn—half again as large as the others, and with short-cropped hair that framed large dark eyes—smiled, an expression that shone with moonlight. "We are not long returned to the seas, and have found the Serpent quiet. I will seek him out, and tell him more than we were wont to, when last we swam the world's salt waters."

Máire said, "Lady," in a voice of longing, and extended a hand toward the speaker. The siryn considered it, then gestured an acceptance. Máire curled her fingers, calling the wall of water closer, until the siryn's hand touched hers. The siryn transformed, stepping gracefully from the water onto Kate's back, where she stood above Máire and brushed her fingers over her hair.

Human, she was Amazonian in proportion: taller than Grace and broader of shoulder and hip, thicker of waist and so strongly muscled that even relaxed, she spoke of danger and sensuality. Grace might have elbowed Tony for gaping, save that she could no more draw her jaw up than he could. Máire, though, shone with joyful tears, and the siryn brushed them away. "What a creature you are," she said to Máire. "Caught between so many worlds. Born to a witch, loved by a human mother, blessed by the most ancient, and made half of our element. Child, you will be some time in finding your way, but there is a thing in you that is also in us, so know now and always that you have a home amongst the siryns; so says Ninanak, who is queen among them."

"Thank you," Máire whispered, and then again, helplessly, "thank you."

"I think someday it is we who will thank you." Ninanak bent and kissed Máire's fore-head, where a silver imprint lingered a moment and faded. Then the queen leapt back into the sea, and as if her weight bore Máire's walls down, they crashed back to the water's surface, carrying laughing siryns with them.

The siryns left them as Janx's island came into sight, diving deep into the sea and disap-pearing. Grace, silent with wonder, watched them go, and when they finally reached shore, said to Kate, "I thought they were all lost."

"They were, until I found them." The half-dragon, human once more, spoke with neither pride nor humility. "You're not the first one to take something from my father's hoard, lately."

"Someday I'd love to hear that tale."

"Someday it might be mine to tell." Kate stepped out of Grace's way, gesturing to the vol-canic island before them. "He's waiting for you."

Grace turned her attention from daughters fraught with power to the greenery and stone rising in front of her. "I don't suppose you'll give Grace the key to the front door."

Kate laughed. "He'd rather you found it yourself."

"Fecking dragons." Grace eyed the mountain's blown-off top, so long used to its changed shape that trees and bushes swept over the volcanic edge. "Up there?"

"It is the *obvious* way to enter a volcano."

"It is, but Grace hates to be obvious. Stay here," she said to Tony and Máire, as if they had any choice in the matter when she faded, and simply stepped through the rock.

It had never been difficult, the ghosting. Not unless she brought someone else with her. This time, though, it felt like the mountain itself resisted her, making its sides of thicker stuff, harder to traverse. Perhaps it was Janx's power, pushing her away; ghosts weren't meant to truck with the Old Races. Or anyone else, for that matter; ghosts, save for Grace herself, didn't really seem to exist.

Because she wasn't a ghost, only an enchanted human, and the witch who had long since drawn on the Tear's power, weakening Grace's place in the world, no longer did so. Perhaps she was less a ghost than she had once been, and the walls of the world less willing to let her pass. They might soon refuse to grant her passage at all.

Just before that thought turned to panic, she fell through the mountain's inner side and tumbled down a mound of gold and jewels legendary in proportion. She rolled to her backside, stopping her slide with heels dug in, then, laughing, filled her hands with coins and lifted them to drip through her fingers. They sang as they fell, tinking against one another and starting small avalanches of their own, even as the larger number she'd dislodged clinked and tinkled to a stop. Still smiling, Grace rose to her feet and looked around, then lifted her hands again, empty now, as if to embrace it all.

The volcano's inner chamber *glittered.* Light and warmth came from everywhere and nowhere—a dragon's purview—and caught edges of gold, chunks of jewelry, magnificent sculptures and astonishing wonders. At a glimpse she knew a dozen precious items lost to history—even an Ozymandias presided, graceful and enormous, over the chamber, making Grace wonder how many colossal statues had been carved of the great Egyptian pharaoh—and trusted that a hundred more would come to light with a little exploration. She bowed to the ancient king, murmuring, "The world has looked upon your works, O Mighty, and despaired. We remember, king of kings, no matter how little of you we might know. We do remember," before an impatient rumble filled the room. "If you want me to laud you, Janx, you'll have to come out where I can see you," Grace called.

Gold shifted beneath her feet, slowly at first and then with greater speed, until to remain standing on it she had to ghost, stepping only lightly in the world. It felt natural, not forced as it had through the mountainside, and she thought perhaps it had been Janx's power after all. What good was it to be a dragon unable to dissuade people from approaching a treasure?

He burst out of the gold like a column of lava, all fiery red and jade-eyed, and let go a roar to shake the foundations of the earth itself. Gold and jewels rained down from half-spread wings, slid down his spine and caught on his scales until he shone as brilliantly everywhere as his gold-dipped claws did. He towered above her, stories tall in height, and had she not only recently spoken with the Serpent, even Grace might have trembled before him. Instead, as full of lightness and joy as she could ever remember being, she called, "You *are* gorgeous, dragonlord. Would that the world could see it."

Air imploded, a rush of sound and pressure that would have knocked Grace from her feet had she been ordinarily corporeal, and when it ended a man of red hair and jade eyes, dressed in a slim-fitting suit with a high collar, stood atop the mountain of gold where the dragon had been. Not a man: here, in the heart of his own hoard, Janx made no effort at all to draw in the impact of his presence. He was always larger than life, his attention a weighty thing; Grace had seen it drag people down, slow them, frighten them, even when they had no sense of what they truly faced, and she had seen him transfer that attention in the same swift manner he could transfer his dragonly mass. It made him feel as though he moved too quickly for human understanding, and perhaps in fact he did. But here he made no pretense about it, as he usually did in the human world. Here, although the man stood only a few inches over six feet in height, his *self* filled the chamber as a dragon. It was, in its way, as free as Grace had ever seen him. Stupidly, tears came to her eyes.

"What on *earth*," Janx said, incredulous.

Grace, almost laughing, brushed tears away. "It's been an extraordinary week, love, and the sight of you steals Grace's breath."

Irritation spilled off the dragon in the way a soothed cat might still raise its hackles: he could not resist a compliment, yet resented that it worked so well on him. Grace laughed again and climbed the mountain of gold to stand just below him, her hands spread to encompass the wonders. "I can only imagine this is the crude and obvious selection of your trove, dragonlord. That this is what the dull and ordinary might be shown, all the better to impress small minds with. I envy those whom you hold dear enough to share what you keep close to your heart, and truly treasure."

Janx thrust his jaw out, a small action with the undertones of great force. "Have you been to kiss the Blarney Stone recently?"

"I didn't think of it," Grace said with perfect honesty. "I should have. Tony would have loved that."

The dragon's eyes lidded, and for all that he seemed human, Grace saw the depths of anger and mistrust in his gaze. "You brought him here. A *mortal*."

"A mortal who already knows what you are, and who isn't going to betray your secrets or your hoard to the wider world. Your Negotiator sorted that out, so don't play silly buggers with me, Janx. You may not care about crossing me, but I'd say woe betide the fool who crosses Margrit Knight."

"Margrit Knight is still only *human*."

"Is she?" Grace meant the question honestly enough, and the fact that Janx didn't answer answered it truly enough. Instead he stared down his nose at her, then finally snapped his teeth—she felt the breeze of the gesture, his dragon self only barely hidden—and finally said, "You're here for the Tear."

"I am. Will you give it to me?"

He gestured, an odd twist of one hand, and though he didn't move any more than that—no more, at least, that Grace could see—the Tear was in his hand suddenly, a palmful of opalescent grey. It seemed brighter than Grace remembered, but she had seen it only under Ireland's cloudy skies, and by night, not in the reflective golden heart of a dragon's hoard. A pulse ran through her, less desire than pain, and she had to still her hands to keep herself from trying to snatch it. Janx's lip curled, a breath of thin blue smoke escaping his lips. "What will you use it for?"

"To live," Grace said with a shrug, and, more softly, "to love. I only want to belong in this world again, Janx."

"So," the dragon said, "do we all."

"Then give it to me," Grace said suddenly, impulsively, "and so shall we all. I wish the magic was free in this world, Janx. I wish the magic was free."

The Tear throbbed, a single sudden beat, and erupted into an ever-expanding halo of power.

It hit them first, the dragon and the ghost, and Grace fell backward from the impact. Janx caught her with a lightning-quick hand, and her hand remained solid in his. She flinched, and tried to ghost, and could not.

On the island's shore, Kate exploded uncontrollably into dragon form, the crash of displaced air knocking Máire and Tony to the side. Tony rolled to sitting first, gaping at the young dragon who flailed at the air and sea, trying to right herself again. She had grown immeasurably, the new size unfamiliar and dangerous: Tony ducked as an enormous wing sailed over his head and dragged along the ground, digging a rift of considerable depth. "Kate! *Kate!* Watch it, you're—you're huge! Watch what you're doing! Switch back, you're—"

"Tony." Máire's voice, small and thin, came from the other side of the ditch Kate had accidentally dug. The dragon yanked her wing upward and beat hard at the air, shooting skyward without a foggy mask to protect her. Tony leapt the ditch, concerned for Kate's well-being but more grateful for her departure. Máire sat up where she'd been knocked to, a few feet up the mountain, and extended a hand toward him. "Tony. Tony, *look*..." Her hand was whole, four fingers and a thumb, as if Fuamnach had never nibbled away at her, bit by bit.

Tony took her hand, turning it this way and that, then held it, his thumbpad against her palm, as she thumped her other hand against a leg, now whole and healthy, that hadn't been there for centuries. "What *happened*?"

Máire took her hand away from him, turning it over and back again herself, and shook her head. "The...the magic came back. All the magic she took from me, all the magic she ate in my bones, it came...back."

"How is that even p—" Tony swallowed the question and shot to his feet, swinging around to look at the mountain like he might see through it, into it. "She made a wish."

"She can't have, she—" Máire came to her feet as well, then stared at them, the habit of centuries at war with the instinctive use of a limb she'd once had. "She can't have," she said again, but less certainly. "What did she wish for, to make this happen? To make..." She looked to the sky, where Kate's lithe form made a silhouette between the half-moonlit sky and the wine-dark sea.

The sea beneath her began to boil. Siryns came first, racing higher and farther from the surface with each leap than they had even with Máire's power to change the face of the ocean. Máire made a glad sound, and it came back to them in echoes, the siryns bringing to life a song that had been silent for centuries.

After them, after them came serpents, not many, but some: great winding beasts who broke the water's surface and splashed below again until the sea was a living thing, sinuous and unforgiving. Their iridescent crests split the waves and sent wakes rushing behind them.

Janx, enormous and roaring, burst forth from the caldera of his volcano, spitting fire at the sky, coloring moonlight blue to purple. Kate roared in response and flew to him, their wings beating so hard as they hovered in the air that the wind of it swept down to the island, buffeting Tony and knocking Máire, unsteady on her feet, to the ground again. Laughter rose in Tony's throat as he offered Máire a hand: incredulous laughter that even he couldn't hear under the dragons' roars, which was a noise like the end of the world.

And the water still boiled, surging upward so fast that Tony pulled Máire up the mountainside, looking for safety — safety that didn't, couldn't, exist. Not when a vast head finally broke the surface and rose up and up and up, a crested serpent like the others, glimmering in moonlight and dragonfire and large enough to encircle the world. The Serpent lifted itself from the water until its height was equal to that of the dragons', and Janx, boldest of his kind, swept away from Kate's side to make obsequience, bowing to the Serpent from the heart of the sea. He was so large, so ancient and long-grown himself, that he made measure by the Serpent, while Kate looked barely a speck beside the Serpent's impossible size.

The Serpent greeted the dragonlord with such honor as no other had known: he touched his nose to Janx's, then crashed back into the depths, and the sea came rising, and its darkness swept Tony and Máire away.

Magic pulsed, a power so deep that even Margrit, with only a few sips of Old Races magic in her blood, felt it in her bones, and came awake with a jolt, squinting in the morning sunlight. Alban, nestled like a great stone cat in the corner of their room, woke as well, and for an instant all was still as their eyes met in daylight.

Then the power was gone, and Alban slept again encased in stone, while Margrit sat, breathless, in a world that had changed forever.

#

There is a story as old as time: a story of a lamp, and a wish, and a genie.

The wish was made, and the lamp was cracked, and the djinn, mad with time immemorial spent in darkness, swept out.

Emma, bent over a bit of paper and a smaller bit of spellwork, lifted her head as magic poured across the world. "Oh," she said in delight. "Oh, she did it!"

Jana, as suddenly a dragon as Kate had been, though smaller, transformed back to human and shook herself. "She did *what*?"

"I don't know," Emma said joyfully, "but it changes everything."

A grimoire almost as old as secrets themselves flung itself off a shelf in Baba Yaga's hut. Its spine cracked as it fell open, and a few creatures escaped: a harpy, screeching and howling with rage as she threw herself about the hut and —by chance—out the door; and a vampire, so quick that, even starved, it disappeared before Baba Yaga leapt on the book and slammed it shut again. She caught a selkie's foot as she closed the book, and stuffed it back between the pages with a drop of blood and a cursed spell that had held a thousand years. Iron and blood bound the grimoire closed again, and the ancient witch clucked to her chicken-legged house, calling it to wakefulness.

It shook itself and shuddered, then hopped to its business, striding swiftly across the land until it reached the shores of the Volga, lifeblood to half a nation. There, the book in the crook of her arms, Baba Yaga leapt down from her hut and called her mortar to hand. It flew to her and she stepped within, then commanded it rise and fly her over the river, the swiftly flowing water that no witch could cross.

The mortar flew straight and true. No pain wracked the old witch's bones, and the chicken-legged house jumped into the water to swim along behind her.

Baba Yaga smiled a smile with her iron teeth, and the world began to crack.

THE OLD RACES
will return in an all-new series

THE WITCHES' WAR

Acknowledgments

First, I want everyone to know that tantalizing last line — that the Old Races will return! — is definitely true. Also it is definitely not a promise for something to come out super soon, because as of the writing of these acknowledgments, I have one series under contract and about five self-published projects going on, so I need to catch up on those before I throw myself into new Old Races books. But my thought-goal-plan was always that once the short stories were concluded, the Old Races universe would be set up for more full-length novels. I feel that I've accomplished that goal, so...someday, yes, there will be more novels in this world. I make no promises as to when, but there will be.

Second, there are so many people to be grateful for, for this book. My cover artist, Tara O'Shea, who is infallibly amazing. My friend Paul-Gabriel Wiener, whose story prompt begot "Threnody", one of my favorite stories of this collection. My Patreon crew, who, as a group, have kept the wolf from the door and allowed me to write things like this collection, which I probably wouldn't have been able to justify without their support.

My stalwart friends and cowriters in the War Room helped me get through this book, as they've done with every one I've written for the past nine years. Ellen, Mikaela, Michelle, Sharpie, Laura Anne even though I never see you anymore, everybody I'm forgetting right now... :)

And, of course, my Ted and Henry, whom I love very much. <3

About the Author

According to her friends, CE Murphy makes such amazing fudge that it should be mentioned first in any biography. It's true that she makes extraordinarily good fudge, but she's somewhat surprised that it features so highly in biographical relevance.

Other people said she began her writing career when she ran away from home at age five to write copy for the circus that had come to town. Some claimed she's a crowdsourcing pioneer, which she rather likes the sound of, but nobody actually got around to pointing out she's written a best-selling urban fantasy series (The Walker Papers), or that she dabbles in writing graphic novels (Take A Chance) and periodically dips her toes into writing short stories (the Old Races collections).

Still, it's clear to her that she should let her friends write all of her biographies, because they're much more interesting that way.

More prosaically, she was born and raised in Alaska, and now lives with her family in her ancestral homeland of Ireland, which is a magical place where it rains a lot but nothing one could seriously regard as winter ever actually arrives.

She can be found online at:

mizkit.com

@ce_murphy

fb.com/cemurphywriter &

tinyletter.com/ce_murphy (a newsletter, by far the best place to get up-to-date information on what's out next!)

Special Thanks

I've been running a Patreon for a few years now. Patreon is a modern answer to the Days Of Yore, when artists would have a wealthy patron to support them. Today, **many** people of ordinary incomes help support artists through Patreon and other systems like it. From an artistic point of view, it's a lifesaver. My patrons have helped me through some hard times, and supported me with their encouragement and enthusiasm.

In exchange, I've written two books of short stories, a full length novel, and a couple of novellas for them. All of those books have eventually been collected for general publication, as this one has. They've provided me with the freedom to pursue projects I love, and I'm eternally grateful to them.

My Patreon page and all of the content I've written for it is available for as little as $1/month at patreon.com/ce_murphy. Perhaps I'll see you there!

-Catie

My thanks to the KISS OF ANGELS patrons:

Ailsa Barrett, Alan Bellingham, Alena Franco, Althea
Clark, Amanda Priole, Amanda Weinstein, AM Koenig,
Amy, Andrew Armstrong, Andrew and Kate Barton,
Andy Merriam, Angela N., Anne Burner, Antiqueight,
Auntie Makeel, Axisor, Barbara Eagle, Barbara Hasebe,
Barbara Gallant, Benaets Dorien, Bernadette, Beth Ras-
mussen, Beth Skaggs, Beverly Lee, Brian Nisbet, Briony
Seedhouse, Bryant Durrell, Camilla Cracchiolo, Carl
Rigney, Carol Guess, Carol, Carol Guess, Casse
Williams, Cate Howard, Catherine Sharp, CathiBea
Stevenson, Charlotte Calvert, Chesley Cox, Chelsea
Jones, Christa Bowdish, Christine Swendseid, Christine
Stewart, Christopher Buser, Christy Hopkins,
Chrysoula, Clare Boothby, Coby Haas, Cori Weisfeldt,
Danielle Ingber, Deanna Zinn, Deb Alverson, Debbie
Matsuura, Debra Orton, Deirdre Murphy, Denée Zah,
Denise Moline, Diana Taft, Diane Dupey, Donal Cun-
ningham, Doniki Boderick-Luckey, Doug McGill, Earl
Miles, Edward Ellis, Eleanor Konik, Eleri Hamilton, Eliz-
abeth, Elizabeth, Elizabeth, Elizabeth Bennefeld, Eliza-
beth Wyatt, Elizabeth Thomas, Elizabeth Cadorette, Ella
Ivcp, Ella Peabody, Emily Poole, Emma Pitt, Emma
Bartholomew, Erin Gately, Esther MacCallum-Stewart,
Evil Hat, Gabe Krabbe, Gemma Tapscott, Georgina
Scott, Gienah Ghurab, Glynn Stewart, Heather Knutsen,
Heather Roney, Hugh Shannon, Idria Barone, Janet,
Janis Ossmann, Janne, Jean Diaz, Jeffrey D., Jennifer
Cabbage, Jenny Barber, Jeri Smith-Ready, Jessica Nel-
son, Jill Valuet, Jill Coddry, Joe Fernandez, justadream-
inghufflepuff, K. Gavenman, Kaat Van, Karen Schiller,
Kari, Karyl Fulkerson, Kas, Kate Copeland, Katherine
Malloy, Kathleen Tipton, Kathryn Duffy, Kathy Traxler,
Kathy Rogers, Katrina Lehto, Kaye Soleil, Kaz D'Spana,
Kbrem, Kelly Myers, Kenan Kigunda, Kerry Malone,
Kerry Kuhn, Kes Yocum, Kristine Kearney, Kyle Miller,
Kyna Foster, Larisa LaBrant, Laura Wallace, Laura
Hobbs, Laura Anne, Lauren DeVoe, Lauri Weaver,

LeAnn Haggard, Lesley Mitchell, Lianne Burwell, lies-behindstars, Lilly Ibelo, limugurl, Lisa Soto, Lisa Pegg, Lisa D, Lisa Guertin, Lisa Stewart, Little Snips, Liz Engan, Liza Olmsted, Lizzette Piltch, Lola, Lydia Leong, M A, Margaret Menzies, Maria Lima, Marisha Munroe, Marjorie Taylor, Marnie, Marsha Simmons, Mary D, Mary Anne Walker, Mary Hargrove, Mary Keefe, Mary Baldwin, Maryelizabeth Charlotte, Maureen Gately, Max Kaehn, Megan Pokorny, Michael Bernardi, Mikaela, Nancy Weston, Nathalie Boisard-Beudin, Nicolai Buch-Andersen, Nicole Oldham, Pam Blome, Pam Hatler, Pamela Dean, Pat Knuth, Patricia O'Neill, Patsy Tisdale, Paul Anthony Short, Paul-Gabriel Wiener, Persephone, Peter A., Pierce Rowley, Priscilla, Rachel Sahtout, Rachel Coleman, Rachel Reither, Rachel, Renata Carmen, Rhona, Robert Collier, Rosanne Girton, Ruth Stuart, Saifa Rashid, Sandra Jakl, Sara Harville, Sarah Brooks, Sarah Goslee, Sarah, Scott Shanks, Sean Collins, Shannon Scollard, Sharon Corbet, Shel Kennon, Sherry, Skye Christakos, Sonia Williams, Stacey Slager, Stephanie Boose, Sumi Funayama, Susan P, Susan Baur, Susan Carlson, Susan Shelly, Susan Sullivan, Susan Johnston, Taiyo Lipscomb, Tami Mitchell, Tangled Strings, Tania Clucas, Tanja, Tasha Turner, Tara Lynch, Tara O'Shea, Thomas Withrow, Tiana Hanson, Tiff, Tiffiny Quinn, Tom & Rosie Murphy, Tony James, Tracy McShane, Tracy Davis, Trip the Space Parasite wum wum wum, uninvitedCat, Valentine Lewis, Vathek, Wolf SilverOak, Zach Bertram

CPSIA information can be obtained
at www.ICGtesting.com
Printed in the USA
BVHW072114041021
618139BV00008B/479